JOHN COLLIER

His Monkey Wife
or, Married to a Chimp

INTRODUCED BY

PAUL THEROUX

OXFORD UNIVERSITY PRESS
1983

Oxford University Press, Walton Street, Oxford OX2 6DP

London Glasgow New York Toronto
Delhi Bombay Calcutta Madras Karachi
Kuala Lumpur Singapore Hong Kong Tokyo
Nairobi Dar es Salaam Cape Town
Melbourne Auckland

and associates in
Beirut Berlin Ibadan Mexico City Nicosia

Oxford is a trade mark of Oxford University Press

First published 1930 by Peter Davies, Ltd
First issued as an Oxford University Press paperback 1983

British Library Cataloguing in Publication Data
Collier, John
His monkey wife.
I. Title II. Theroux, Paul
823'.912[F] PR6005.036
ISBN 0-19-281407-9

Printed in Great Britain by
The Guernsey Press Co Ltd
Guernsey, Channel Islands

INTRODUCTION

BY PAUL THEROUX

"THIS is a strange book," the man wrote of *His Monkey Wife*, beginning the review on a small rectangle of notepaper. It was unlined paper but his sentences were set out in an orderly way, as if his copperplate was intended for someone at a linotype machine. He went on, "It clearly sets out to combine the qualities of the thriller with those of what might be called the decorative novel. Like most things which are extremely far apart, these two are also surprisingly near to one another." He continued in this elliptical way for four pages and then found the novelist wildly inexact. "From the classical standpoint his consciousness is too crammed for harmony, too neurasthenic for proportion, and his humour is too hysterical, too greedy and too crude."

On the other hand, this review of the novel was written by John Collier himself in 1930, when the book first appeared. It was titled "A Looking Glass", and one of its more bizarre aspects was that though it was carefully written it was very much a private joke: it was never printed anywhere, nor has anyone ever mentioned it before. Furthermore, it was rather dismissive—it contained faint praise but was generally belittling. It must have been the result of an impulse, but when you think about its backhanded generosity, its self-mockery and its extreme poise it is impossible not to be curious about its perpetrator.

What sort of a man writes a masterpiece and then writes a sniffy review of it and slides it into a drawer to be found fifty years later by his widow? It is not an easy question, because John Collier is one of the great literary unclassifiables—which is another way of saying genius. Collier had a generous man's modesty, and a great imagination, and no airs. Towards the end of his life he said, "I sometimes marvel that a third-rate writer like me has been able to palm himself off as a second-rate writer." He was a poet, editor, reviewer, novelist and screen writer. He was also unknown to the general public. "He eschews fame and has a horror of publicity", Anthony Burgess wrote in his Introduction to *The John Collier Reader* (1972). Like many other people who have no appetite for celebrity, John Collier was a happy man, who lived a rich and contented life. I am not speaking of books but of passions and pleasures. He was an attentive friend and a traveller; he was enthusiastic about boats and food. He liked to cook. He grew roses. He was asked by *Sight & Sound* magazine in 1976 why he had become a script writer. He admitted that he had been "abysmally ignorant of the cinema . . . I had seen scarcely a dozen films in my life." He had gone to Hollywood because he had fallen in love with a fishing boat in Cassis, near Marseilles, in 1935, and so he wrote the script of *Sylvia Scarlett* in order to buy the boat.

There is another aspect to his anonymity that is interesting. He seems faceless and ungraspable and then, after a little probing, one discovers his involvement in all sorts of well-known contexts. Mystery men are often like that. Collier was poetry editor of *Time and Tide* in the 1920s, and in the 1930s published a number of short stories in the *New Yorker*. Collier it was who first suggested that Jack Warner buy *The African Queen* to film—and he wrote the first script for it. Some of his macabre stories were dramatized in *Alfred Hitchcock Presents*, Sandy Wilson made a musical out of *His Monkey Wife*, and it was Collier who introduced "the magical-Druidical element" into Franklin Schaffner's film, *The War Lord* (1965). He also wrote the script for the film *I Am A Camera*. So, though he may have been somewhat hidden, the fact remains that he spent the best part of his life working magic.

*

"John Henry Noyes Collier was born May 3, 1901", his widow Harriet wrote to me, when I asked for the details. "His parents were John George Collier and Emily Noyes Collier. His great grandfather was physician to King William IV, a great uncle was a physician connected with the Hospital for Nervous Diseases, and there were other doctors, artists, and an Uncle Vincent, who was an unknown novelist (he published *Light Fingers and Dark Eyes* in 1913), who tutored John and was a great influence on him and his career. His mother, a teacher, taught him to read at the age of 3, and he read an average of a book a day for the rest of his life. Except for kindergarten, this was the extent of his formal education. He read at the Bodleian and spent a great deal of time in the Reading Room of the British Museum."

His early writing was poetry and reviews. This was in the 1920s—in 1922 he received the poetry prize from *This Quarter*. In the 1930s he published thirteen books—poetry, novels, short story collections, an edition of John Aubrey, and a piece of collaboration entitled *Just the Other Day: An Informal History of Britain Since the War*. His early life divides almost by decades, for after his literary beginnings in the Twenties, and his assured and varied writing in the Thirties, he was occupied in the Forties with films—"a mixed bag", one critic wrote, for they included *Elephant Boy*, *Her Cardboard Lover*, *Deception* and *Roseanna McCoy*. "I suspect that what I wrote was far too wordy and far too literary", Collier once reflected, with his customary humility. The 1950s were the beginning of a happy period that lasted until his death in 1980. During this time he wrote more stories and more movie scripts, and bought a house, Domaine du Blanchissage, in Grasse, France.

His last project was his favourite, a movie script of

Milton's *Paradise Lost*. In an interview, Collier said, "I think the theme of *Paradise Lost* is singularly suited to attract a wide audience, and especially the young audience, of today. It is quasi-religious, quasi-scientific, and deeply humanistic, being the thrilling story, with which we can all identify, of how innocent, vegetarian, Proconsul or Pithecanthropus was caught up in the guerrilla war waged by Satan against the authoritarian universe, and how he emerged as moral and immoral, curious, inspired, murderous and suffering Man." The film was not made but the script was published as "A Screenplay for the Cinema of the Mind" in America in 1973. It is an astonishing thing—not quite what Milton intended—and Satan is the hero.

*

Collier loved unlikely heroes. His stories are full of them, and so are his novels—not only Willoughby Ollebeare in *Defy The Foul Fiend*, but a whole marauding gang of savages in his novel of our tribalistic future, *Tom's A-Cold* (the American title was *Full Circle*)—set in the 1990s. And what is less likely than the main character of *His Monkey Wife*?

"The chimp is civilized"—the flat statement appears in the first chapter. Very soon we begin to realize its implications, for Emily is no ordinary chimp. The laugh is on the scientists "who have chosen to measure the intelligence of the chimpanzee solely by its reactions to a banana". Collier implies that it might be far better to test a chimp's reaction to the poetry of Tennyson or Frances Crofts Cornford. Emily is tremendously well-read—no one in the novel, not even the aesthetes or writers, is so knowledgeable as she or possesses her range of reference. She knows she has no dowry but "she brought with her the treasure of a well-stocked mind . . . which, all the books said, was infinitely to be preferred". She has a good nose for literary style, finding in the prose of the divorce laws a stark simplicity of greater merit than the exoticism of the marriage service. On the ship to England from Africa the other passengers want to feed her nuts and they urge her to smoke and do tricks. She tries to engage them in a discussion of Conrad's understanding of the sea. She can't win.

That she is a monkey is of small significance to the other characters. (She is not, we know, a monkey, but rather an anthropoid ape. Collier uses the words interchangeably, and I have followed his example.) There are many references to the fact that Amy, too, looks like a chimp. I once heard that in the seventeenth century a monkey was found in the north of England and was hanged by the locals, who suspected the poor beast of being a French spy. Emily is taken to be Arab or Chinese or Irish; most onlookers conclude that she is probably Spanish—dusky and hot-blooded. On several occasions men try to pick her up. It is the humans in the book who behave like monkeys, gibbering and indulging their frivolous passion for fancy dress. This has the effect of making Emily a deeply sympathetic character and of giving force to the love story in the satire. If Alfred Fatigay were not so clownishly obtuse and such a jackass in all his dealings with Emily, it might even have been a touching love story.

Throughout the novel all the real feeling is Emily's and all the insincerity belongs to the humans. After reading a letter Amy has written to Alfred, Emily understands the bogus nature of Amy's sentiment—but Alfred remains blind to it. Soon we cease to expect any subtlety or surprise from the humans in the book; they are stick-figures, being held up to ridicule, and they come out very badly in comparison with the chimp.

It is not only the subtlety of Emily's understanding that is impressive, but also her ability to express it. It is Emily's bookishness that fills this novel with literary allusions. (One of the great games *His Monkey Wife* inspires is guessing the sources of the numerous quotations.) I have mentioned F. C. Cornford and Tennyson—'Locksley Hall' is a special favourite of the chimp, presumably for its own Alfred and its own Amy and its own view of love. But there are also poems by Vaughan, Donne, Dowson, Coleridge, Wordsworth and Blake. Emily is romantically inclined and eager to give Alfred the benefit of the doubt. Love has made her literary, and so has contempt, for when Amy treats her like a slave Emily feels "like something out of *Uncle Tom's Cabin*". Collier made her presence especially effective by giving her thoughts but no voice. What might have sounded pompous or improbable in direct speech is persuasive and vigorous when rendered as ruminant thought. One of the funniest scenes in the novel also depends on a literary classic for its effect. This occurs when Emily brandishes a knife and a copy of *Murders in the Rue Morgue* in Amy's face, just before the wedding ceremony. It is unexpectedly fierce of Emily to threaten anyone (love is her excuse), but even so it is the Poe that makes the point.

His Monkey Wife has been described by Osbert Sitwell (in his Foreword to Collier's *Green Thoughts*, 1932) as an allegory about "the growth of the soul, from beast to man", and other critics have suggested that it is a satire against the New Woman. Anthony Burgess described the book as a "wayward masterpiece" and a "sport" and said that thematically "anything will do". It is a highly adaptable fable, but will anything do? The book is so funny and bright it does not need critical explanation. Sitwell's thesis about its illustrating a kind of moral evolution is not very interesting, and mentions of Virginia Woolf and Mrs. Pankhurst and gibes at George Moore hardly create enough wind to fill the sails of a feminist argument.

But not anything will do. The book is a laugh, yet it is also a great satire about human weakness. The chimp is weakest at her most human, and strongest and most resourceful at her monkeyest. There is not a human being in the book who is not deficient and deeply silly in a crucial way. Collier's writing is in the tradition of English satire in being cheerfully misanthropic, and not long after writing the novel he declared, "I cannot see much good in the world or much likelihood of good. There seems to me a definite bias in human nature towards ill, towards the immediate convenience, the ugly, the cheap . . . I rub my hands and say 'Hurry up, you foulers of a good world, and destroy yourselves faster.'"

Fatigay is perfectly named—he is limp and clapped out, always the solemn fool, and not a patch on "his sensitive pet". It is one of the ironies of the novel that none of the characters has any idea of how wonderful Emily really is, or what a good mind she has. This is particularly true of Alfred. He never discovers how perceptive and high-minded she is. The chimp is civilized, an omnivorous reader and a woman of the world, but it is for her pet-like qualities that Alfred admires her. He comes to love her at last for her being a good pet, for her constancy and devotion. Human love is shown to be no more than selfish condescension. Emily is the worthiest character in the book. If this were not so, the satire would be quite different. The last irony is that a novel that delights in being unphysical ends on a note of triumphant carnality.

Among other things, the novel is a chronicle of Emily's success. In the course of four years, Emily rises to such a highly paid position as a star dancer in London that she is able to transform Alfred, who has been brought to a pitiful condition—gnawing cauliflower stems for sustenance and chattering in Piccadilly. It is when he becomes most monkey-like that Emily shimmers out of the Ritz and offers him a new life. Redemption is the proper word but it is out of place in a discussion of this glancing novel. At important points in the narrative Emily takes the initiative—saving Alfred from Loblulya, learning to read, managing the marriage ceremony, and carrying Alfred away from the brink of oblivion. At last it is she who suggests that they return to Africa together. One of my favourite asides in the book is Collier's mention that Alfred is the only person ever to have returned to Boboma after having once left it.

From the first sentence of the novel the reader is aware that he is in the presence of a magician. This is Collier's strength as a writer. He casts a spell and he does so always with a smile. His style is effortless, always enjoying itself as it weaves its magic. The book is full of asides, parodies, half-quotes, and Collier's literary rope tricks, in which before our eyes he levitates a number of clauses and then he disappears leaving a long sentence dancing in the air. The second paragraph in Chapter XII begins with a sentence of 354 words.

If *His Monkey Wife* is a disturbing book it is because the chimp is so innocent, so winsome, so undemanding, relying on the power of romantic love in an atmosphere of human failure. She is civilized in the way man ought to be; she is Man before the Fall, before Satan and God hatched the idea of sin. She is also a terrific vaudeville act. The ending—one of the greatest last paragraphs of any novel—is a good shock; it is perfect, in fact. It gives order to the disturbance, and it reminds me of Collier's remark about his script for *The African Queen*, in which he chose to deal with Allnut and Rose in his own way. "A happy end?" he said. "Bet your life it was."

*

As a footnote, here in its entirety is the review John Collier wrote of his novel:

A LOOKING GLASS

This is a strange book. It clearly sets out to combine the qualities of the thriller with those of what might be called the decorative novel. Like most things which are extremely far apart, these two are also surprisingly near to one another. In order to reach the one spot on the globe which is twenty five thousand miles from me, I have only to turn around. Similarly, it is not necessary, nor I think desirable, to circumnavigate the novel-world, passing through the warren continents of character and zeit-geist, in order to link the most highly coloured aestheticism with the penny dreadful. They stand back to back on their small island of complete arbitrariness.

In penny dreadfuls, the Wembleys, or the earthquakes of the mind, an astonishing amount of unworked beauty is to be found. And this beauty, while it can be no more absolute than beauty of any kind, may perhaps give us the illusion of being so, for it has this accidental advantage, that being cut off from mental habit by a frame of improbability, it is perceived in its purest and most electric state, as in a modern picture.

Violence and extravagance do not prohibit beauty and subtlety, as Webster's plays and the penny blood lives of the Borgias demonstrate, but beauty and subtlety will prohibit violence and extravagance if they get there first. The aesthete, then, must go more than half way to meet the thriller, lest he should vitiate his material into mere charm and fantasy. The sea serpent is a shy serpent, and if we do not go far enough in search of him, we may find ourselves with only a pretty toy snake in our hands, of which we could have bought a dozen at Mudies.

The problem is an amusing one, and, if successfully worked with, it should yield a very downright sort of story, which would be at least a holiday from the mass of serious and yet facile psychology which lends a sameness to most of the better sort of fiction of today. How far has Mr. Collier been successful?

The plot he has hit on is certainly bizarre enough, and if he does not keep entirely clear of that mental slackness which we are tasteless enough to call "charm", he very consistently avoids fantasy; that is, he insists that we meet his extraordinary characters on their own terms and do not send out merely the childish survival in us to deal with them.

Viewed as a story, this novel is an emotional melodrama, complete with a Medusa villainess, an honest simpleton of a hero, and an angelic if only anthropoid heroine, all functioning in the two-dimensional world of the old Lyceum poster or the primitive fresco, where Chinamen walk haloed in infernal green, where an angel may outsize a church, and where a man may marry a monkey on a foggy day.

The simplest novel, of course, must exist on other planes than that of its action. In the mere choice of words something of the writer's attitude to life must leak through. Mr. Collier's positively squirts through, too insistently at times. This makes for variety of interest, but not for harmony. This point inevitably marks the widest divergence of this type of novel from the true penny dreadful, whose author generally has a very simple and unobtrusive attitude to life. He expresses a dislike of villains, and a liking for chums and sweet girls. But the aesthete founds his existence on a complex system of likes and dislikes, and Mr. Collier, if he is all sensationalist in his plot, is all aesthete in his counterpoint of personal expression.

He seems to dislike almost everything and everybody in life, and to love everything and everybody as soon as they have been transmuted into a comedy which is sardonic and unjust. The sentences that carry in the melodrama are loaded, sometimes overloaded, with phrases which insist on this transmutation: they kick out like mules with their hinder clauses, their blows falling alike on the cultured and the uncultured, the chaste and the unchaste, the ambitious mind and the loving heart. This, though it adds richness to the texture, prevents the writer from attaining the important part of that classicism after which he seems to strive. From the classical standpoint his consciousness is too crammed for harmony, too neurasthenic for proportion, and his humour is too hysterical, too greedy and too crude. For example: "*The snow's a lady* . . . and like the rest of her sex, though delightful in her fall (to those who enjoy her), once she has fallen her effect is depressing, particularly in Piccadilly."

HIS MONKEY WIFE

CHAPTER I

If thou be'st born to strange sights

and if you don't mind picking your way through the untidy tropics of this, the globe, and this, the heart, in order to behold them, come with me into the highly coloured Bargain Basement Toy Bazaar of the Upper Congo. You shall return to England very shortly.

The tall trees on the edge of the clearing have here and there, it seems, lifted their skirts of scrub, giving us the same sickening drop from our expectations as shop-window ladies do, when their dresses are opened at back or placket, and we see only wire and emptiness. So dead are these vistas into the dark jungle, that if there emerged from them, into the sun's spotlight at their entrance, one of those sights we still absurdly expect ; an elephant, say, with a leopard hanging as banderillo from his slatey shoulder, but sliding down, leaving red tracks grooved in that slatiness, sliding down to be crushed of course, we should feel that it was just a turn, *Great Xmas Treat*, materialised from some dressing-room-like pocket in space, and not native to those scaffoldings and canvas backs, with hanging ropes and sterile floor and darkness. There are birds, naturally, of all sizes and qualities, whose penetrating whistles and clockwork screech and chatter add to the illusion, whichever it is.

This path leads straight to the bungalow of Mr. Fatigay. You see, he has introduced some English plants into his garden. His is the only white man's house in Boboma, and it must be admitted that the large man, with his round schoolboy jacket and his honest puzzled eye, appears to greater advantage alone here among the infant blacks, to whom it is his vocation to bring literacy and light, than he would if there were other white men about, whose coarser codes he might too readily take on. But that is the way with most of us. Sitting on the wide verandah, however, almost alone, his personality expands naïvely, and something quite poetic appears in the twilight of that hour and of his nature, like the sweet but inconsiderable bloom on a ragged nocturnal weed.

I have said *almost alone* in order to prepare you, lest, hearing his voice rise and fall with more point and direction than a man employs who idly mutters to himself, and noticing, as we draw near enough to see into the shadows of the verandah, that no other white-clad figure is stretched out there, you should conclude that he is mad. This is not quite so. Like Vaughan, he is *least alone when most alone.* He has not noticed it, but he, whose shyness limits his conversation to a string of Empire-builders' clichés when he is in the company of his compatriots, he becomes positively fluent and individual when only in the presence of that which moves in the corner behind his chair. He becomes quite a chatter-box. What is it that moves? Look: it's Emily! Here she comes!

Do you wonder, when you see her emerge into the shaft of lamplight, smiling her Irish smile, brushing the floor with the knuckles of her strong capable hands, do you wonder that the branches of the great tree, that which shades the bedrooms from the aching moon, are sometimes torn asunder, when a dark face juts out over a straining hairy torso; Henry's face, who has shared her arboreal infancy, a face all convulsed in the puzzled clown-grief the Prologue speaker plays on us in Pagliacci: *A word! A moment. . . .* But no word comes, naturally, and the moment is lost, and the heavy boughs press inward and close, drowning that dark face in a flurry of white blossoms and shining leaves, as if it were in moon-breaking water. Can you wonder that on the silvered grass-patch her mother and sisters sometimes stand, tangled in each other's comforting arms till they look like a Laocoon group cut from a briar root, wondering if she sleeps well, that winsome baffling creature who has left them for a life farther set beyond the scope of their simple minds than is that of Hollywood from the film star's folks', Momma and Poppa in some little wayback home-town on the prairie.

Can you wonder that, *petite*, dark and vivacious, she is the life and soul of the lonely bungalow, so that the passing trader or Colonial Office man has no sooner thrust out his legs into the cool comfort of his evening's rest, than he says, "Now then, old man, where's that chimp of yours? Let's see Emily. Ho! Ho! Ho!"

But as she ambles forward on such occasions, turning a somersault, perhaps, as slowly and gravely as day and night, see! her smile dawning at the end of it has something of trouble and strain splintering under its sensitive flexibility. Loyal in her support of Mr. Fatigay, quixotically hospitable in her determination to give such guests what they are most fitted to enjoy, she is none the less ill at ease. Yet she masks it. This generous hypocrisy is the first strong sweet ferment of the noble savage heart. It is civilisation. This chimp is civilised.

She had not been so before she had come into the possession of the good schoolmaster. That was a year ago, before her captor, an anthropologist, whom she had revered rather than loved, had exchanged her to Mr. Fatigay for the more conveniently portable possession of a magnificent pair of antlers. Then, though eminently deserving of that second-rate sort of praise implicit in such adjectives as *well-grown*, *sagacious*, *a fine specimen* and the like, she gave no sign, and was herself unconscious, of any claim to esteem in terms less niggardly and low. What seeds lay latent in her of qualities with such a claim, sprouted only under the sunshine of Mr. Fatigay's smiles, and the gentle warm monotonous rain of the evening monologues, in which, when work was done, he expressed his hopes, dreams, ambitions to the friendly dumbness by his side.

"Ah, Emily!" he would say, with something of the gesture as well as of the onomatopoeism with which he habitually strove to make English clearer to the piccaninnies, "How nice to be at ease again!" lolling his head, and then, in mild explosion, "What a day! What a day!" And he would continue with a monosyllabic expressiveness which I, who have never taught the blacks, am quite unable to imitate. From simple allusions to physical fatigues and pleasures, he would proceed to higher matters, and would sometimes have daubed in a very fair self-portrait, rather larger than life, before an awareness of his reflection, small and gesticulating, in the dark mirror-bright eye of the chimp, would bring him back to self-consciousness.

"Why, Emily!" he would say fondly, but with an uneasy titter, "One would think you understood every word I said."

And, indeed, Emily had soon come to understand the more concrete terms he used, her comprehension falling back only when he soared into abstractions beyond her experience and his expressiveness. Yet it was in the course just of these, she noted, that his rare fits of enthusiasm would come upon him, and having seen him thus transformed and shining, she longed restlessly to know what it was he said then. She had seen the same light play, but rather more coldly, like an aurora borealis, over his prism and silent face when he sat sometimes with a puzzlingly dry and unattractive object in his hands, and evidently voyaging through strange seas of thought, alone.

She was, after all, a schoolmaster's pet, and on the frequent occasions on which she had accompanied him to the schoolroom, she had seen enough pictures of cats with the letters C A T printed beside them. Is it so hard to understand how she came to a comprehension of the function of books, and even, perhaps, of the abstracter functions of language ? Our scientists may think so, who have chosen to measure the intelligence of the chimpanzee solely by its reactions to a banana. They suspend the delicacy from the ceiling of a cage, and assess the subject's mentality in terms of the number of boxes he or she will pile one upon another in order to secure it, failing to see that nothing is revealed except the value which that particular chimp chooses to set upon the fruit. And, beyond a certain low limit, this surely is in inverse ratio to intelligence. What boy of ten would not pile up a dozen boxes in an attempt to climb within reach of it ? How many would

Einstein clamber upon? And how many less would Shakespeare? Emily, though a fruitarian by instinct, would have disdained an eagerness capable of more than two and a jump.

If you would arrive at a juster estimate of the potentialities of her race, study Emily's conduct following upon the shrewd hypothesis she had made. She now never missed an opportunity of following her master into the schoolroom, where her attention became most concentrated, though unostentatiously, during the high proportion of elementary reading lessons. With her, the first steps were more difficult by far than they were to her sooty classmates, but the later ones were less so. She was stimulated, however, in the powerful effort demanded of her in the early stages, by a new sensation, a feeling of being slightly inflated by a gas lighter than air whenever certain thoughts or memories crossed her mind. These were always connected with Mr. Fatigay. The chimp was awakening to love.

Full consciousness of it, like motor headlights suddenly leaping up behind one in a private and violent dawn, came on her one sultry afternoon.

'What makes the lamb love Mary so?'
The children all did cry.

chirruped the piccaninnies in voices in which still echoed so strongly the hollow clicks of their tribal lingo, that they sounded as if sticks were being drawn along a wooden paling. And

'Oh! Mary loves the lamb, you know'
The teacher made reply.

came Mr. Fatigay's virile tones in response.

A choking gurgle, sadly out of tune, arose from Emily's corner. The sound of that voice, rough and sweet to her as wild honey, took possession of the wilderness of her heart like a John the Baptist. The words, freely translated as to sexes and species, seemed to fill the desert with a message optimistic as the Jordan slogan. Her spirit, a caged lark which hears another in the sky, beat madly against her bars and roof of dumbness: it seemed that only one more effort was needed and her heart would spirt forth a clear low wood-sweet voice to harmonise with that world-creating, world-filling bass. A blank agony of concentration resulted. The striving creature dared not abate it, even to inhale. At what seemed the opening of realisation, darkness crashed down upon her, like a cloth flung over a bird-cage, and she fell forward in a momentary swoon.

As she came up out of it, into the light of consciousness and memory, she paused a little before opening her eyes, in order that she might reassemble the potent impressions which had immediately preceded her collapse. A different, and a sweeter, dizziness was superimposed upon the physical one. Still she kept her eyes fast shut, waiting, like the Sleeping Beauty, and it seemed for a hundred years, for her Prince Charming tenderly to awaken her. Then, far away, falling as from a height infinitely above the near unnoted stridulations of the little blacks, she heard the awaited voice.

"Drag her out by the legs, and throw a bucket of water over her."

Emily swooned again, and this time more deeply, her spirit, like Ibsen's wounded wild duck, clinging to the cold dark mud in the depths below her consciousness.

The impact of the cold drench revived her, and, having now nothing to wait for, nor finding any pleasure in arranging her returning thoughts, she rose to her feet in uncertain haste, and staggered blindly from the arid playground, heedless of the hoots and guffaws of the leaping little coons who had all too eagerly administered the restorative. For what was such infantile derision to one on whose bowed and nakedly twitching head the laughter of the whole universe was being poured?

The chimpanzee cosmology is highly animistic, and it seemed now to Emily as if the slumbering personality of things had awakened and stood up a moment, to jeer and laugh. The bungalow grinned and looked out of its windows at her; the grass huts were doubled up and shaking. The very airs joined hands and danced in their mean mirth, and the trees threw up their top branches and rained down on her the silvery tinkle of a myriad sun-echoing leaves. For the sun's brazen laughter was the worst of all, and to escape it the poor chimp shuffled in under the cascade from the quivering trees. Like the water of certain high falls, however, this had broken up in its long descent and had become rain, then mist, then nothing, before it reached the ground.

Here, in the dark dry-rottenness of the lower jungle, Emily found escape from the externalised form of her reverse. Here, with the powdering log, and scaley life, woodlouse and small serpent, the bright hot blood fountains from her wounded heart congealed, and soon their brittle larva flaked away, each sob loosening a little, leaving the subject anæmic but sane. It was a suddenly mature chimp that came home from those anti-febrile shades, but, tight-lipped and steady-eyed, neither a shattered nor an embittered one.

There is a satisfaction in the bankruptcy of hope and self-esteem, if only it is complete enough. With only the unassailable core of the ego left, one is eased of the intolerable unconscious burden of the debt one's faultiness owes to fortune for preserving its absurdly disproportionate, and nervous, superstructure of greed and pretension. The chimp was aware of this, having heard the school children sing, *He that is low need fear no fall*, and, indeed, having seen some of the elder ones demonstrate it very heartily, in one narrow interpretation at least.

Who would have thought, seeing the trim little brown figure trip so self-containedly through the village, or describe such a suave arc on the end of the swinging bough that landed her pat, here, back again at Mr. Fatigay's feet, as he sat at dinner on the verandah: who would have thought, seeing all this, that beneath that rather Charlotte Brontë surface, there was, actually, a Charlotte Brontë interior, full of meek pride, hopeless hope and timid determination. At one moment, in fact, it became positively Emily B., and that was when Mr. Fatigay, swallowing the last mouthful of his yam, said, with unwonted coarseness:

"Well, Emily, here you are again! Why; I thought you'd got skittish. Thought there must be a Tom about, you know, and you'd gone off for the night."

And, in his blindness, the foolish fellow actually hummed a bar or two from the suggestive chorus of his latest syncopated record, *Those BABoon Blues*.

Emily turned her face to the wall. She little thought, as neither did Mr. Fatigay, that this unusual gaucherie of his was expressive of his pleasure at seeing her safely back again. She tried to concentrate on the idea that he, like lesser men, was at heart just a great big boy, with a boy's capacity for the sudden careless blow. This, while it assisted, but perhaps unnecessarily, in repressing any impulse towards anger, did little to salve the new hurt in the barely stanched wound of that afternoon.

As she sat motionless in the gathering darkness, and watched her childhood's home, the jungle, she pondered once more the advisability of withdrawal.

The cloudy, smoke-blue billows of that forest washed up almost to where they were sitting, as the sea did to the palace steps in *The Little Mermaid*, and with the same tremendous appeal of depth on depth on depth to dissolve in. It appeared to go on so far that the actual horizon was lost in it, and the moon, which then began to lift directly opposite them, rose like a silver bird from a twiggy blue nest. As the moon rose it got smaller, and time, which it took up with it, got smaller also, and the forest swept on infinite and eternal beneath. Large enough to be a grave for sorrow. A timeless cloudy sea to melt memory away.

"Switch on the light," said Mr. Fatigay, and it was gone.

Before the chimp was a white painted handrail, a bamboo table with pipes, a whisky and soda, and the *Overseas Daily Mail*. Beyond these was a wall of darkness in which the moon hung like a word of reminiscence which must pass unnoticed. The white rail and the table stood at the threshold of a new life, stretching beyond her vision, but full, as far as she could see, of strangeness and of pain.

CHAPTER II

Dust hath closed Helen's eye

Six months slipped swiftly by in the little clearing of Boboma. The seasons, as we know them, are of course tangled up in that locality, caught as they are in the sun's heel, which passes over twice in the course of the year. Spring flew overhead without settling, like a wild bird, tardy migrant! on its way to Hampshire. But Boboma, all unconscious of its distinction, had a little private Spring going on in its very centre. The new world, which Emily had visualised as opening so aridly before her, had in fact contained one element more than she had bargained for, and that of such aureate quality as to shed a glow even upon the stark and forbidding outlines of her relationship to Mr. Fatigay. Literature this was, in its wider aspects, that made the future seem incredibly rich, not in colour and sensation merely, but in possibilities. And at the thought of these possibilities the living principle awoke, like sap, in Emily's heart, so cramped and contracted by an iron resolution she had made, to feel and hope no more. This, as when the spring grass cracks stone-slabs of pavement, was a signal instance of the futility of the strongest anti-vital contrivances, when pitted against the forces latent in even the very softest of living tissue. Mr. Bernard Shaw would have been delighted.

So was the chimp. The dawn, culturally speaking, had come for her when she had passed from reading the flavourless simplified passages in the children's lesson books, to groping at the tough and prickly sweetness at the core of her master's little stock of well-chosen classics. The dawn, we must remember, is remarkable for its high and transitory colours, and its deceiving mists. Emily's mind was in many important respects too unsophisticated, too unsuspicious, too generous and eager, for her to estimate at their true worth the various pictures of life which she found in Mr. Fatigay's favourite authors. She believed them all. The world that lay before her was irradiated by Tennyson and Bernard Shaw, by Georgian poetry and Michael Arlen, and, worse than all combined, by love.

But how, you will ask, had she gained so quickly this command of letters, and what did Mr. Fatigay think of it ? She had gained it by sheer concentration, and Mr. Fatigay thought nothing of it at all, for, despite his monologues, he was completely unaware that his pet, or plaything, had understanding of any words beyond a few simply spoken commands.

"*Something better than his dog, a little dearer than his horse!*" thought Emily, with a momentary bitterness. But it was, she at once admitted to herself with all the warmth of generous self-reproof, largely through her own weakness that he continued unmindful of her prowess.

On a day very shortly after her rebuff, and in the first impetuosity of her resolution to become worthy of his regard, she had tried to reveal her intelligence to her master in the classroom. She had taken a place at an empty desk, instead of her usual one beside the master's stool, and when the piccaninnies saw her clutch pencil and paper in imitation of themselves, and glance eagerly upward to where Mr. Fatigay stood ready to inscribe model letters on the blackboard, they had cried out with delight. At which Mr. Fatigay had turned round, and, seeing what was afoot, he had said, smiling:

"Come, come, Emily! If you are as clever as all that, you must be sold to perform on the Halls."

At once the frightened chimp had relinquished the implements of clerkliness, and crept trembling to her old place of subjection. How it all recurred to her when later on she read that Mrs. Virginia Woolf had been denied admittance to a university library! From that moment she gave no sign of possessing an intelligence higher than that with which she was naturally credited. To be debarred from doing so was very grievous to her, less on account of being denied the pleasures of innocent display, which interested her only so far as the impression she made on Mr. Fatigay was concerned, than because she was thus prevented from any opportunity of learning to write, for she could not partake unnoticed in the writing lessons as she could in those on reading. Afterwards she thought that perhaps all had been for the best, for, in her over-wrought emotional state at this time, she might have been tempted to fritter away precious hours in the production of a sonnet-sequence, to the detriment of her more instructive studies.

So she learned nothing but to read, but, since she was well able to concentrate, which the school children were not, she learned it at least a hundred times as fast as they. Before the six months had passed she was tolerably conversant with most of the books that a mild idealist takes to the jungle with him in these days, and on these, which help most of us to forget that we are human, she founded her innocent theory of what human life should be. Perhaps, in view of her sex, this was just as well.

There were, in this world she visualised, which must have something resembled a stiff and formal Rousseau wedding group, over which some European tree alarms us by the painter's memory of equatorial frondage, and among which a small hairy non-human figure is set, smouldering destructively in its juxtaposition to these starchy nuptials; in this world there were certain elements which seemed alien and antagonistic to its central principle of domestic bliss. These were, to put it bluntly, women, and the chief of them was that woman of thirty, on whom G. Moore delivers himself with all the gusto of an egoist and a bachelor. Reading his rhapsody, the chimp was impressed in spite of herself. She recognised the enemy of her faith and her hope, and she hated, yet admired. She toyed with the thought of making this creature her model, and shrank in innocent alarm from even the playful girlish whim. She was repelled, fascinated, and, on Mr. Fatigay's account more than her own, she was filled with vague fears.

"Woman!" she thought, thinking of herself and the negresses, who were the only human kind she had seen, "Woman! The meek hairy shadow, or the glossy black caricature of man! Surely they must be of this second strutting kind who can be imagined as thinking and acting thus!" And, shaking her head, the perhaps old-fashioned chimp had replaced the disturbing volume on the shelf. But for some time this odalisque lay across her path, smiling.

Such forebodings, however, occupied only the more speculative of Emily's reveries. Most of her time was filled, more happily, with the enlarging and remodelling of her conception of her beloved, for, as new ideas expanded the maiden demesne of her heart and mind, so the image of him who was destined lastingly to fill both grew within them, and was ever to be newly explored and additionally loved. That deeper and more work-a-day grain, which is only to be won by the recognition and cheerful acceptance of blemishes, now marked her feeling for him.

At first, as an apparition from another world, and unrelated to any background, he had possessed for her something of the flat and arbitrary luminosity of a saint in a stained-glass window. Now, seeing him more in the round, she was conscious of certain little weaknesses and blindnesses in him, such as are knit in the fibre of most of us, and while these made him less of the god to her, their earthiness made him more the man—one might say, the mammal—to be reached, to be loved possessively. She, who had longed to burn out her heart before him as one renders up the complimentary uselessness of incense to a deity placed high above needs and desire, was now possessed by a more practical tenderness, not less lofty for being practical, as it was not less becoming for being out of date: that is, to strengthen him against the world, to amuse him against himself, and to protect him against treacherous mischance. An opportunity soon came.

Emily was one day with her master in the little arbour which he had made at the end of the garden. He sat at the table, busy writing at some report or other, while his faithful pet was seated high above him on the strong cross-beam which held the structure together. She looked down lovingly upon his rather palm-treed head. Its very untidiness seemed to her expressive of all that was boyish, ingenuous and enthusiastic in his nature. Its colour, debased Nordic, was the æsthetic affinity of her own rich chestnut. How she longed for the right to stroke it caressingly, and to supervise, in her motherly way, its entire well-being!

Suddenly a shadow pitched into the doorway, and in such an inexpressibly business-like fashion that one could imagine that the black figure, which had clicked into being there, had flung down this outermost skin like a gauntlet. The air at once became tense. Yet it was only Loblulya, wife of the head man of the village, carrying fruit.

Who . . . what is she? Ten years ago she was still the reigning toast of Boboma, though she had already had three husbands, each of whom had been ruler of the little village in his time. No sooner did one of them dwindle and die than she married his successor. Mr. Fatigay, when he had arrived there, had heard of this, and had felt it incumbent upon his unofficially magisterial position, to call her before him and put certain questions to her. But on his asking her if, by any chance, ju-ju or potent vegetable decoctions had played part in the premature demise of her successive spouses, she had replied, with a sniff, that while she would have scorned to deny having taken such measures if brutality or neglect had rendered them necessary, the fact was that the deceased had all of them been very good sorts of men, on whom she had never laid hand save in the way of kindness, and therefore she could only attribute the decline of each of them to some insidious weakness of his own. This was received rather dubiously by Mr. Fatigay, as he was aware that tribal custom decreed the position of head man only to the strongest champion in each particular community, but he felt himself unable to press the inquiry any further.

Loblulya had now been for some years a grass widow, the reigning chief, her fourth, having been accosted by a spirit while he was walking in the wood some two months after their marriage, and this spirit warned him that the tribe would perish to a man if he did not confine himself to a solitary hermitage in a mountain range some miles distant from the village, and if his wife did not, at the same time, take upon her the vows and restraints of a vestal. The village elders, feeling that the fates recently attendant on the dynasty lent much weight to this pronouncement, decreed that he should want for nothing in his retirement, and that a penalty of painful death should await whoever imperilled the village by disregarding the second of the supernatural edicts.

This obedience had brought a double prosperity upon the settlement. Blessed by the unique possession of an absentee and cheaply maintained head man, it grew peaceful and rich, and its tranquillity was singularly undisturbed by malicious manifestations on the part of those spirits which usually play the very devil with the peace of mind of the blacks. Indeed, save for one, which occasionally pursued young men on their way home from feasts or drinking bouts, the wood demons seemed entirely to have withdrawn. And among themselves the villagers lived in a state of goodwill, only corroded by the strong vain of shrewishness which had gradually developed in Loblulya.

That beauty, as she grew older, reflected the steatopygous ideal as if in the convex surface of a spoon. Less and less grew the danger of any hot-blooded young warrior incurring the death penalty by violating the taboo placed upon her charms. And less and less, by the way, grew the danger of the sole remaining wood demon's pursuit. It seemed slower of foot with every passing year, though those young men who were occasionally so fuddled as to be caught by it, testified that the horseplay to which it subjected its victims grew more irresistible, more violent and more protracted. No man it had once seized in its clutches was ever quite the same again. But for some time, now, it had caught no one.

Loblulya stood in the doorway of Mr. Fatigay's arbour, with her basket of oranges and plums. This, clutched against her mighty bosom, was dwarfed there to the likeness of a large and tasteless brooch.

When Loblulya laughed, it was like war in the village. When she was sombre, it was like witchcraft. But when she smiled, a powerful odour of musk filled the room.

Mr. Fatigay had stretched out his hand, courteously to examine the fruits she set down on his table. Loblulya advanced a pace, and took his hand in hers, and smiled. Emily, silent upon her perch, felt the hairs bristle upon her neck. Mr. Fatigay breathed deeply, then dizzily retreated a pace. Loblulya, with that gracefulness often noted in stout dancers, circumvented the table, and, still smiling, approached still nearer.

"What does this mean?" said Mr. Fatigay, whose wits now rallied to his sense of outrage.

"Om tsang bu t'long umbawa!" thickly replied the charmer, smiling still.

"Begone this moment," said Mr. Fatigay, "or I'll call for help."

"Insensible monster!" returned Loblulya (whose remarks are here translatable into English). "Ingrate, lost equally to the chivalry of a gentleman and to the sensations of a man! Beware! for no sooner shall you raise an outcry impious to my honour and menacing to my life, than, I assure you, I will do likewise, and visit that punishment upon your treachery, which, but for your vicious insensibility, you might by this time have deserved, but not received."

On hearing these words the chimp, paralysed, remained suspended, but Mr. Fatigay, with a meaning glance at his cigar, on which an inch of ash had developed undisturbed, opened his mouth to summon assistance.

But at that moment, the terrible Loblulya, who

had followed his eye, struck the Havana evidence from his hand, and, tearing the kerchief on her bosom, she soon towsled herself into an invidious disarray, while her shouts for assistance rang perjurously through the grove.

Within a minute or two, the sound of running feet was heard, and into the arbour burst three or four of the gigantic elders of the village.

Pale and trembling, Mr. Fatigay gasped for breath, looking the hard-breathed simulacrum of red-handed guilt, whose first stammering denials were drowned in the outcry of his twenty-stone accuser.

"Oh! the beast! the filthy beast!" she cried. "Scarcely had I set foot in this arbour when he offered me bribe, marriage and violence simultaneously in word and deed."

Not Judge Jefferies himself ever looked so blackly on the shrinking wretch in the dock, as did then the fanatical elders upon poor Mr. Fatigay, helpless, alone, remote from any possibility of aid.

Alone? No, not alone, for at that moment something stole up noiselessly behind him, and into his nerveless shaking hand was pressed, by a hairy one, his cigar.

It was hot in his hand. Looking down, he could scarcely believe his eyes. There, upon the end of it, was the full inch of ash which he himself had seen shattered, two minutes before, into a thousand pieces.

Enheartened, he drew himself up, and faced his accusers, collecting all his dignity into a frowning brow.

Imposing silence, demanding attention, with the forefinger of his left hand, he slowly raised his right, and displayed to the astonished elders the fine old testimony of the unbroken ash.

In the breathless moment during which the significance of this simple final proof dawned upon the blacks, the smoke of the Corona rose straight up towards the roof of the arbour.

Manly apologies followed, smiles and invitations were exchanged, and within a few minutes the elders had closed upon the gasping Loblulya and had borne her off, instantly to begin her execution. Mr. Fatigay was alone.

Alone ? Yes, alone, for, at that moment, Emily, who had crept out unnoticed after placing the cigar in his hand, was being violently sick in the obscurest corner of the garden. It was she, who, seeing the invaluable evidence destroyed, had with a present and inspired mind swooped down upon the cigar, and, taking it into a corner, had so vigorously inhaled its unaccustomed fumes, that by the time Loblulya had completed her tirade, the ash was reborn, blushing as ought the snows on Hecla.

"Oh, Emily! Emily!" murmured Mr. Fatigay, hastening to find his pet. "For this, you shall have a new collar with a gold medal, and your name on it."

CHAPTER III

Thou shalt hear the 'Never, never.'

NOTHING is more sudden than nightfall in the tropics. It resembles the swift transition, in a pantomime, between the fade-out of the principal boy, effulgent in his golden spot-light, on a last dying fall or expiring parrot scream, and the sudden appearance on the other side of the stage, in a silver ray, of the principal girl, with her chorus of fairies star-foreheaded.

On the edges of glades, under bushes white with nocturnal flowers, the long, towsled grass is torn and drenched with blood, black as a hole in appearances. The acetylene moonlight, like a local anæsthetic, freezes pain, and the gorilla, standing, staring at the reeking pieces of leopard still clutched in his iron hands, feels the white-hot scratches on his chest and thighs, equally with the sharp grief which from the meek hate-empty detachment of those dripping fragments bursts his puzzled heart, to be part of a problem remote cold and complete as some jig-saw mathematic.

Emily crouched, petrified, staring at certain phrases scrawled on a sheet of letter paper, gobbets of a mental organism, oozing and steaming with personality, the mind's blood, felt much the same.

This is what had happened.

Days of peace followed upon the nerve-shattering Loblulya episode; days steeped in that golden classic quality in which our summer arrests itself towards its final end, and with the same doomed illusion of eternity. Emily, in her brief periods of introspection, could not help feeling that her action had set a modest hall-mark on her development into something far removed from the naïve sylvan creature, dazzled by a first glimpse of civilisation, which she had been a few months before. And since, to her, knowledge and experience seemed the greatest addition by which a personality can be enriched, she would not have exchanged even the more melancholy strata of her deepened nature, not even that the rich deposit of suffering which caused her suffering still, for all the blind confiding delight of her tree-top childhood. For, rating its effects so highly, as she did all that conduced to enlargement, how could she but believe that its fruition in every glance and gesture must gain for her her protector's deeper regard ? She had yet to learn that it is not through suffering herself, for this conveys but a very bourgeois sort of distinction, but through being the cause of it in others, that a woman becomes fatal and fascinating to man. But who would grudge Emily this innocent, if ill-founded, optimism, in the light of the bitter experiences through which, like a tot of brandy, it was to be her only support.

Moreover, Mr. Fatigay himself exhibited certain marked changes of demeanour towards his humble admirer, and if these were slight in comparison to the construction she placed on them, yet let him who would laugh at this poor heart's simplicity beware, for to-morrow may find him running his errand in high fettle, and building up Heaven knows what fantastic castles in the air, all because his fine wife, with melting in her voice, and a rose in her cheek, and a note in her bosom, good humouredly speaks to him as Mr. Fatigay did to Emily, as if he were not a beast, that is, but a human being. Yet our hero was as honest and good hearted a fellow as any, and a very modest one too, so that he had no suspicion of the true state of Emily's feelings, and much less any intent to inflame them by the occasional terms of endearment which his affectionate nature proffered, in this solitude, to the nearest deserving object.

"Come, my dear! Come, my pretty!" he'd say, scooping her up on to his knee. "You and I are going to set off to England together very shortly."

And once he added, staring at the desolate wide forest that stretched away on every side: "Yes, by God, I've been a bachelor long enough!" And, biting his lips in a nervous frenzy, he crushed her thin arm in a painful grip. Overcome, she sank her head upon his shoulder.

Her new hopes gave her the happy feeling of a completeness she never before had known. Under their influence, her appearance improved vastly.

Her eyes seemed larger and more lustrous than of yore, her smiling face dimpled provocatively, the curves of her slight figure became a shade more rich and ripe.

Her crescent radiance was reflected in her surroundings. When, with her airy tread, she entered the squalid hut of some sick native, and, setting down her little basket of nourishing soup or cooling jelly, she proceeded to shake up the pillow and to lave the fevered brow, the stricken black (the motion of whose rolling eyes, relative to that of his rolling head, it would take four pages of mathematical symbols, or one line of poetry, to describe) would address her now as B'hlongba instead of, as hitherto, B'tongba. At the sound of that dear epithet she would lay her finger on her lips and shake her head at the speaker in smiling reproof, but she could not resist treasuring in her breast the thought that her new status was mirrored, as in a japanned coal scuttle, thus exaggeratedly in the simple sincerity of the blacks.

Mr. Fatigay provided, also, further iridescent materials for the dream palace which thus rose about his gentle pet, in that, now his return to England was decided upon, he began, for certain purposes of his own, to school her in graces of deportment, and in the manners and customs of civilised society. An easy carriage and an upright bearing were now imparted to the chimp, and instruction also in the proper method of entering a room, proffering cakes and tea cups, and making a curtsey. So meticulous was the schoolmaster in his training of her in this last respect, that poor Emily began to wonder if she was to be presented at Court, an idea which she would have laughingly dismissed as presumptuous to the point of absurdity, but for a sentence which she read at about that time, which said: "In England the Primate takes precedence of all but Royal Dukes."

The society paper in which these words appeared contained several photographs of personages prominent at Court, and these, combined with its axiom, frequently repeated in one form or another, that nothing was more to be envied than direct descent from an ancient stock, however barbarous, strongly supported the misinterpretation which the innocent creature, unacquainted with the hierarchy of the Church, placed upon the words. She saw herself as one of "this year's brides," and in order that she might be fitted to maintain her husband's dignity in such a position, she attended with her utmost concentration on his instruction.

Why did she not now reveal her talents to Mr. Fatigay? From this delicate motive: so that when he met her, barefooted as it were, at the altar, and there bestowed upon her apparent nothingness and poverty the right to clothe herself henceforth in his material and mental grandeur, she might then surprise and gratify him by revealing that she was not altogether so dowerless as he had supposed, since, though she came to him bare of gold and jewels and securities, she brought with her the treasure of a well-stocked mind, a possession which, all the books said, was infinitely to be preferred.

And as she sat rapt in the contemplation of that moment, she heard him say:

"Come, Emily, shoulders back, please. You mustn't sit all hunched up like that, you know. That would never do in the position you are going to hold in England."

And shortly after, he set the gramophone to work ("What'll I do ?" the song was) and, advancing towards her, he raised her by the hand, and motioned her to follow his movements in sinuous response to the music.

"What'll I do
When you
Are far
A-way,
And I
Feel bloo
What'll I do ?"

One, two, three. One, two, three.

The dolorous words floated off, winged with the poignant notes of the saxaphone, blue into the blue darkness about the verandah. From the trees on the slope below, the strain was echoed, more poignantly yet, in a succession of deep, not unmelodious howls.

"That," thought the chimp, pursing her lips, "must be Henry."

It was he, most persistent of the admirers of

her sylvan days, to whom she had given this name; he who haunted the foamy tree beneath her bedroom window.

The kindest of hearts, when happy in devotion to one being, may be inclined to rate a hopeless passion, bestowed on itself, as over shallow and too easily compensated. Modesty, forbidding too clear a realisation of one's power to arouse such a feeling, plays a great part in this, and a still greater perhaps is played by the desire to imagine the whole world as happy as oneself. Emily, prompted thus, took advantage of their next circuit of the dinner table, and, taking a banana from the dessert dish, she flung it in a graceful arc over the rails, with much the careless movement of a dancing film-actress disposing of her cigarette ash. For a moment the embittered harmony was stilled. Then, humming like an angry insect, the skin of the banana shot across the verandah, and crashed upon a pane in the window just behind their heads.

"Good God!" said Mr. Fatigay. "What was that? A bat?"

And the gramophone needle scratched and scraped fretfully as the melodious sorrow came to its end.

Emily stepped aside, as he hurried to lift it from the record, and, picking up the banana skin, she dropped it flatly over the balcony.

All in a moment a cloud had veiled the moon. Something lay chill at Emily's heart. Had she sinned against love, she wondered wistfully, in the slighting attempt to silence even its intrusive vehicles by the carelessly flung fruit? Though this had not altogether been rejected, something ugly had crept into the Eden of her inner life, and ugliness, where all else was tranquil beauty, was in itself foreboding.

Next day dawned hot and blue, and the passing mood was forgotten. After lunch Mr. Fatigay cried out for his horse, and, smiling at Emily, he said:

"I'm going to ride down to meet the mail boat. There may be a letter for me. You, Emily, must stay at home, as it is such a long way for the horse. I shall be back in time for dinner."

When he was out of sight, Emily turned from the window, and began to wonder how best she might employ her time till evening. Suddenly she smiled: an idea had come into her head. She would devote the long hours of waiting to the practice of a branch of her reading which hitherto had been sadly neglected: the deciphering of manuscript. This, she felt, would be of essential importance in the social life that lay before her.

Sauntering across to her protector's bureau, she opened the blotter which lay upon it, and took up some sheets of letter paper at which Mr. Fatigay had been busy all the morning. Frowning slightly, she peered hard at the crabbed writing. Frowning still more, she peered still harder.

At last the fatal words conveyed their message to her.

"My beloved darling Amy."

It was the draft of a love letter.

Aghast, the stricken chimp reeled back, one hand pressed to her brow. Her dream world lay in ruins about her feet, and, with the deathly faintness which now spread over her, it slowly began to revolve around, evoking a sensation not unlike (yet how unlike!) that procurable on the Joy Wheel at the Fun Fairs and Luna Parks of the carnal capitals of Europe.

"Good Heavens!" she tried to say, "What deceit! What treachery! God! What a fool! What a blind, trusting fool I've been!"

And she crushed the letter and dashed it to the ground (as if that could prevent it clinging to her heart like a fly paper!), and in one leap from where she stood she had sprung out and over the verandah, straight into the branches of a palm below, the near end of one of which she caught, which bore her on an inverse arc to the next tree, and so, like a small boat swinging out on the billows of an hurricane, dizzily on into the jungle.

Lovers' lane is said by some to be a winding lane, but the path of despised love is as straight as a Roman road. At the moment of disillusion, a red-hot coal smoulders where the heart has been, and the victim is impelled forward, heedless of obstacles, bearing with him, like a cow with a thorn under its tail, the very gall he runs so madly to escape. When poetry has fully civilised us, and brought us accidentally into that heaven where the true and the chosen vision are one, and pain and pleasure are no longer divided arbitrarily by superstition, as good and evil once were, we shall find, in this long urgent avidity for relief, a pleasure higher than that now associated with successful love, in that of all appetites this lasts longest, and endows us with an intenser life, or more reality, the while we attempt to satisfy it.

But Emily's torment was not shot, as it were, by this weft of superior consciousness; it was pure agony, white-hot, that she experienced as she described a bee line of many miles, which ended, not because the hell-spark in her heart was quenched, but because it had burnt out, temporarily, all the fuel which her cindered nerves had contained. These, like the filaments in a worn-out electric light bulb, could glow no more, so that the spark ceased to act as a motor, though it burned hot as ever, numbly isolated in her bosom, as she sank, fordone, beneath a mighty tree. From whose branches, some hours later in the night, peered down the dark and eager face of Henry, who had witnessed her rout, and followed, with lesser speed, in hope of advantaging his unrequited desires.

From an ashy sleep, the chimp awoke to see him drop like a vulture, hitting his mark, yet staggering where he landed.

How repellent they seem to us, when the bright Eden where dwells our loved one casts us forth, and we must return to them, those other ordinary people, acquaintance and kin, whose sottish good humour and tasteless tragedy seem drawn by some Dutch realist, after the crisp exaltation of the Hellenic illusion we have lost! Shall we bow our spirits into profane forgetfulness, and turn in with them, pouring their tallowy kindness into our wounds, bemusing sorrow in the treacley vintage of their mirth and their passions?

> *I*, in short, *to herd with narrow foreheads, vacant of our glorious gains,*
> *Like a beast with lower pleasures, like a beast with lower pains!*

This was what Emily thought, as her persistent admirer shambled towards her, holding out both his hands, in clownish imitation of the truly biped life of which she had tasted. Yet—he loved her. To love, and to be loved; these, the hemispheres of happiness, how rarely they coincide! Would it not be better, she thought, better for all concerned, to let them follow one upon the other, as some take whisky and then water, and to complete her experience lopsidedly thus, since it was fated never to be a perfect whole?

He loved her. And let happiness curl its cruel lip as it may, those who have loved in vain will know, only too well, that when love has consumed mind, tastes, standards, character itself, till the victim has become only a void in which that desire functions abstractly, then the elements of choice are gone also, and whose hunger has been raised by one particular dish of all in the world, will, if he starves long enough, be satisfied with any. "And that," thought the poor chimp, "without forgetting the least aspect of the truly beloved object, but rather trying, in the final despair of constancy, to inform the husks to which one turns with something of its image, as the families of wild Irish do, who cram their bellies with earthy spuds and fix their eyes on a herring slung out of reach above the table.

I have been faithful to thee, Cynara! in my fashion.

But, as the serpentine quotation writhed in the blasted Eden of her mind, she remembered that the poem had a Latin title, and, whether it was a womanly suspicion of words she could not understand, or whether it was wisdom of that deep kind which circumambulates the guileless, she had a profound distrust of all poems with Latin titles, and this straw, wedging across the gutter, stayed, not her drowning, but the torrent in which she was submerged. She raised her eyes, and gazed indecisively, inquiringly, not untenderly, on the supplicating visage of Henry, who had halted, as halts a tom cat, some feet from where she was crouching. Something in his tortured eyes, something that might have been a spark of her own misery, gave her further pause.

Was it fair to him?

This is a question which takes so long in answering, generally, that the majority of her sex take their conscience's sullen dumbness for assent, but Emily was of different fibre.

Of his misery, wanting her, she could not doubt, for, save for her pestered impulsiveness in the matter of the banana, she was incapable of dismissing lightly any sincere feeling on the part of another, however disproportionate it seemed to its cause. Poor Henry! At that moment it seemed that the only thing left for her to do was to make him happy. Yet how?

For not all the craving of her torn and aching heart for something to hold close and snuggle up to could betray her into the sophistry that she would bestow happiness in bestowing an affection which, like a caged lion, must ceaselessly pace up and down, or sit staring into nothingness, heedless and unresponsive in its obvious longing for its ever-distant ever-present home. That would be worse than sending him away. Was there no solution?

There was. Behind the suppliant swain the tall grasses waved, were parting. Looking over his head she caught a glimpse of a sinewy spotted back, cautiously drawing nearer.

Perhaps it was all for the best. Holding her breath, she held also Henry's attention with her eyes. Time slowed up, as when a clock gaspingly gathers up its powers to strike.

Then, all simultaneously, in one flash, in one scream, in one leap, the leopard was upon poor Henry, and Emily, as if she had been sitting on the other end of a see-saw, was shooting towards and clinging to the bough above her, and ere the long scream had, like a withering fountain, sunk to a gurgle, she was swinging madly on, as if to leave love and death and warm life forever behind her.

Let her go as far, though, and as fast as she may, her blind and mind-shut rush is foredoomed to a limit, as that of a rocket is, which, urged by a similar fire, must, unless it flies clear of the earth's field of gravitation, fall back in exhausted fragments, with a plump exactly proportionate to the momentum of its break-away.

Mr. Fatigay, we know, was all the world to Emily, and a world of which the gravitational attraction was so far-reaching that there was no practical possibility of her ever flying clear of it. It was hopeless for her to try to escape from jealousy by "going native," for the moment inevitably arrived when, like the dog in Tennyson, she *rose*, *twofooted at the limit of her chain*, *roaring to make a third*.

This occurred some days later, when she had travelled exactly a thousand miles, by the way, and, running out along a broad bough, she stopped as suddenly as if she had been pierced by an arrow.

She stood, staring into vacancy, seeing, as if it was flashed upon a cinematograph screen before her, a vision of herself and Mr. Fatigay walking slowly home from the schoolhouse, through the long and treacley beams of the evening sun. It's very strange, how at the moment that one's blind flight stops, it is generally no really important aspect of the dear one that abruptly arrests us, opening up like a firework in the blank behind the fixed neuralgic business-like mask we have put on, but some detail of the background, seeming to have slipped past the censor by virtue of its obvious unimportance, that brings home to us, and us home, to the dearness we have lost.

Emily visualised Mr. Fatigay's mildly sloping shoulders just before her, and her closed heart opened in such a quick ecstasy that it seemed that if she could only see just that much just once in reality, it would be enough. We do not ask at such moments—"enough for what ?"

But, turning with the shaking eagerness of the long-starved, we run helter-skelter back again, and, as we stumble blubbering into the presence we have hungered for, we scarcely notice at first if it is warm or cold, any more than a famished man does when his porridge is put before him.

So Emily stood motionless, for a moment or an hour, staring before her, with one hand on her heart, which ached now like a cramped limb to which the blood returns, and then she made one slow step back, and then another, and a few doubtful paces, till suddenly she broke into a run and soon was swinging back along the airy forest road as quickly as she had come. And, in effect, as blindly, for the thawed stream in eager spate is as far from clear as it was when set blackly in the cruellest frost.

What thoughts she had, as she toiled in sobbing haste up the long tangled slopes; or stared from their crests as if, ere she had gone a tenth of the way, she hoped to see her goal; or plunged madly down from tree-top to tree-top on their farther sides, were hardly thoughts, but rather the beams and timbers of the dam she had built up against emotion, and these, now that the torrent had broken through, reversed their purpose, and, if anything, hurried her faster down the swirling race. She longed to feel again, to *know*, the very wound against which she had clenched her mind ; it was, even in the very killing of her, life, and, compared with it, all that she could fly to was desert and dead beyond bearing. Besides (and here she took wider leaps) there might be some unimaginable misunderstanding. Perhaps he was writing a novel.

At last the last mile was traversed, and, looking out from the hateful forest, she saw before her the clearing of Boboma, yellow in the afternoon. She paused. It was so much the same, and so unconscious of her, that it seemed as if she was in another world. She almost expected to see her own shape emerge from the schoolhouse. Her lips trembled, and a great booby tear rolled down her face.

As she watched, feeling empty and impotent as a ghost, the singing ceased in the schoolhouse nearby, and the children began to come out, racing and screaming as if no chimp had ever existed. Emily stared at the door, her blood standing still in her veins. Ten minutes crept by like a glacier. Suddenly the well-known figure appeared, and, see! he looks anxiously up and down as if in hope to see the absent one. Emily's eyes, which had yearned so for the sight of him, were blinded with happy tears. Springing to the ground, she totteringly hurried towards him.

"Emily! Emily! Where *have* you been?"

CHAPTER IV

Thus vent thy thoughts;
Abroad I'll studie thee,

A POISON cup, if one is sufficiently thirsty, will yield a momentarily invigorating draught, and at the first renewal of the life-giving contact, Emily was deliriously, thoughtlessly, happy. It was not long, though, before thoughts of the future began to gnaw at her.

At first she tried to postpone dealing with them, but as they became more insistent, she realised that the situation must be carefully weighed up, and a course of action chosen which would be neither a cowardly abandonment of her struggle, nor, on the other hand, an idealistic attempt at a self-sacrifice high-pitched beyond the ability of her flesh and blood to maintain.

For if there was one thing which even this scarcely tutored chimp had a contempt for, more than any other, it was the type of woman who, having made up her mind to sink differences and accept disadvantages in living in the presence of her beloved, sets out at the first check to infect him with her own discontent, as if she was one of those burnt envenomed lechers Donne refers to, who hope to become sound by giving others their sores.

"Never," said she to herself, "shall his tender heart be tortured by the consciousness of a passion which it is not in his power to return, nor his blithe spirit be oppressed by sullen mood or hysterical outburst of mind. But can I achieve the necessary restraint if I remain beside him? Can I bear to go away?"

"I can see no light whatever on the first question," she continued, "but that is the greater reason, not the less, for preventing the unhesitating 'no' with which all my being responds to the second, from influencing my decision. What, now, would be my chief trials in the Tantalus life to which my instinct, but not yet my reason, inclines me?"

The first and greatest would be, she decided, the future Mrs. Fatigay. At the thought of her, the chimp raised her hands to her cold damp forehead, and feeling there the garland of scarlet blossoms with which her rejoicing master had laughingly crowned her, she bitterly tore it away, and rent its gaudy beauty to nothingness, as an image of her rival flashed upon that inner eye which is said to be the bliss of solitude. Calming herself at length, she began to realise how important it was that she should at once obtain some definite idea of this woman's personality. But how?

From the letter of Mr. Fatigay's which she had read, it had been apparent that he regarded his inamorata, not as a woman, but as an angel. Emily felt, though, that she could not accept this figure, much as she would like to, as literally correct, and for all she knew it might be the very wildest hyperbole. And then: "What a fool I am!" she thought. "That letter must have been part of a long correspondence, and, beyond any question, he has treasured up all that he has received from her."

Brushing aside conventional inhibitions with a weary smile, Emily descended to Mr. Fatigay's bureau, and finding at the back of one of the drawers a packet of letters carefully secured by an elastic band, she withdrew with these into a private nook, intent on learning all she could from their contents before her master returned from school.

Compressing her lips, the dreary-hearted chimp drew the first missive from its envelope. The letters were neither many nor long, but she read with such concentration that Mr. Fatigay was already approaching his home before she had replaced the last.

She descended to greet him, and both then and while she sat opposite him at tea, there was a something, not of contempt, but of that which we express by "Well! Well! Well!" in her curious regard. For it was now very clear to Emily that the woman whom he had addressed with such passionate adoration had very little sincere feeling to offer in return, and not even enough respect for him or his love to prevent her from parading her indifference with all the needless cruelty common to people of a certain type when they find themselves in possession of the whip hand. So that Emily could not understand, and stared at him as if to read the riddle in his face, now partially eclipsed by a tea cup, how this man, kind, wise and just as she knew him fundamentally to be, could have poured out his heart in slavish devotion to one who wrote, without affection, without respect, without a decent hypocrisy even:

My darling Alfred,

It's lovely to take out your letters, and read them over before answering them, as I do now. It's like going into a quiet dell, away from all the wild glitter and stress that one's restless mind urges one into. I wish, for your sake, I could be simple and wholehearted like you, instead of suffering this tearing hunger to do and do and do—oh, a million things! This month, and last, have been full of people and things—new ideas that seem to remake the world for me, and, side by side with them—the craziest fun you can possibly imagine. Its been so crazy that I daren't describe it to you, as I should feel even in writing it down that you would never understand, and I should see your "schoolmaster" look come between me and the paper.

That's why I missed writing rather longer than I ought, but you mustn't write reproachful things about it, for it makes me feel all hard inside when you do, and then I feel that I *can't* write. It makes me feel as if I wanted to do something you didn't like—flirt or something equally meaningless and mad—out of sheer cussedness. It *is* meaningless—truly.

I feel the same sometimes when you are extra possessive in your letters—stressing the "my own" element—you remember our talk about it before you went away. Don't do it, sweetheart. I can't help being a wincing jade whom the first hint of a fetter makes keen on nothing but bolting. It makes me feel, too, that you've forgotten all you promised then about my personal development—or didn't mean it, perhaps ? ? ? I just can't be anybody's in the way you mean. So that's that.

Don't misunderstand this, dear, or think, as you hint not very kindly in your last two letters, that I am reluctant to keep my promise. I only suggested that you should sign up for the extra two years because it's so clear it would give us a firmer foundation to begin on, and give me time to accustom myself to the idea of being tied up. But having given my word, I should certainly keep it, if you insisted. I haven't time to go into all the pros and cons now, as it's a Ballet night, but I'll write you a long letter about it by the next mail.

I think also, dear, that you are being a little selfish about not getting married in a church.

It's not fair to say I don't respect your ideas—I do—but I have to think of mother's feelings as well. But, after all, such details are still very far off.

Well, good-bye now, dearest. Don't frown. I think of you always. I enjoy your letters so much, more than I can possibly say. I love them. This is a short, poor letter, but I'll write again soon. Forgive your mad bad sad girl.

All my love, darling,

AMY.

Now she knew why he had so often stopped short while they were walking together, particularly, she recollected in days following the mail boat's arrival, and had fetched a great sigh, looking distractedly about him, or had ground his teeth like a bound man who has been struck a blow in the face. Probably it was the bitter sense of humiliation engendered by the coarsely flaunted indifference in such phrases, that had prevented him from including some account of his love in the long discourses on his work and ambition which he had so often drifted into as they sat on the verandah. Knowing him as she did, she could guess how cruelly such treatment must have eaten into his warm heart and his proud spirit.

For, save for the glibly extravagant endearments at the beginning and the end, each of the letters had for its core the insistence that the writer was accepting Mr. Fatigay, partly to satisfy most economically an emotion she despised and distrusted, and partly because his devotion rendered him the most tractable partner she was likely to get.

"In these letters," thought Emily, "the mean is hardly the product of the two extremes, as it is, when, in love as in arithmetic, so-and-so is to so-in-so as so-in-so is to so-in-so."

This revelation, while it made her painful choice the heavier, left it still undecided, for how, more than ever, could she bear life with Mr. Fatigay when he was married to this woman, and see him, not merely loving another, but being tortured and debased? And how, more than ever, could she leave him now, and know him, not only lost to her, but lost to happiness and to himself?

"How can he? How *can* he?" groaned the unhappy creature, feeling her heart grow hot within her, while she dashed the scalding tears from her eyes with the knuckles of her clenched hand: "How *can* he crawl thus on his knees to his own destruction, crushing in his blind eagerness the heart that loves him so unutterably. So unutterably: that's the curse of it, for, if I could but speak, would I not set maidenly modesty aside, and, taking him frankly by the hand, represent to him the waste, the folly and the pity of it all? Then, perhaps, though it would be but an outside chance (fifty to one? twenty to one? thirty-three to one?), he might awake suddenly, and, dashing the poisoned sweetmeat to the ground, turn breathless towards me, with "Emily, my good angel! My twice preserver! My consolation! My love!"

And, intoxicated by the picture she had conjured up, she fell to wondering if only she might effect this by a combination of eloquent signs, and of thrusting the paltry letters before him, and of putting out of books open at telling and relevant passages.

Is it well to wish thee happy?—having known me—to decline
On a range of lower feelings and a narrower heart than mine!

This might do as a revelatory conclusion, bringing about the crescendo of exclamations which now pealed like wedding bells on her inner ear.

But then, shaking her head at herself in sad admonition, she dismissed the wild plan from her mind. This was not, it is to be understood, from any tardy revival of old-fashioned conventionalism. Emily considered herself to be as modern, in the worthier sense, as any of her sex, and though she deprecated the way in which many of her contemporaries appeared to fling away all regard for graciousness and responsibility, and even for the true development of their lives, in order to loot and ravage a few masculine privileges, she was capable, as in the case of Loblulya and of her sane benevolence towards Henry, of acting with complete decisiveness and freedom whenever she felt it to be genuinely necessary. It was the harder achievement of applying cold reason to her day-dream that now restrained her.

"How could any clumsy interposition of mine turn aside such a love as his?" she thought. "Is love less strong in its defence, or more so, when it is bestowed on the unworthy? And even if I could convince him that chivalry does not bind him there whence reason calls him insistently away, and could bring him to obey that call: what hope have I that he would forthwith turn to me? Did the black on whom he once so unflinchingly operated, without anæsthetics, endeavour to kiss the steel which sawed at his gangrened limb? No! He would certainly spurn me as a self-seeking malicious intriguer, none the less cruel in act because I protested that it was for the best. If he turned at all to another love it would almost certainly be some coal-black mamma, or mammas, he would take to his bosom." Here she shuddered.

"It is more likely, of course," she proceeded, "that he would become a recluse, a hermit, and bury himself here in Boboma with his shattered ideal forever beside him, and that . . . yes! yes! that would be even worse. I would a hundred, nay, a thousand times rather that he found solace in some association which, however degraded, was at least healthy and natural, than that he should thus gratify the vilest and most selfish motive that has ever stirred in my breast." And she curled her lip as she crushed for ever the scarceborn wish to spoil for others what she could not have herself, unaware in her innocence that just there, perhaps, lay her closest point of similitude to the human female.

Who treads down an ill motive is generally elevated in the very act to a tall strong generosity, which may bring him too recklessly to engage himself in the opposite direction. Emily had spurned the selfish thought almost before she had properly conceived it, but the bare reminder of such mental processes summoned up all the noble forces of her nature, and she now faced the prospect of a life-long battle with herself with something of the bellicose confidence of a nation during a period of military manœuvres. And as if her own weaknesses were an insufficient foe, she bristled more and more eagerly to defend her beloved against those of his future wife.

"Let the future bring what it may," she thought, standing very erect and earnest in the middle of her little white room, "my place is beside Mr. Fatigay, and who knows but that even he may come to be grateful to the humble chimp, when the dawning sense of her love and constancy shines as the only light on the dark path he seems fated to tread."

And, going down to his study, she took from the shelf a pocket encyclopædia, and soon was deeply immersed in an account of the divorce laws of England, which she read, not from vain hopes of its future practical utility, but for its prose, which struck her, in its stark and Puritanical terseness, as being far superior to the more exotic phrasing of the marriage service.

CHAPTER V

Behold! behold, the palace of his pride!
God Neptune's palaces!

Not long after this there was a great bustle in the schoolmaster's pleasant house. Bags were dragged out and packed, live-stock and garden appurtenances disposed of, crates filled with curios and souvenirs. Blacks thronged the garden path and sat all day upon the steps. Every time Mr. Fatigay appeared at a window he was cheered to the echo; every time he appeared at the door he was swamped by clustering natives, thick as flies on a roadside fragment, who first loudly, and I believe sincerely, implored him not to go, and then, on his smiling persistence, pressed upon him yams and what not.

"Here," they cried, piling these up into his arms, "let us exchange mementos."

And off they went, calling out his praises; one carrying a pair of old shoes, another a collection of used razor blades, yet another a rain-spoiled pith helmet, and a fourth that fine piece of earthenware which had stood beneath his washstand. They gave him all their old rubbish and he gave them his, and everyone was content.

The school children marched up with flags and music, and performed a masque in his honour on the lawn. In this, the seven deadly sins were mimed with such energy that the pair who enacted Anger were carried gasping to the infirmary, Gluttony was sick on the spot, and when it came to the seventh Mr. Fatigay was obliged to step down and marry the actors before they had completely finished with their parts.

This interposition, however, in no way marred the effect of the whole, in which it had been arranged for an impersonation of himself to appear and to redress the assembled vices, transmuting them by his mere presence into the corresponding virtues. And, as they thought he was honouring them by taking up his own part in their play, nor did it bear ill-fruit afterwards in tying together two adolescents who were yet too young for the cares of domesticity.

"Good-bye!" they cried at the end. "Bless our dear teacher. Hurrah! No more school! Hurrah! Character rather than Intelligence! Hurrah!"

"Good-bye, dear friend," said the headman of Boboma, who, shortly after the execution of Loblulya, had been told by the spirit that he must return to the village.

"Good-bye," replied Mr. Fatigay, "I suppose you don't want to get married again before I go?" For he would have liked to see the whole world married.

"No, thank you," said the head man. " After

my last dear wife . . . I shall never marry again. *Mais*," he continued, unconsciously quoting George II, for he had worked in his youth in the French Congo, "*j'aurai des maitresses.*"

"Good-bye," cried all the servants, their faces so wet and smiling that one instinctively looked for coal-tar rainbows there. Not only the good and faithful ones, but the idlers, thieves and wastrels among them, even Topsy, the fat cook, found now that they loved Mr. Fatigay and wished he would not go.

"Good-bye," said an old tin can, from which, Emily remembered, as she caught sight of it lying forlorn upon a dung-hill, she and Mr. Fatigay had had some delicious pineapple for her name-day tea.

"Good-bye," murmured Emily's heart to it. "And good-bye,village. Good-bye, Arcady. Good-bye, summer. Good-bye. Good-bye."

And the jungle opened up its track, parting like the waters of the Red Sea as they rode away. Mr. Fatigay's ardent heart went on before them, in alternate cloud and fire, on this journey through what wilderness he knew not, to a Canaan other than that of which he dreamed.

Half a day's journey away, lay the rotten little pier head, blistering in the mud, where once a month a tiny hiccuping river launch put in an appearance. Sitting on the shakey planks, surrounded by either twenty-five or twenty-seven packages, they stared into the grey heat-haze where the river curved, and the leaden trunks and streamers of the trees, prolonged by reflection in the shining slime, muddled the distance as if by a frowsy bead curtain. Space and time hung about the place like grey shoddy garments, infinitely too large for man and his shrunken activities here.

After a long wait, a mean and weakly chug chug was heard, and the dirty launch had suddenly appeared to mark where the trees were after all divided. Emily stood up in her skimpy cotton frock and watched its approach with fluttering heart. This then was the steamship, a major factor in Tennyson's dictum, *Better fifty years of Europe than a cycle of Cathay*. She was glad she was not going to Cathay.

Its poor appearance, however, did not damp her excitement, for the splendours of the civilisation she was now going to visit had been too strongly impressed upon her in her reading to be negatived by the shortcomings of a little African mailboat. Nor were they entirely cancelled by the prospect of a life of unsatisfied emotion, which was all she had to look forward to.

"For," said the sensible little creature, "mind is still mind, whatever may befall the heart; perhaps the more so. I will visit Madame Tussaud's and the Tower of London, and become as well-informed as any of my sex, if not as happy. I will drain each new experience to its dregs, as far as is consistent with proportioned and virtuous conduct, and, since my life is to be a tragedy, I will see to it that it does not descend into mawkishness through a deficiency of intellectual content."

And, reminding herself that this was her first journey by water, and the beginning of a new life, she looked keenly about her as she tripped up the gangway.

"I hope," she thought fervently, "that I shall not be sick."

Soon the packages were all stowed away on board, and the captain, in accents which boredom rendered as flat and colourless as the mudbanks among which he sailed, declared that all was serene. Ropes were unhitched, the engine strove and stank once more, and they were off. If Mr. Fatigay had been less absorbed in his own thoughts at the moment, he might have noticed that the tall fringes of the jungle were festooned with the innumerable dark faces, like gigantic plums, of a host of chimpanzees, mostly Toms, who had come to look their last on this Helen of the jungle. Darkest Africa would be the darker for her going: this she could not doubt, who saw it written so unmistakably in those crowded mournful faces, so simple and sincere.

Day after day the little boat ticked its way through the uneasy stupor of the Congo, under high bluffs where vultures sat, soaked in metallic light, on the gallowsy branches of dead trees; over shallow places where reeds, swarming with filthy larvæ, poked up from the mud like mangey hair; past sand-banks hideously alive with the scuttling panic of crocodiles; past squalid settlements where nothing stirred but a scream, or, worse still, a laugh, and on down to where the great estuary began, and the port sweltered behind the roll of hot flashing breakers at the ocean bar.

The boat on to which they were to exchange for the sea voyage was due to sail on the day of their tardy arrival, so that Emily, who had been looking forward to her first sight of a town of size, had to content herself with an inspection of the quays, and with but a distant glimpse of white buildings and tin-roofed shacks dancing in the quivering air. Her disappointment, though, was soon forgotten at the sight of the crowded ship, and at the thought that now she might come into contact, more or less as an equal, with the sort of people among whom she was to live.

It was, as she afterwards discovered, through the generous consideration of her master, that she was not disappointed of this pleasure also, and forced to spend the three weeks of the voyage penned in a narrow cage between decks, in disgusting proximity to crates of serpents and the reeking young of the greater cats.

Mr. Fatigay could not endure the thought of his sensitive pet languishing in such hateful confinement, and his desire for her presence beside him, no less than his fears for her health, had prompted him to apply to the Company for a special ticket, that she might share his stateroom on the voyage. To this they had agreed, providing that she was to be suitably attired, and that he would take all responsibility for her behaviour, and that the full passenger's fare should be paid. As to her good conduct, he had no doubts at all, for she had proved so apt a pupil in even the subtlest points of the etiquette in which he had instructed her; besides, he knew that a sweeter-natured creature had never drawn breath, than Emily. The fare had been a serious consideration, for his savings amounted to no great figure, and he had an instinct that Miss Amy Flint, his bride to be, would be ill-content at any rash expenditure on his part. But here, he felt, Amy would agree that he was justified. As for dress, it had been a simple matter to purchase a plain cotton frock and a shady, if unmodish, sun-bonnet from the village store.

Emily was pleasedly conscious of her outfit as, holding tightly to his strong hand, she accompanied him through the bustle and life of the promenade deck in search of their cabin. She wondered what all these tall bronzed men and elegantly costumed women would say to one another about her, and she thought it possible that the simplicity of her dress, and the modest way in which she bent her head as she passed among them, might commend her to their good graces as one who was not inclined to presume nor to give herself airs because her talents had raised her to a milieu so widely different from the condition into which she had been born.

"Who can that dumpy little brown creature

be?" was what they actually were saying. "The one going along with that shabby fellow there. One of these women anthropologists, I suppose."

And as such they accepted her, taking the silent nods and smiles with which she acknowledged their formal good mornings as resulting from the shyness and reserve of the dowdy student, until a day or two later, when Mr. Fatigay, on being asked if his wife was not a great traveller, since she stood the sea so well, replied in surprise:

"My wife? Excuse me, but I have no wife. At least, not yet. . . ."

"Then who, pray," demanded his interrogator, for, being the wife of a Cape magistrate, she considered herself responsible for the morals of all who met her, and not responsible for those of the lost legion who did not, "who, pray, is that lady in the sun-bonnet over there, who, I am told, shares your stateroom, sir, where, for some reason, she always takes her meals?"

"Oh!" said Mr. Fatigay. "That! That's not a lady: that's Emily."

Then suddenly aware of his interlocutor's puffed and purpled visage, he made haste to add, "That is to say, she's not what you might call a woman at all. She's my pet chimpanzee."

"Oh, really!" cried the lady, the storm which had been gathering on her brow now melting into an expression of astonishment and interest. "Really! In that sun-bonnet, and the way she walks, everyone has taken it for granted she was your wife. How extraordinary! Please call her over here, I must have a good look at her. Steward! Some nuts."

And Emily was summoned to make her curtsey before this proud wife, and to listen to the bland and patronising comments made upon her appearance and manners.

At once the news spread like wildfire round the promenade deck. Cries of "Good heavens!" and "Oh, momma, ain't she cute! Won't you buy her for me, momma?" were heard on every side, and soon the embarrassed chimp stood nervously in the middle of a ring of grinning faces.

It says much for her native good humour, and for the training she had received from her protector, that she lost neither her temper nor her outward self-possession, but making a stately inclination or two in acknowledgment of the attention bestowed on her, she gently pressed her way through the crowd and sought the quiet sanctuary of the stateroom.

"You must not mind her shyness," explained Mr. Fatigay courteously. "She is very unused to the society of a large circle of white people."

"Bring her out. Go on, man! Bring her out," shouted the young subalterns and planters, going home on leave. "Will she smoke a cigarette?"

For the two or three days following this Emily's life was little better than a torment, for no sooner did she venture on deck to take a breath of fresh air than she was surrounded by an inquisitive crowd, to whom the least and most ordinary of her actions was a source of loud amazement. When, in the hope of turning aside their derision, and even of enlisting the friendship of two or three of them, who appeared more intelligent than the rest, she ventured to nod approval of some remark they made, or handed them, for example, the Conrad she had secured for herself, with one finger marking a fine descriptive passage, while with the other hand she indicated the appropriate sea around them, they would merely burst out into crueller laughter than before.

"Ah!" thought the chimp, "though it is bad enough to be mocked on account of unfashionable clothes and perhaps superfluous hair, these are, after all, admittedly defects. But why should they laugh at me for my understanding? Perhaps they think it ridiculous for one of my sex to aspire to culture. It would be different if I were a tom."

With this, she drew into her shell a little, and as there was little entertainment in the sight of even a chimp sitting hour after hour staring at a book, the fickle interest of the voyagers soon slackened and was diverted. A seaman was discovered to be a woman masquerading in man's clothes, and a stewardess to be a man in woman's. A fancy-dress ball was promptly organised, and in the general excitement the chimp soon ceased to be an object of remark.

"We must go to the ball," said Mr. Fatigay, and Emily's heart bounded with joy. After all, she was young and spirited, nor could she, any more than the rest of her sex, resist the peculiar thrill of the prospect of appearing in the most bewitchingly suitable costume, and among an admiring crowd.

"Perhaps I might go as Carmen," she thought, "if only I could beg a Spanish shawl from someone, and a red rose to hold in my lips." And she looked anxiously to where Mr. Fatigay was eating a dish of Irish stew, to see if there were any bones in it which might serve as castanets.

"*To-re-a-dor!*" The quickening strains stirred in her mind, making her blood tingle as if they had been struck up to hail her entrance into the ballroom.

"The question is," said Mr. Fatigay, "what shall one go as?"

"Or perhaps Elaine, the lily maid of Astolat." True, it was, strictly speaking, a part for a blonde, but after all, there were tiger-lilies. And a white sheet, pinned here and there, would do for the basic part of the costume. "And I might carry his rowing shield," she thought, "and be polishing it! In a way it wouldn't suit me as well as Carmen, but supposing he realised that he is my Sir Lancelot, and *she* his hard exacting Guinevere!"

"Of course, I make a very good pirate," murmured her protector.

"Or supposing I went as Ruth," she thought, "dipping my morsel in the vinegar. A smile or two, bestowed generally, would reassure the company that no slight was intended. . . ."

"By Jove! I've got it," suddenly cried Mr. Fatigay, slapping his thigh with a crack like a pistol shot. "Where's that green velvet smoking-jacket mother sent me? It'll be just the thing. I'll go as an organ-grinder, and I'll get the stewardess to run up a little suit for Emily, out of some red stuff, and she can be the monkey. Perhaps we'll get the prize."

Emily gazed at him in consternation. Her first fancy-dress ball! Why should he demean himself by appearing as a paltry mountebank, and how *could* he force her to appear in the most humiliating of all possible rôles? A hot tide of anger and rebellion surged up in her heart, and she, even Emily, raised her foot to stamp in ungovernable rage.

Yet even in the very act she hesitated, and, struck by a new thought, she remained in that stork-like posture, while she considered the matter more seriously.

"After all," she said to herself, "Mr. Fatigay is a man, and no doubt he knows best. To me this evening's gaiety seems highly charged with glamour and romance, but it is clear that to him, since he elects to behave farcically, it must be a matter of very little importance. His serious attention is, of course, reserved for higher things than this, and though his good breeding forbids him to remain insolently aloof from the company, he saves his dignity by joining them only in a jesting way.

"Or, perhaps," she continued, bringing her right foot gently to the ground, "it is possible that he considers the Comic muse to be as worthy of reverence as any other, and all the worthier, perhaps, in this degenerate age, when romance is bedecked in the tinsel of Wardour Street, and sentiment is become the pandar to every weakly sensual instinct. Then, when all caricature is good, self-caricature is best and most salutary, for our vanities may survive being mocked as ours, but to see another mocking them in himself must leave us in no doubt as to either his sincerity or his knowledge of the subject. Well, if I am to be a jest, I'll see to it that I am a hearty one. I'll dance the can-can. *Ride Pagliacci!*" and she promptly obeyed Mr. Fatigay's eager beckoning, as he set off to gain audience with the stewardess.

That night the lights of the *Stella Mundi* shone bright on its first-class nordic chivalry, on brave women and fair men. They all looked very vulgar.

In the silence which followed the second dance, a trivial and wispy tune tinkled outside, and the door flew open, revealing the broad shallow steps of the companion way, and standing on them was Mr. Fatigay, cold-coloured in the outside starlight, which was very blue, and he was wearing the velvet smoking-jacket, and a pair of tight trousers, and a little hat. Before him hung a child's hurdy-gurdy, and as it dropped reluctantly each strained unearthly note, the tune being the *Barcarolle*, Emily, from where she crouched at his feet, arose in her scarlet jacket and trousers, and, shrinkingly brazen, kissed her hands to the company, and began to execute the postures of her dance.

"Oh! how beautiful it is," she thought, as she skipped with exaggerated skimpy care from one extravagant attitude to another, "that this jot of quintessential humour, expressed in an almost meaningless abstraction, should be capable of entering differently every different mental structure that beholds it, and, like a radium needle, can disintegrate each cancerous collection of experiences into pure laughter and virgin chaos."

"One will think of his career," thought she, revolving, with an appearance of painful conscientiousness, upon one leg, "and another perhaps of his love or of his god. Laughter and new beauty must fuse together in the only aqua regis which may dissolve these golden illusions." And, bending down, she turned a couple of somersaults very gravely and precisely.

And as she solemnly high-kicked there between the rottenly phospherescent seas without and the rottenly shining faces of her audience within, she exulted in her conception of a renascent humour, remote from the funny as Picasso is from Louis Wain.

"Bless my dear Mr. Fatigay," she murmured, painfully attempting the splits, "for thus weaning me from my cheap and inartistic romanticism.

Garbed according to my original ideas, I could have at best been reflected, albeit glowingly, in the shoddy consciousness of my beholders, but now I am breaking up that consciousness, and shedding a clear and bitter light on the dark deeps below. How they will love me!"

But at that moment a couple of sharp raps were heard, and a volcano of treacle buried all subtleties under the strains of *Maggie! Yes Ma! Come right upstairs.*

"Look here, old man," said a subaltern, approaching the suddenly arrested work of art in the doorway, "are you coming in or staying out ? "

Like broken instruments of music the disconcerted pair stumbled in. Not a hand! The dancers shot forward, marked time, and shot back again as hydrometer insects do on the surface film of water. Each pair of eyes was fastened, as if by some quickly grown fleshy tentacle, to the pair opposite, and not so much as even a casual glance was bestowed on the discomfited performers.

An interval followed, and then another dance, then another and another, and still no response was accorded by the feminine element to any of Mr. Fatigay's shy smiles, nor did Emily hear, as still she half hoped to, any manly bass voice at her elbow, murmuring excuses to her partner, and entreating of her the favour of a dance.

Indignation now began to mount the chimp's bosom, less on her own account than because of the effect, becoming increasingly marked in her master's dejected bearing, that their cold reception and this almost pointed neglect was having upon him. It seemed as if he was beginning to feel himself a failure.

All at once an idea came into her head. Unostentatiously she slipped from his side, and quietly left the great saloon. In a few moments she had gained the upper deck, whence she clambered perilously down a stanchion till she could gain footing in the porthole which lit the stateroom of an American heiress. She leapt noiselessly to the floor, and peeping behind the curtain of a hanging cupboard, she drew forth the object of her search, a magnificent scarlet shawl which she had once noticed that lady to be wearing.

In this she hurriedly draped herself, and, taking from the dressing table a pair of large jade earrings, she screwed these on, and hastened from the room in search of a rose and a low-crowned black hat.

In the saloon the heat had grown intense, and the dancers halted more and more frequently for refreshments. Stewards glided easily among the flashing throng, bearing claret cup, Cydrax and iced lemonade. Champagne was to be purchased at a sufficient price. Bright eyes now shone with an extra brightness; the hot blood bloomed in every cheek. Masculine murmurs, tapping at the heart as a neurologist taps on the patella reflex, or Moses on the rock, elicited silvery laughter in sudden fountains all about the saloon. The bandsmen paused a moment, leaning back to mop their foreheads, yet even without the music the mounting spirit of the evening went on, up to the moment of full tide.

"Now," said the M.C. to himself. "Now's the time for the balloons."

But before he could leave the room to call for these, the doors sprang apart, and there stood Carmen, glowing dark and deadly as a poppy, drawing all eyes by her fatal Southern attraction; her lips, behind the crimson flower, curving in a smile wherein passion and scorn slumbered lightly side by side.

"Carmen!" The word burst forth simultaneously from every male throat in the saloon. The conductor, an artist to the finger tips, instantly gave the word to the band, and, as Emily advanced towards the spellbound assembly, the opening chords of *Toreador* blazed out into the vibrant air.

"Carmen!" Subalterns, civil servants, diamond smugglers, judges, motor salesmen, confidence men, all that well-tubbed clean-limbed throng advance to do her homage.

"Carmen!" And as the band rises once more in the modern and almost equally appropriate notes of *Valencia*, the crowd, in one eager husky murmur, entreats her to dance.

But now, with a superb and tigerish gesture of contempt, she passes through their dividing midst to where a single solitary figure droops disconsolate against the wall. Plucking the hot-hued blossom from her lips, she laughingly flings it at his feet, and extending a graceful hand, she has drawn the suddenly awakened Mr. Fatigay into the whirling mazes of the dance.

CHAPTER VI

We drifted o'er the harbour-bar,
And I with sobs did pray—
O let me be awake, my God!
Or let me sleep alway.

THE steamer now drove out of the Gulf of Guinea, and turned her bows to the north-east and home. Mr. Fatigay, who had till then been yearning to starboard, for his love lay there, now felt his heart swing with the swinging needle, and he yearned proportionately to port. Ah God! the moment when, in its changing course, the swift ship pointed, stern to stem, straight to "The Woodlands," Stotfield nr. Haslemere, where sate Miss Amy Flint, all this particular microcosm's desire!

When, said his pocket compass, that moment had arrived, Mr. Fatigay, for just so long, was accorded the ineffable bliss of being able to yearn as it were, full-steam ahead. How his poor heart then rose up in his breast, and began to throb and strain to burst free, that it might fly with the velocity of a cannon ball (but it was as soft and spicy as a plum pudding) straight to the bosom of his beloved!

But they were to call at Gib, and the course soon fell away some degrees to starboard, so that our hero's heart lost the added impetus of the steamer's straight direction, and it settled into an uneasy stillness again, as a dog's does when his master turns away from the warren.

Now the waves took on a brisker blue, and smokes were seen everywhere on the seaward horizon, and the sails of fishing fleets towards the shore. Electric light cables, dwarfed to the likeness of one-strand wire fences, switch-backed along the undulating coast, corks and orange peel met them on the oil-streaked tide: they were entering the English Channel. Everyone ran suddenly to the side. "There! That's it! There! England! Home!"

"Never forget this day," said a white-haired old commissioner to his son, a bright-faced lad coming home from South Africa for the first time, to begin his education at one of our great schools. "That," said he, pointing to the coast of Devon, "is England."

"But, daddy," replied the youngster in amazement, for he had read his Phillpotts, "it looks like those huts on the gold-fields."

A group of South Africans, full of patriotic nostalgia for their colony, stared frowningly at the tactless lad.

"Our Motherland," replied his father, with a dignified glance at these, "may possess neither gold nor fields, but always remember, my boy, that it leads the whole world in building sites."

"If it reminds you of a mining camp," he added,

"you must bear in mind that a camp is the most fitting home for heroes, and that it is from surroundings like these that men have risen to go forth to battle, scornful of the horrors of the trenches and careless of the imminence of death."

"Good-bye, dear," whispered a number of straight-limbed clear-eyed young matrons, glancing tenderly at their well-tubbed squires from under their level brows. "We had better say good-bye now. I expect my husband will be waiting on the quay."

Now the port lay immediately before them, and the hum of life in its narrow streets drifted out on the April breeze. The intermittent nature of this vehicle made the medley of wheels, taxi-horns and voices appear to rise and fall, like the breathing of some vast organism. Emily, feeling incredibly small and brown, peered forth timidly from her niche in the great wall of the floating palace. The crowd on the quay surged forward like a gathering wave, a thin surf of handkerchiefs breaking out upon its crest. A broken spray of self-conscious shouts leapt weakly at the steep side of the liner and drizzled back on the upturned faces whence it had sprung.

A tiny shudder ran through the vast bulk of the ship, and it died happily, and, as the strongest appear weak and small in death, when we are put in mind of the lives they have come through, so it suddenly became a cockle shell that had come five thousand miles, across waters in many places over a mile in depth. And its blissful end, and the pathos of its delivery, and the slackening within each passenger of some strain, which had, it now seemed, all the while been nervously seconding the efforts of the engines; all this moved their hearts so deeply, that if a hymn of thanksgiving had then been struck up, there is little doubt but that many would have joined in under their breaths.

Sirens, which seemed severely meant for everyone, now began to sound, quiet words of command were issued, a rattle of gangways was heard, cries of "There he is! Jim, *Jim!*" arose, and the crowd on the boat and the crowd on the quay rushed together like mouths in a ravenous kiss.

Now up and down among the cleaving throngs ran Mr. Fatigay, dragging Emily tripping and stumbling behind him, and he was looking into every face like a dog that seeks its master.

"Amy! Amy! Where can she be? I say! I wonder where she can be."

As he runs back and forth, growing white and breathless, banging into people, trying to look cool and collected, then not caring how he looks, risking a faint coo-ee, covering the same ground three or four times over, rushing up to distant figures of the most impossible shapes and sizes, getting something in his eye, whispering intently to the grim custodian of *Ladies*, and performing a hundred heart-breaking mad tricks that he will blush for to his dying day; let us despise not him alone, but all of us, both those who are capable of such besottedness and those who are not. For the heart is, in a sense, like the Prince of Wales; we would not have it cut in stone, yet how pathetic it is, when, as at Wembley, we see it modelled in butter.

When he had sought her until he was ready to drop, he acknowledged despairingly that she could not have come aboard, and he made haste down the gangway on to the quay, where he commenced his search anew. Soon he saw a Cook's man standing magnificently apart, and, hurrying up to him, he said:

"Excuse me, but have you seen a lady anywhere —a small dark lady—young—looking for anyone ?"

"Well, sir, there's a good many," replied the humane official. "Can that be her, perhaps ?"

But Mr. Fatigay, turning to follow his glance, saw only Emily, hastening to overtake him with all the speed she might.

Shaking his head sadly, he reached out, and, grasping the poor chimp by the hand, he scurried her off with him. At last, having given up all hope, he drifted out under the entrance arch, to where cars and taxis were ranked in the dock road. And there, in a taxi drawn up by the kerb, sat Miss Amy Flint, waiting her love's appearance.

"Amy!"

"Alfred! How brown you're looking! And yet . . . just the same. Have you had a wonderful voyage ?"

"Amy!"

"Well? Have I changed so much? Do you think you'll still like me? Have you got lots to tell me?"

"Amy!"

"Well, if I haven't changed outwardly, I've altered a good deal within. You'll have to be very nice and kind and understanding with your wayward girl. But what a time you've been! Most of the people seem to have come out half-an-hour ago. I was getting quite anxious."

"Why, I've been looking for you everywhere inside," stammered Mr. Fatigay. "That's where everyone was being met. I thought you must have met with an accident or something."

"Ah!" said she with a smile. "Just the same old Alfred! Didn't you guess how I'd feel about the public scene? Never mind: you're forgiven. Hop inside!"

"But who . . .?" she added with a stare—"But what on earth's this?"

Emily, unable to breathe even, looked up supplicatingly at her protector.

"Well," said he, "ha! ha! Well, the fact is . . . I wondered, er . . . I thought perhaps you might like a chimp."

During the pregnant silence that followed, the taxi clock rose thrice.

"Good heavens!" said Amy at last. "Is *that* the wonderful present you've been hinting at in all your letters? A monkey! Darling! My poor old boy! What in the world could you have been thinking of? What should *I* want with a monkey? Covered with fleas, no doubt, and sure to make a filthy mess about the house! You'd better shoot it, or give it to the Zoo or something. *I* don't want it."

"Her name's Emily." said Mr. Fatigay, very cast down.

"Anyway," he said, seeing that this communication elicited no response, "we'd better be getting along to your hotel. Get in, Emily."

"I don't want the filthy creature in along with me," cried Amy. "Let it sit beside the driver, or ride on the roof. Oh! I don't know though. Anything is better than being made a public spectacle. Perhaps we'd better have it inside."

Emily had heard little of all this. She stood amazed. To be given away! She felt like something out of *Uncle Tom's Cabin*. And to be given by him, for whom she had renounced all, for whom she had come so far, asking nothing but to watch over him—to be given by him to her! She had expected a disillusion to result upon the first sight of Amy, but it seemed to be happening in the wrong quarter.

"Get in, Emily." The words percolated at last, and she automatically obeyed. Taxis were new to her, and seeing only the back seat within, for the others were sprung back against the partition, she naturally took her place on this, not as one wishing to presume, but because she saw no alternative.

This aspect of the matter did not perhaps occur to Amy, for, seeing the chimp occupying one of the better seats, she took offence, and demanded that it be turned off at once, and be made to sit upon the floor.

"Emily shall sit upon a front seat," said Mr. Fatigay, and he smiled at her reassuringly as he pressed one down.

"You see, my dear," he resumed, as the taxi jolted forward, "Emily is no ordinary chimp. She understands almost everything that is said to her, and, as for having fleas and being ill-trained for the house, why she is as clean and neat and well-behaved as any human being. I have trained her, thinking of you, to bear herself with the utmost decorum. She has her own knife and fork, and her own little bed, and she is not only completely tidy, but also very helpful about the house."

"Then she had better be sold to perform on the Halls," said Amy Flint.

At this the poor chimp started violently, and turned her eyes imploringly on Mr. Fatigay. She had a violent prejudice against the stage.

"But, darling," said he, "that wouldn't do at all. I really couldn't bear the thought of parting with Emily to anyone except you. Why, once she saved my life. I thought that might make you look favourably on her, and take her as a novel sort of maid, and if you could only bring yourself to do so, I'm sure you would soon grow to love her for her own sake. My dearest hope," he added, "apart from yourself, has been that you two might come to understand one another, and be friends."

Now, as he said these words, a look of grateful adoration shone from the eyes of the chimp, and Amy, in a flash of feminine intuition, had realised that the humble creature had lost her heart to Mr. Fatigay. And while well-founded jealousy bears no proportion at all to the love on which it feeds, but only to the possessive element in it, there is a certain fanciful and ill-founded variety which thrives inversely in relation to the strength of what affection may lie beneath it, just as some mountain weeds bloom most flaringly where the soil is thinnest. Of this kind, is the sort which is often to be noted in cold and sterile natures, the sort which is most inflamed, not by their beloved's loving elsewhere, but by their being loved, regardless of whether they return it or not. And if this unsolicited gift of affection should glow so warmly as to put their own emotional impotence to shame, as it does the more unmistakably the colder and more sterile they are; then their vindictiveness is sharpened to a surer point than has ever been known among our hot-blooded *señoritas* or ukelele ladies.

A feeling of this description now arose in the bosom of Amy, and, born with all its teeth, it soon fastened on the best method of chastising the impertinence which ventured to love with a strength of which she was incapable.

"Very well," said Amy, "I'll keep the creature, and if it has any intelligence at all I'll train it to wait on me. Otherwise it must be sent away. I suppose it's my only chance of having a maid of my own."

CHAPTER VII

. . . when, sick for home,
She stood in tears amid the alien corn,

the chimp's sad heart was charmed by no nightingale, for the bird had not yet returned to Stotfield, and what corn was showing was but a scanty acid-green, ragged among the flints of those chilly fields. It was the black-thorn winter, and Emily, who had been sent out to gather primroses, found the thin stuff dress she now wore, designed by Amy to resemble the drabbest of charity child's garments, to be but a miserable covering against the cruel east wind. A thin and lonely song trembled among the telegraph wires, where the road ran up between the tilted ploughlands. It was a disillusioned scene, embittered by the default of spring; yet the primroses seemed loath to leave it. Their crowded sickly faces peered up anxiously at Emily as she knelt shivering beside them and tried to loosen their stems from the tough grasses to which they seemed desperately to cling. A variety of small brown birds, blowing about like dead leaves, uttered cold and colourless notes, much like the whetting together of flint stones.

Cum, Somer, cum, the suete sesoun and sonne !

thought Emily, wondering how long it must be before the warm and scented weather came to save her. Perhaps her wistful plea was taken as an impertinent complaint, for the sky darkened forbiddingly, an icy gust made the black-thorn branches rattle against one another, and a sudden rain lashed through her fluttering, shoddy dress. Her fingers were too numb to pick any more, and, as it was, many of the stems were broken off too short, so she crept through the hedge and took the field path towards home, for she felt incapable, in her present dispirited condition, of bearing up under the curious glances of the village people.

The path ran out desperately to the shoulder of the hill, then bent and scurried down to where two or three red-brick houses formed a modern and genteel suburb to the village. Nearest of these was "The Woodlands," where Miss Amy Flint, when she was not in town, lived with her mother. This handsome villa of pre-war construction formed a delightful residence with gabled elevations, detached, on two floors, affording seven bed and dressing, two servants', two bath, three reception rooms, sun loggia, cloakroom, bright domestic offices, detached garage, surrounded by choice well laid-out grounds of just over one acre including shrubbery and tennis courts.

Poor Emily stumbled down the path and slipped into the cold house through the back-door, as she had been bidden, and, hurrying past the kitchen, whence emanated the rude titters of the cook and parlour maid, she knocked timidly on the door of the drawing-room, and entering, found Amy and Mr. Fatigay at tea.

"Hullo, Emily," said Mr. Fatigay pleasantly.

"Here it is at last," said Amy, and, addressing the sensitive creature briskly rather than unkindly, she said:

"Well, where are the primroses? Show me."

Emily shrinkingly proffered the meagre bunch.

"What? Is that all?" said Amy. "And see what miserable little stems you've got to them." And privately she gave the chimp an angry look.

Further than this, however, she did not choose to go, for though her relationship to the poor chimp was founded, almost entirely, on the feeling that she deserved a good sharp slap, Amy was never brutal to animals, nor was she inclined to appear severe before Mr. Fatigay, who might have been provoked to a defence of Emily, which would have puffed up the chimp undesirably, as well as wasting a quarrel. Amy did not believe in being too prodigal in this direction. "Quarrels with a fiancé," as she put it in one of her witty sallies to her intimate friends, of whom she had many, for she was considered by a large circle to be the Queen of Haverstock Hill, "Quarrels with a fiancé, though frequently tonic and diverting, should never be indulged in for wanton pleasure. They are too useful for that, and will be found just as thrilling if saved up till a time when, in the warmth of reconciliation, some important concession is to be obtained."

Amy therefore contented herself with being firm, and with sometimes laughing at Emily, and even this she confined mainly to two occasions, of which the first was when she laughed at her for being a chimp, and the second was when she laughed at her for behaving like a human.

So this time she said no more, and raised no objection when Mr. Fatigay poured out a milky cup of tea for the half-frozen creature, and bade her bring her little stool to the hearth-rug, that she might toast herself before the fire. It had been in Amy's mind to dismiss poor Emily to the solitude of her fireless little garret, but now watching her settle humbly into her place, her ingenious jealousy suggested a more satisfactory way of chastising her impudence, which was, by allowing her to remain in the room while she continued her conversation with Mr. Fatigay.

"Come, love," she said softly, stretching herself upon the sofa with a voluptuous grace, modelled on that of Goya's "Maya" (clothed). "Come and sit here on the pouf, and go on telling me what you did, and thought, and felt in Africa."

"Africa?" said Mr. Fatigay, with a touch of that conversational elephantiasis which should surely be listed among the commoner tropical diseases, "Africa? Why, I may have *done* things there, but as for thinking and feeling—how could I think or feel in Africa when my mind and heart were here with you in England?"

And with a tender leer he possessed himself of his lady's hand.

"No. Tell me," she said, in a velvety purr.

"What I thought!" burst out Mr. Fatigay. "What I felt on those long hot nights! Ah, some day I'll tell you. Some day I'll make you understand."

"Tell me now," murmured Amy, who had an infinite capacity for conversation of this kind.

But, alas, Mr. Fatigay, whose feelings had hurried him beyond the limits of his verbal expressiveness, had passed his arm about her waist, and seemed eager to carry out the second of his projects.

"Now! Now! Remember your promise," said she, feeling well pleased that the chimp should witness this display of ardour, but in no way inclined to round it off by any considerable response. "Sit up properly and talk."

"Oh, Amy!" cried the poor fellow, who had been set back in this manner over a score of times since he had come to Stotfield. "Can't you see I'm dying for you? Don't think I am being too physical, dear: I wouldn't, for I know you hate it. But the fact is—after all, we are grown up, aren't we?—I've lived so long out there with only your image, that when I see you in the . . . in reality, I don't know what to do. Can't we be married at once, darling—do say 'yes'—instead of waiting so long?"

As the tormented water sinks into a momentary quiescence when the cold egg is cast in, so Emily's seething heart subsided into a hot stillness at these words, that she might better catch the answer. "Yet how," thought she, "can anything but assent be given to such a plea, and from such a man?"

"Oh, Alfred!" said Amy, in tones more of sorrow than of anger. "You promised not to pester me till I myself felt ready. I thought you understood how necessary it is to me to be just myself for a little longer. Besides," she went on, to punish him for having forced her to show a reluctance which she could neither overcome nor bring herself to acknowledge, "Besides, it's so long since I've seen you, that you can hardly expect me to be quite sure of my feelings till we've been properly engaged for a few months. It wouldn't be fair to you to let you tie yourself up with someone who wasn't quite sure of herself."

"And you ought to have time," she added, "to think over your own feelings. These are your first weeks in England, and you've not seen a white woman for years. Can you be sure that this, joining up with our old feeling for one another, is not making you think that you feel what, perhaps, after all, you don't?"

All this was perfectly reasonable, and even benevolent in its thoughtfulness for Mr. Fatigay's welfare, nor could any objection be raised to it except, perhaps, by those churlish fellows who are beginning to cry out that women, who have long ago broken in such emotional spontaneities as tears and frowns and smiles to their own use, are now attempting the same with sweet reason, which, if it makes a good master, is a confoundedly bad servant, though an obedient one. "Women," such boors remark, "are unreasonable enough when one wants to argue with them, but when it comes to other matters (as needs it must, if health and good spirits are to retain their seat) then up springs this same forgotten reason, like a garden rake one treads on when picking flowers, and hits you on the nose."

Beside such scurrilities, Amy's words stand arrayed in sweetness and light, except for the trifling fault, since nothing can be absolutely perfect, of being a little insincere. It is extremely difficult for a tenderly nurtured young woman of our race and generation, especially one who is diligent in keeping abreast of contemporary science, to say in so many words, "I like nothing more than being wooed, and nothing less than the prospect of being won," and this must be the reason that so few say it, while so many evince that attitude very clearly in their behaviour. Not, indeed, that this is true of every woman, or that there is really a lack of healthy physical instinct among the cultivated shes of to-day. On the contrary, there is an ample sufficiency, the only trifling criticism to be advanced being connected with the distribution of it, for half, like Amy, have none at all, and the other half have perhaps twice too much.

But, be that as it may, the fact remains that Amy expressed herself thus, and Mr. Fatigay, when he had well pondered her words, began to shake and tremble at the prospect of delay, as if he had been sentenced to a second turn on the rack, and, getting up from the pouf, he took a fling or two about the room.

"Amy!" he cried at last, "Heaven knows I am unwilling to pester you, as you call it, and still more so to obtrude on your notice that side of my nature which your purer one finds so repellent. Do understand! I am not incapable of the higher sort of love which you rightly require of me, but in spite of that, I am, in short, a man. And if, so to speak, I am repressed much longer, I fear I shall become totally unhinged, and perform, in some awful aberration, a desperate act, which, when you hear of it, will make you hate and shun me. Have pity, therefore, on what is, after all, only the agonising nature of my sex."

"It may well be the nature of your sex," said she, "in animals and in those men who are nothing more. Doubtless the monkey that sits there could bear you out in that. But I cannot think that any *true* man, least of all you, Alfred, to whom I have given so much, could be so utterly lacking in self-control. Why, George Weeke," she said, "was engaged five years to Adeline Chili, and . . . " But when he heard these names, which were not unfamiliar to him, Mr. Fatigay uttered a strange sound.

"I see," went on Amy, with some asperity, for she could not bear to hear her friends disparaged, "I see that I am right in resolving to know you more certainly before I entrust my life into your keeping. And if you are that sort of man, who puts *that* before everything else, it surely cannot matter whom you marry. You had better think very seriously before you tie yourself to one who has a life of her own to lead, and can't put that thing first in importance."

Hearing these words, Mr. Fatigay was very cast down, for to him Miss Amy Flint was the way and the life, and what disagreed with her least opinion, though it might be the very foundation stone of his being, was not long in appearing to him as both inferior and offensive.

But Emily, on hearing this admonition to him, to take thought, could have sprung from her seat, and going up to Amy, have shaken her warmly by the hand, for she had no idea of the process which fishermen describe in the phrase, "giving him line."

Mr. Fatigay went to the window and watched the dark and rainy wind shake angrily at the numb bewildered boughs, which might have expected by this time to be flecked with translucent green. "The buds," he thought, "seem actually to be retreating."

As she saw him standing there so dismally,

drooping in the sudden vacuity of a complete non plus, staring at the window-panes, which, piteous with the cold trickle of raindrops, seemed a fitting mirror for his suddenly colourless and weeping soul, Emily thought to herself, "This pain of his, though it throbs at my heart's root, is perhaps all for the best. Amy spoke the truth, and for better reason than she knew. This deluded ardour of his, the monstrous product of five years' incubation in loneliness under the African sun, must soon dwindle and disappear now it is brought face to face with so manifestly disproportionate an object. While it continues, my master must value this woman's qualities as the highest, which means that his standards must be in utter chaos. But when the bubble is pricked by some word too sharp or prospect too thorny, they will reassert themselves, and he will realise that it is best to give his heart where the warmest return is to be expected. And then . . . who knows ? "

"Perhaps he is on the point of revolt now," she continued. "He has reason enough, I am sure. Or perhaps he must have time to see something of normal women before he regains his mental balance."

For poor Emily, in her innocence, believed Amy to be a very chimera of wrath and treachery and greed, and all because she knew how to stand up for herself and was not disposed to be treated as a mere chattel. She thought of her as a cold-blooded variety of that terrible "Woman of thirty," whom she regarded as an apocalyptic monster, absolutely transgressing all that Tennyson and the loving heart laid down as beautiful and good. It would be unfair to Amy, however, not to correct this by saying downright that she was, as far as these things can be co-existent, a flower of England's womanhood, beautiful, intelligent, high-principled; a charming companion, a devoted daughter and the best imaginable comrade.

"He will be a lucky man, on whom Amy bestows her love." So said the dozen or so, each of whom regarded her as their closest friend. But it must be admitted that the male section of these, though they valued her friendship more than anything else in the world, only found it possible to maintain it at the pitch of high intimacy she set, by making the most of certain other acquaintance they had among the ladies of Bohemia and the Café Royal.

And now Amy stretched out her hand, and said with a frank and tender smile:

"Come now, old boy! Don't be furious with me for a little plain speaking. After all, we've both said more than we meant, no doubt, but it's a sad case if being honest with one another should estrange us." And she gave him a melting smile, the glutinous sweetness of which he devoured with the avidity of a diabetic who swallows a fatal spoonful of jam. And, not pausing to analyse her words; nay, only too eager, in his trembling desire for reconciliation, to make every surrender he could, he sprang towards her and caught her yielding but elastic frame in his arms. As he was kissing the silky curls at the back of her neck, a process which in itself made the corresponding hairs on Emily even more stiff and straight than usual, Amy peeped out underneath and gave her a glance, and this glance said as plainly as any words might:

"You see?"

CHAPTER VIII

And at night along the dusky highway near and
nearer drawn,
Sees in heaven the light of London flaring like a
dreary dawn;

To the outer, if not to the inner eye, this was rather reversed when Emily first approached the metropolis, for they all went up together on the morning of the first of May, a day so bright in the country, and so conspicuously clouded by London's smoke pall, that it seemed as if they were travelling in time rather than in space, and approaching the outskirts, not of the town, but of yesterday's bad weather. It follows that the highway along which they were being drawn became dusky only as the grey streets engulfed them, for, on the washed hills outside, unpunctual Spring had arrived with a rush, all hot and shining, and the railway lines glinted above the hot shingle of the track, as, with a blue glance, she made them her mirror, while she powdered her face with chalk dust and dandelion pollen.

The downs through which the line ran were torn everywhere by new roads, long angry scratches, along which buildings in every stage of erection stood like clots of the earth's red-brick blood. Clustered under the railway embankment, a few white rough-cast villas were being built, the completed ones being already occupied, and, when the fair-haired, bun-faced, bare-armed young matrons came out to pin napkins on their clothes lines, they seemed from one angle like Piera della Francesca angels, against their background of rough-cut chalk road-way and roofless walls, and, from another, like advertisements for a labour-saving soap.

Inside the carriage, the heat was bewildering rather than intense. The dust, which had lain congealed all the damp winter, awoke in the cushions behind their heads, issuing out at the least movement to tickle the inflamed membrane at the back of Emily's throat and nose. She had a slight cold, which at once heightened and confused her impressions: she seemed lost among many speeds, many times, many states of existence. Her companions' faces, which had a waxy and artificial look, lolling weakly as dolls' heads, seemed to survive only by a miracle the sudden leap and snap of signal boxes, which flattened themselves on the windows with loud smacks; unsmilingly they still wagged after the temporary annihiliation of tunnels, and bobbed like corks on the terrific entrance of concertina-ing hilly streets, volleying into the carriage with the whirr of a watchman's rattle.

But through it all Emily was conscious of a feeling of renewed life and anticipation. London certainly proffered a dawn, though it might be a dreary one. After the icy midnight of "The Woodlands," the prospect of seeing the world's largest capital, rich in public buildings, monuments, stately thoroughfares, and, above all, in associations of the many distinguished figures whose lives and opinions she had read, was one which she could not but find exhilarating.

"Besides," thought she, "my dear master will now have an opportunity of meeting other women, both good and bad, and in the first he will see what his beloved should be, and in the second he will see, with eyes unclouded by love, what she is. He will recognise faults which are the true cause of his present discomfort, and which, in his unhappy blindness, he imagines to be resident more in himself than in her."

"Suit-case," said Amy peremptorily, and the chimp reached up a slim but strong right arm to take it from the rack. Mr. Fatigay began to gather up hand-bags and papers.

Victoria Station! Emily completely forgot her cold and her problems as she pattered along after the engaged couple, nor did she allow the heavy suit-case with which she was burdened to prevent her from peeping eagerly in all directions. Most of all, of course, when she was once embarked on her first taxi-drive through London, she was impressed by the appearance of our marvellous police. She thought them simply remarkable. For the rest, though the reflections of an untutored chimp are scarcely worth the setting down, she was mostly struck by the appearance of abject misery which was apparent in all the passers-by, especially in their sickly complexions, their peevish or anxious looks, their slave's gait, and, most of all, in their rare and rickety smiles.

Do not think, however, that she jumped at once to the conclusion, as some more superficially observant stranger might have done, that the great city is on the whole a nasty mistake, and that it would be better, all things considered, if Highgate Hill were to turn Vesuvius, so to speak, and obliterate, to put it bluntly, all the ugly ant-heap at its feet. No: she had experience of her own enough to know that happiness is like some of the lower forms of life, of which, if one of them is cut into pieces, some inconsiderable fragment or other is sure to survive. Thus she had little doubt that, among these hurrying millions, most of whom looked to her (though she knew little of homes and offices) as if they had been both crossed in love and condemned to penal servitude for life, many had compensations, which, however small they might seem to the indifferent spectator, must in logic be so great to each individual concerned that they compensated for the toil, the illness, the worry and the emotional starvation marked clearly in his face, for they demonstrably withheld him from suicide. "What a wonderful thing a stamp collection must be," thought Emily, "or the construction with one's own hands of a home radio set!"

By now their taxi had reached Haverstock Hill,

where Amy had a little upper maisonette in which she spent the greater part of every year. The rooms, unlike the larger, but more stereotyped, apartments of her mother's house, were furnished to express her own personality. The furniture was modern and artistic, but not lacking in occasional evidences of a charming feminine touch. Under a large coloured reproduction of Van Gogh's sunflowers, an expensive doll, dressed to represent Polly Peachum, flopped tipsily against the telephone. There were bulb-flowers, faded during the owner's absence, a drawing by Augustus John, and a huge witch ball.

While her escort set down their burdens, Amy went forward, and flung the windows open, letting in the warm and living air from outside, where a man was selling brown wallflowers.

"Have you everything you want, my dear," said Mr. Fatigay, "before I rush off to the bank ?"

"Yes, indeed," said Amy. "Except for a little peace and seclusion. I always want a spell of solitude after staying at home. And now, with you as well as mother and everyone else—well, I'm sure you'll understand, dear, if I want a quiet evening with one or two old friends."

"Why, of course," replied her lover, his face falling a little, for he had hoped that she would go that evening to the theatre with him. Will you come out somewhere with me to-morrow ?"

"Well, let's see," said Amy. "To-day's Friday, isn't it? Why not come round on Monday even-

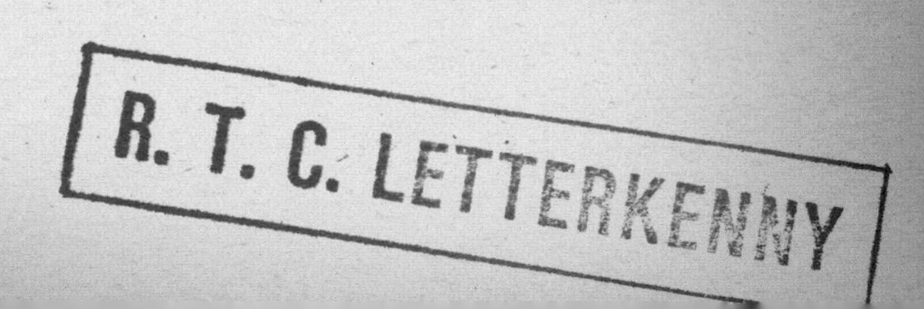

ing. I'm having a few friends in then; people you must meet. Till then I really feel that I must be alone. I've such a head, dear." And she passed her hand wearily over her brow.

"All right," said Mr. Fatigay after a moment's pause. "Perhaps I may look in in the morning for Emily, to take her for a walk, and perhaps see you for a moment at the same time."

"Of course, she'll have a good deal to do in helping the char," answered Amy, who noticed with disapproval the sudden beaming of the chimp's ingenuous countenance. But she felt it would look rather bad to refuse without good reason, so she added, "Still, she might be able to go with you in the afternoons. Only I don't want her spoiled. One must begin as one means to go on. Well, good-bye, dear. I'm really terribly tired."

And with that Mr. Fatigay took his leave.

Emily had not done looking after him, nor had Amy done peeping here and there in the uneasy aimlessness which overcomes one when, returning after a long absence, one re-establishes one's rapport with a confusing sunny room, when that black daffodil, the telephone, pealed goldenly through the dusty shafts of sunlight, and Amy (no mother hearing her only child squall could have moved on a quicker instinct) swooped down upon it, and took it to her bosom. The rapid but quite natural transition from nerviness and fatigue to a pleasureable excitement was perhaps a shade too frankly realised: a hint of lingering lethargy would have been a seemly compliment to Mr. Fatigay, and to—not so much to the sincerity of her plea of weariness, for it was sincere enough—but to its depth and stability. What had been important enough to occasion the rather curt dismissal of her lover should hardly have evaporated so quickly at the prospect of speaking to a friend. But Emily, who, not coming of a gregarious stock, had no conception of the thrilling beauty of the telephone, through whose ebon and Plutonic lips our friends address us in voices revived from non-existence, Lazarus voices cold and earthy as those of the temporarily awakened dead, Emily felt that Amy had been shamming her headache, and eyed her frowningly. It was hardly the first time, nor was it destined to be the last by many, when the puritanical chimp, seeing Amy at her most ordinary, set her down as being positively criminal instead of simply womanly.

"Now, Emily," said Amy, replacing the receiver, "two or three friends of mine are coming round to tea, and they will probably stay to dinner, and there may be some other people coming afterwards. This means that every single piece of glass and china in the place must be thoroughly washed before tea time, for the dust settles on it. So you'd better start at once."

Emily nodded obediently, for she had no desire to accept Amy's hospitality without giving her ample value in labour in return, and, taking off her sun-bonnet, she held it out, and looked about her in a manner expressive of a desire to know where to put her things, that she might prepare herself immediately for work.

"You'd better come up here," said Amy, who had found out some time ago that the chimp understood all that was said to her, though she continued to address her in a few monosyllables except when they were alone. "This is where you'll sleep. You can use the straw in that packing case in the corner." And as she said this, she pushed Emily into a pokey little garret where lumber and boxes were stored.

"Come down now, and I'll show you the scullery," she went on. "You can boil some water, and begin, while I go out and get you some black dresses and white caps and aprons to wear in the afternoons. Then you'll look more or less respectable when you open the door to visitors. I think, by the way, I'll call you Smithers in future. Emily sounds hardly suitable for one of your species and position."

Emily followed with a sigh. She remembered those distant days when she had studied so absorbedly under Mr. Fatigay's tutelage for the position he had said she was to hold in London. So this was what he had meant her for! The poor chimp sighed once more, then, shrugging her shoulders, she took up the kettle and turned to the ugly sink, accepting, as a now chronic condition of her heart, that painful bursting feeling from which no amount of sighing could afford any real relief.

The next day, though, when her spirits were just at their lowest ebb, Mr. Fatigay appeared shortly after lunch, and said he had come to take Emily for a walk, at which the world seemed suddenly transformed for her, and the enraptured creature, having hurriedly pulled on her shady bonnet, trustingly put her hand in his, and they set forth in the summery afternoon to see the sights of London.

It was that day, of all the year, when the barrow men who sell sickly roots of daisies do their briskest barter with the sentimental wives of Camden Town, when husbands lean out upon window-sills, and the bugs crawl out upon walls; that day when children swarm in noisy dirtiness on the first hot paving stones of the season, and when the grimiest scrap of newspaper, trundling in warm idleness before the smelly wind, seems to move in a sensuous ritual dance.

The bus they mounted, being either late or sensitive to the spirit of the day, swung wildly down into Camden Town, and before long Mr. Fatigay, who had not Amy's keen perception, and had not guessed in over a year what she had seen in less than a month, the extent of Emily's understanding, but who, nevertheless, partly from his natural openness of heart, and partly in unconscious response to her intelligent glances, always spoke to her as if he was aware of it, was pointing out scenes familiar to him in his youth.

"Look, Emily!" he said. "There is the 'Horse-shoe.' What a place! When I was at London University, that's where we used to foregather. What a time that was! Well! Well! Well!"

Emily fixed her eyes on the sacred spot. A vision of our hero in the first flush of his youth, ingenuous, idealistic, rose before her.

A young Apollo, golden haired,
Stands dreaming on the verge of strife,
Magnificently unprepared
For the long littleness of life.

As the appropriate lines recurred to her, she saw him, blushing a little in the attempt to overcome his boyish self-consciousness, kindling the divine fire in the ardent, though lesser, breasts of his admiring companions, as he told them in ringing tones of his determination to leave the world better than he'd found it. To that inspiring picture succeeded a softer one, and she saw the band of young students sitting pensive and enthralled, as one of their number, probably that same one, sang the old sweet song, with which, as she had read in *Trilby*, the Paris art students were wont to melt each others' tender hearts—"My Sister Dear."

"What would I not have given," thought Emily, "to have been one of that golden company: to have shared their studies, their vicissitudes, their evenings of grave discussion or innocent mirth! To have been, perhaps, as far as modesty permits, the dear platonic friend of each of them, and, as time went on, something more to one! For the day might have come, when, suddenly breaking off in describing the generous Utopia of his latest dream, he would have hesitated, and, all his swift rhetoric gone, would have said, bluntly and clumsily, 'I need you.' And I, meeting his eyes. . . ." But here the bus jolted on, and Emily awoke from her reverie to hear him say:

"And here's the Charing Cross Road. This is where all the second-hand book shops are. Many's the hour I've spent poking about in some of these places; standing, sometimes, for the whole of lunch time, reading some book I couldn't afford to buy. Yes, you can stand there as long as you like, reading, and no one says a word."

Emily heard his words with something of a thrill. She determined to avail herself at the first opportunity of the facilities of this enlightened, courteous street.

"How appearances deceive!" she thought, looking at the tall fronts of the dwelling-houses, greyly lustrous in the sun, which rose like cliffs of mud above the sluggish ditch through which they were crawling. It revived memories of her trip down the Congo. A few old book-lovers, looking like those dull and crippled water insects which resemble bits of old dry stick, which, again, are exactly like book-lovers, hung precariously at the shop fronts, as if in fear of being swept away by the slowly drifting scum, for this is a great street for actors. Here a policeman, dark, shining and clumsy as a huge dytiscus beetle, hung stationary in the middle of the hot colourless stream. Billy and Bertie and Kitty and Gertie coming from rehearsal in their cream and vermilion Mercedes, open and shallow, looked like four pale electric grubs in a water lily. High above the mud banks an aeroplane, or loud dragon-fly, split in relatively wide freedom the limited ashy blue.

"And the palpitations of this slime," thought Emily, "are the effects of mind! The rich silt of all the mental progress of mankind is collected here, radio-active with the living truth. Decidedly I must come. Perhaps," she thought, "I may find a priceless first edition among the musty contents of one of those boxes marked fourpence. I should like to do that."

And so they came to Trafalgar Square, where Emily smiled, for she was no prude, at the statue of Lord Nelson, and where she gazed with regret, though of course she had never stayed there herself, at what was once the site of Morley's Hotel.

And so they went down Whitehall on the open-topped bus, and on into the sun's eye, their different figures black and ragged in silhouette as they advanced, on their high and jolty car, solemnly and slowly into that radiance, till at length they drew up in Pimlico, from which they were to start out for a walk along the Chelsea Embankment.

Looking forward, it is possible to catch other

glimpses of them, on various of the afternoons when Amy was engaged with her friends. They are either strolling under the sugary flowering chestnuts of Bushey, their slightly unfashionable attire lending a stiff verisimilitude to the beauty of the avenue, or skipping, hand in hand, hurriedly across Fleet Street on their way to Saint Paul's, or emerging, blinking and feeling pale, from the hot maggoty darkness of an Oxford Street movie show, or, what they did more often than was really worth while, passing from show-case to show-case in some museum or other, happy in virtuous headaches and the silent friendliness between them.

CHAPTER IX

Stone walls do not a prison make,
Nor iron bars a cage,

thought Emily on certain thundery afternoons of hot July, when, after lunch, Amy now regularly hurried her upstairs, and locked her in the narrow lumber-room where her poor straw bed was, before going out herself to concerts, matinées or picture exhibitions, or perhaps to tea with a party of friends. For Mr. Fatigay's brief holiday was over, and he had leisure no longer to take the chimp for walks in the afternoons, and Amy, when he had hinted that she might occasionally do this, had replied woundingly that she did not usually take menials about with her, even when they happened to be human, and that since the apes at the Zoo managed to exist very comfortably without exercise, she saw no reason why Emily should not do the same.

"And what's more," she had added, with a stern glance at the poor dumb creature, who was powerless to contradict, "Emily does not show, in the sweeping and scrubbing she sometimes has to do, such an excess of pent-up energy as might indicate any pressing need for additional exercise. No, Alfred! The chimp is mine now, and though, as you know, I am incapable of cruelty, even to the humblest and least prepossessing of God's creatures, I don't see why I should make an exhibition of myself by dragging her about with me, especially into the company of my friends. And I won't: and that's that!"

To which Mr. Fatigay had nothing to reply, and Emily, though she had much, was, of course, unable to put it into words.

It was, therefore, without the satisfaction of having been able to point out that she would far rather spend her afternoons quietly in her room, than in the company of Amy, even at the most famous of London's places of interest, that she was now guided, under the humiliating appearance of compulsion, to the very seclusion of her choice. And such is the suggestive power of a conventional standpoint, which can make a terror out of a long period of free board and lodging, that, on the first afternoon that Amy locked her up, Emily felt quite dejected at her confinement, and was actually hurt at not being held fit company for a person for whom she could feel neither respect nor liking.

As the key turned in the lock she could not prevent herself from standing close to the door, facing it, on the inside, as if appealing that it should be opened; an attitude which exposed her fully to all implied in its forbidding blankness and in the grinding turn of the key. She had to bite her lip very hard to repress a flood of irrational tears.

"After all, though," she said to herself, "I am not a child, though I may not be as old as some people are, and I ought think shame on myself for behaving as such. What wish could I conceive, of all that are handy and practicable, more to my taste than that a locked door should be interposed between me and my oppressor, and though if I had the locking of it, and stood upon the other side, it might be somewhat longer before it was opened, the present arrangement is a very tolerable second best, and if the gusto with which she thus suits my convenience springs from her belief that she is making me miserable, why, what a fool I should be to make it a reality merely because she imagines it to be one!"

And with a cheerfulness considerably restored, the agile creature bounded lightly about the room, indulging in a series of hand springs, pirouettes and somersaults, which would have proclaimed clearly, to anyone with an eye to the inner significance of dancing, that she felt herself empress of at least this nutshell, and had no intention of becoming a prey to heavy dreams.

When her girlish high spirits had abated a little, and something of her usual pensiveness had reasserted its sway, she sat down soberly in the middle of the floor and surveyed her bedroom in its new light as a hermit's or a prisoner's cell.

"And what though some would consider it to be the latter?" she reflected, for her race-consciousness made her unusually sensitive to the suggestion of being caged, so that the idea stuck like a burr to her thoughts, "Even if it was, I should be no worse off than the divine Pankhurst, a martyr to the rights of women."

And gazing around her, she examined, with a pleased interest, the miscellaneous contents of her room. All that Amy thought least of was jettisoned here, she noticed, as if waiting her arrival to head the corner. She could not but feel sympathy and affection for the rest of this Salon des Refusées. They were mostly objects of still life. All schools seemed fairly represented, as, she remembered was the case at the Tate. In one corner a dismembered bedstead and a chalky plaster cast suggested an excellent Chirico; in another the blurred pale raspberry-pink and silver of an old suspender belt, and the tenuous mistiness of a few discarded stockings seemed newly soft from the palette of Marie Laurencin. Van Gogh, in an early period, was represented by a pair of crumpled boots, sad upon a broken cane chair; Picasso, by a shattered mandoline and a dusty soda-water syphon disposed upon a sheet of newspaper in the fireplace. A strong Camden Town influence emanated from the faded flower-patterned wall-paper and the pale indecent marble of the mantelpiece, for this room had never been redecorated by Amy. A Japanese parasol with a broken rib stood in the corner, and Emily, who had a weakness for these particular trifles, took it up, and, opening it, unconsciously stepped into the place of honour as a very charming Goya.

After a turn or two, however, the caged bird folded this bright wing, and, betaking herself to the window, she threw up the sash and craned forth her head to stare down between the house backs, where the rank sycamores greened the yellow afternoon into the likeness of water deeps, down to the weedy gardens at the bottom, which were cheaply gay with straggled marigolds and precarious virginia stock. An enervated subaqueous life persisted on this submerged floor. Protruding from the lush and wetly shining foliage of a thicket of michælmas daisies, the dark head of a cat, pressed to the ground, stared up like an angler fish at the small shoals of mud-coloured birds that skimmed to and fro. Beside it, and near a summer house, battered and faded as a fragment of some sunken ship, a ghastly plaster figure hung on tip-toe, in the erect and weightless posture of a woman drowned. No anchor was to be seen, but two enormous shells lay half buried in the weeds. The stray notes of a piano, converted into something rich and strange, floated upwards towards the light, bursting, as the luminous deep-sea fish do, when they reached the lesser density of the roof level.

Down the sides of the houses ran the encrusted drain pipes, soft puce or dead blue, relics, it seemed, of some abandoned dockyard undertaking. Down the side of the house, riveted firmly to the wall, circular and of six-inch, graspable diameter, ran an iron drain pipe, straight down into the deserted garden, divided on one side, by a low wall only, from the side street, and from liberty, London, Life, Adventure, Romance. This exhilarating cup, which now flooded up like some divinely effervescent Bethesda pool, and from an ineffably low ebb, up to the very window-sill where Emily rested her chin, caused a delicious chill of excitement to run through her veins. To revisit, lonely as a cloud, in pensive but by no means vacant mood, those scenes with which she had first become acquainted in the company of Mr. Fatigay, perhaps to explore others, to get to know the great city, its highways and its fascinating by-ways, to scan its changing countenance, to lay fingers on its mighty pulse, to auscultate, however dimly, the eccentric beatings of its mysteriously located heart; this prospect intoxicated the chimp, and, always impulsive, she lightly flung a leg over the sill, in order to descend at once into the magic world whose troubadour voice invited her sweetly from below.

Here, however, she paused a moment. She had learned pretty thoroughly by now the one positively useful lesson which suffering and Geo. Moore have to bestow. This is, that the few pleasures of life are not to be gulped down in bumpkin haste, but savoured as a rare claret should be; anticipation, like the voluptuously inhaled bouquet, being the best part, and to be long lingered over, providing only that one has the cup very surely in one's hand.

The chimp accordingly flung herself down upon her wretched pallet, and passed the long hours until Amy's return in a most agreeable reverie, stewing gently in the languorous garret heat and happily staring at a low and tawny ceiling, now cinematographically frescoed with images of the adventures which lay before her.

It was therefore not until the next afternoon that she uttered the inspiriting lines which have been mentioned, and she did so as she thrust over the sill a foot, resplendent in one of those very crumpled boots which Amy had discarded, and forthwith she embarked upon the descent with a confidence born of her aboreal youth and of the fact that she had prudently borrowed an old pair of Amy's gym bloomers. A moment later she was over the wall, and stood upon the gritty side walk, beneath the caterpillar-eaten limes. Putting up the parasol, which she had brought down gripped in her teeth, she strolled through the gold siesta of stucco and wistaria, moving with almost the bodiless freedom of a dream, except for the occasional pinches by which Amy's boots obligingly reminded her that she was awake.

Emerging upon Adelaide Road, she took on a brisker step, and passing swiftly through the loud and broken streets, she arrived at the spot which, she had decided, must certainly be the object of her first pilgrimage in the great city. To most of her sex this would have been Bond Street or the most super of all cinemas, but Emily, though feminine, was not a woman, and even at the risk of being thought a blue-stocking, she gave the British Museum precedence over modes and movies. She had observed, while dusting Amy's writing desk one day, a ticket for the Reading Room lying neglected in a pigeon hole, and since Amy had sternly forbidden what she chose to call "monkey-tricks" with her own books, the chimp felt justified in borrowing this ticket in the interests of that intellectual urge which it is everyone's duty to forward by all the means in their power.

Emily was not entirely a stranger to the Museum. Mr. Fatigay had taken her there one afternoon, and had even penetrated with her as far as the inner door of the Reading Room, to indulge her with a glimpse of that vast hive, and the swarm of busy creatures engaged in manufacturing a further and diluted yield out of the very honey that gorged its cellular lining. Into this hive, tingling with the apprehensions of an alien wasp, come to contribute nothing, but to carry away all she could, Emily now entered, and, timidly taking a seat, she glanced about under her dark lashes to study the procedure of the habitués.

It was not long before her keen and analytical intelligence had grasped the connection between the consultation of a catalogue, the filling up of an application form, and the subsequent arrival of books. Marking her place with the bright parasol, which, she now realised with unerring judgment, seemed a little too smart and Ascotish for her austere surroundings, where, it appeared, all such sumptuary blossoms had been rigidly nipped in the bud, in order to produce a richer crop of beards and horn-rimmed spectacles, Emily trotted up to where the catalogues were shelved, and, having hoisted DA-DEB on to the shelf, she stood upon tip-toe to peep at it, in search of Darwin's *Origin of Species*, for she was a great believer in beginning at the beginning. But when she came to fill in the form, a most humiliating hitch occurred; humiliating more because she had so stupidly overlooked it than because of the shortcoming from which it derived, for the chimp was by no means an intellectual snob. She was, of course, unable to write. For a moment she was quite overcome.

"It serves me right," she murmured. "What business have I, a mere chimp, to insinuate myself into this Elysium, and by using someone else's ticket, too?"

Then something of the sterner fibre asserted itself, and remembering that the writing of many others, which was but little better than her own, not only had its birth here, but its end and its immortality also, she plucked up heart, and, "After all," she thought, "perhaps, in my humble line, I can do as well as these, and by the same means, by careful copying."

And this she proceeded to do, but, alas, her efforts were attended by even less success than that which usually crowns such methods, for what appeared a passable copy of the English characters to her private eye, seemed to the official behind the grating to be an inscription in some Eastern alphabet, so that, conscientiously approaching the self-conscious chimp, he asked her, "How d'ye do ? " first in Arabic and then in Chinese. On receiving no reply beyond that melancholy and fatalistic smirk with which one naturally disclaims understanding of an unknown tongue, he regarded Emily with great purpose, and observing her parasol, her prognathous jaw, and a nuance of superfluous hair, he addressed her in the dialect of the hairy Ainus of Japan. At this Emily spread apart her hands, as if to cast to the idle winds a soul ignoble enough to lack understanding of so thorough a courtesy.

Perceiving the pinkness of her palms, the official then spoke to her in Persian, and as this elicited only a further gesture of self-reproach from the embarrassed chimp, he tried her next, having noted also her dark complexion and diminutive stature, with the four cardinal dialects of the Deccan. All was in vain. For some moments the two gazed at one another, with much genuine liking and respect, across the linguistic gulf which lay between them.

Suddenly Emily conceived a plan. Taking the kind official by the sleeve, she led him to the catalogue, and putting her finger upon the title of the book she desired, she implored him with her most bewitching smile to fill up for her the form which she proffered. Touched by the sincerity in her eye, the good man, a true friend to all attempts at learning, brushed aside the stifling bonds of red tape, and benevolently made the desired exception to the rule.

How happy was Emily at that moment! She could scarcely contain herself until the book was fetched, and when it arrived she buried herself so earnestly in its pages as to win smiles of sympathy and approval from the blasé veterans of the Reading Room, to whom, for more years than they cared to count, the first glance at the book they had ordered had begot nothing but a dyspeptic desire for yet another. So smiles the jaded gourmet upon the hearty youngster whose naïve appreciation plays disproportionate havoc among the dishes of *hors-d'œuvres*. The officials, too, were appreciative of this single-hearted application of Emily's. One reader at least, they felt, seemed unlikely to add, by a capricious craving for change, to the burden of their hot and swollen feet, and they too smiled upon the eager young student. So smiles the waiter on observing that same youngster settle down to a substantial steak and chips, innocent of the need for titillation which calls for all the porterage of a seven-course meal.

Emily had won the good opinion of the Reading Room, and she had not revisited that spot many times before her demure and sober graces evoked a still warmer feeling from certain of the respectable gentlemen who regularly sat in her section. She was, they unanimously decided, the Belle of the British Museum, and under that title she became the reigning toast of the tea room, where more than one of her hirsute admirers contracted a mild tannin poisoning from drinking, with no heel taps neither, to those dusky charms which had set so many hearts ablaze.

It must not be assumed from these casualties, however, that her influence was mainly of a disintegrating kind. Though one or two of the frailer spirits lost many precious moments in gazing surreptitiously at her unconscious form when they should have been deep in their work, there were others who found in her compelling charm a new stimulus to energy, and scribbled more fiercely than ever in order that they might finish the gigantic works they were compiling, and emerge before her eyes from the dull husk of the reader into the dragon-fly iridiscence of the famous read. And one and all were conscious of a new spirit born within them, a renascent brightness which blossomed here in a new attaché case, there in a bow tie or a little amateur topiary for a straggling beard, and, in some, in a sparkling vivacity, surprising alike to each speaker and his friends, in their tea-time conversation.

"Here's to those bright eyes!" cried one, sluicing a steep wave of tea through the curved baleen of his moustache.

"Here's to her bewitching smile!" "To her orange ear!" "To her wee nose!" clamoured others. "And here's to the day she first came among us!" struck in a fifth.

"I remember it well," said a converted editor of Schopenhauer. "I think it was I who saw her first. I thought, 'Another woman!' Yes, that's what I thought. When I came in and saw a parasol lying on the desk beside mine: 'Another woman!' I thought. I always think that. There are too many . . ."

"Then I saw her before you did," burst in a biographer. "I saw her at the doorway. *She stood —a sight to make an old man young!* Well, I don't know, but tl e effect on a middle-aged one was startling. Perhaps you wouldn't believe it, but my indigestion—Well, you know it was a sort of bowel indigestion before—starchy. From that day to this, believe me or not, just as you like, it's changed. . . ."

"Who is she, I wonder? Where does she come from?" said someone else, not for the first time.

"Irish, if you ask me," said a Teague who was present. "She's Irish; Irish with a touch of dusky Southern blood—the passion and magnetism of old Spain."

"Not a bit of it," said a Fabian. "Those eyes are Oriental eyes, bright with the pain of young life born amid fated glories, like a palm tree springing up through the floor of a crumbling palace. They have the meekness too, of Oriental eyes, the eyes of a slave set free from the tyranny of an old exhausting beauty, meekly awaiting the commands of that inexplicable liberator, Western Civilisation."

"She walks, it is true, like one accustomed to the courts of India, rather than to those of Wimbledon," said a belated essayist on the Woman Question.

"My ideal!" exclaimed an earnest looking man, who had never uttered a word before, and he nodded with emphatic approval at the last speaker, before he sank, blushing like the setting sun, behind the wide horizon of his teacup.

"Well, I like her," said a simple fellow, "because she's a little woman. A bouncing little woman. I like them like that. My first wife was a bouncing little woman. My second wife was not. I was deliriously happy with my first wife. With my second—not altogether so. I like a bouncing little woman."

"Well, gentlemen " said the senior member of the company, who ignored the last remark as being the probably carnal utterance of one whose work was merely the compiling of a cyclists' encyclopædia. "Well, gentlemen, we had better make a move if we're to catch a last glimpse of her, for like all that's best in life, she comes late and departs early, Heaven knows where."

And, rising fragrant-breathed from their tables, the lowing herd wound slowly from the tea room, and lumbered in clumsy haste, goaded by a small and naked child, to their places in the Augean barton within. But, of the nine, only eight were thus urged home, for one, prodded too painfully perhaps, had jibbed at the gate, and now lurked, restless with uneasy purpose, in the entrance hall.

This was the earnest man who had spoken but two fervent words in the course of this, and all foregoing conversations, and from whom even those two could only have been elicited by the extreme force of his approval of the hint that Emily was an old-fashioned woman, much like his mother, of whom his memories were scented as with lavender, and like a dearly beloved aunt, on whom he had had a boyish fixation of the libido. Like most of the silent kind, he was a man of action. Careless of consequences, he had left his attaché case and his MS. derelict upon his desk.

"What," he thought, "is mere property, and the fruits of dry pedantic labour, compared with new-born romance?" "Nothing," he decided, "but the material for a fantastic sacrifice, like that of the beggar who, having come by a ticket in the Calcutta Sweep, flings his last penny into the river or upon the bar, in order to wait, in shiveringly expectant nakedness, for the advent of the capricious Goddess."

"*She is coming, my own, my sweet,*" he murmured, as the door swung glassily at the end of the corridor. "And now to follow her home, and find out where she lives."

Fate, whose initial gifts to lovers are supplied as generously as those free meals an angler offers to the fish, decreed that he should not be disappointed, for in a few seconds the outer door opened, and surely enough it was Emily came through, her rapt eye and parted lips proclaiming the student not yet wholly emerged from the magic spell of literature. Peeping out from behind a rack of post cards, he saw her cross the entrance hall. He followed.

"To think," he reflected, as his unconscious quarry turned out of Great Russell Street, "that I should be following an unknown woman up the Tottenham Court Road!" He was relieved when they had ascended into the less compromising air of Chalk Farm.

"To-night," he decided, "I will rest content with finding out the house in which she lives, and to-morrow I will shift my lodgings into apartments as near to it as possible. Then it will be hard if I cannot find some means of making her acquaintance. I might perhaps venture to address her as she leaves the house, saying, possibly, something like, 'Excuse me, madam,' lifting my hat and bowing with a grave formality which should appeal to one of Eastern origin, 'but have you seen my cat?' I must get a cat. It would be terrible if she found out that I had no cat. But if I had a cat, and she is a cat lover, she must become quite interested. She will very probably express a fondness for the animals. At once I will reply, 'But I have another cat, a little one. Some consider it beautiful. May I, dare I . . . beg your acceptance. . . .' " And, lost in the sweet reverie, he smirked and bowed upon the empty air.

At that moment, Emily chanced to look behind her, and received all the impact of the quivering blandness which her pursuer was bestowing upon her image.

"Good Heavens!" she thought. "Is it possible? Am I loved by D.17?"

The idea was distasteful to her. While she saw no reason to doubt his moral integrity, and felt indeed a deep gratitude for the honour he bestowed upon her, she knew only too well that she could offer nothing in return but a sincere friendship and a lasting esteem, and there was that in the way he had held one hand to his heart when she glanced at him, which suggested he would find such a response worse than nothing. Besides, her present situation was altogether too ambiguous, too unconventional. So the chimp bowed her head and hurried on.

"Did she see me?" he thought. "Provocatively thus to fly? Ah! The witch!" And, quickening his pace, he followed her up Haverstock Hill.

Emily, already late, had no time to make a detour in the hope of giving him the slip. When they reached the quiet turning beside Amy's house, she took a hurried glance about her, and seeing no one but her impassioned follower, she made a sudden leap at the wall and was over in the twinkling of an eye.

"Oh!" cried the astonished man, and he stood rooted to the spot.

"Oh!" he cried again, for the dainty figure had come once more into view, nimbly ascending the drain pipe which led to her high attic window.

The poor fellow could scarcely believe his eyes. His dream was shattered before it had well begun. To think that one so modest, so prim, almost, to the outward eye, should be such an arrant little tomboy in reality! Biting his lip in deep vexation, he hurried down the hill, cursing himself under his breath for having been an infatuated fool. On the bus top, in his hasty retreat to recover his work, there spasmodically burst from him at every few hundred yards:

"... modern women! These modern women!"

Now this incident, which was not without its whimsical side (and, indeed, in later life Emily would frequently shake her head smilingly at the recollection of it), this incident was something of a calamity at the time it occurred, and for a good reason: that Emily now felt that it would be too embarrassing and perhaps too dangerous to return to the British Museum. Even if she could have borne the proximity of one puzzled and outraged consciousness, and the possibility of gossip and curious glances from all sides, she dared not incur even a remote risk of some further pursuit or other complication which might result in her exposure to Amy. Reproach, humiliation, mockery, corporal punishment perhaps, and certainly a very strict confinement in future, would follow. And although a glimpse she had caught of her pursuer's face during her ascent of the drain pipe gave her grounds to hope that his passion was already much abated, she knew from her own cruel experience that, even supposing love to have been wiped out completely by some incident or revelation, it was more than probable that, at the next concurrence of the elements which had produced it, it would be produced again.

She felt, therefore, that it would be better for all concerned if she went no more to the Reading Room, and since the decision, like all thus qualified, was a painful one, she could not entirely banish a rather gloomy expression that evening.

"Emily seems to be frowning rather," said Mr. Fatigay, who was dining there that night. "I wonder if London strains her eyes at all. Perhaps she should wear glasses."

"What nonsense, Alfred!" said Amy.

CHAPTER X

I am become a name;
For always roaming with a hungry heart
Much have I seen and known.

"Tennyson, *Ulysses*," Emily thought; and though as a matter of fact she had not yet seen as much as she wished of the city, she felt now that she had too embarrassing a knowledge of the hearts of men, to permit of her mingling easily with the general crowd. Beside her experience of yesterday, she had frequently heard Amy recite to Mr. Fatigay detailed accounts of languishing glances or even ardent approaches inflicted on her by complete strangers, sometimes of military or artistic appearance, in the thoroughfares of the town. She had concluded, moreover, from his reception of these accounts, that he resented extremely those happenings to one whom he loved, whereupon she thought to herself, "It is a duty to avoid them, also, on the part of one who loves him."

It happened, therefore, that after a busy morning of sweeping and scrubbing, during which she had had no time to take thought, she effected her escape from confinement, and stood upon the sidewalk with no definite notion of where she should go. The hot walls, the hard stones and the sharp-edged dust, roused by their unfriendliness a keen nostalgia in her, and as a parrot screeched from a foody basement nearby, the poor exile closed her eyes and shudderingly inhaled a sharp whiff of her longing for her native land. For a moment she felt herself dispread in shafted twilight in the still heart of some great tree, sprawling on her back along a monstrous bough, with one sunspot, perhaps, making a jewel of the green-plush lichen an inch from her pensive cheek. From a drooping hand half an over-ripe fruit might fall away, splashing in luscious purple another branch forty feet below, along which a tiny pink and silver monkey would scuttle to seize upon it.

What if, her body thus peacefully reclined, her heart within, straining like some overworked engine, pumped out sorrow equally with blood? There, at least, that sorrow, sprouting from her bosom like a rank and cancerous orchid, would unfurl its deadly beauty unhindered and in quiet. Here, her grief, even, was debased and stunted under a petty oppression, frayed by the sharp meaningless detail of an alien world, brought down from tragedy into shapeless misery by her own thwarted attempts at intellectual development.

"And how," she thought, "am I helping my dear Mr. Fatigay by holding myself an anguished spectator of his decay? Would I have not done better to have remained cloistered in some vaulted grove, weeding all thoughts not of him from his green grave in my breast? Creeping out sometimes, perhaps, to follow, softly as the great moth, ghostly as the white bloom, the leaf-mould track to the clearing's edge, whence, looking to the lighted verandah, where his strange successor sat with bottle and magazine, and bright lamp whereunder the shattered beetles died, I should see as it were the opening of the path along which he had gone, leaving no trace on that gateway hardness, but only, in the deep jungle outside, his divine footprint eternal on the desert earth of my heart."

It was not natural to the poor chimp to long for a life of sterile sorrow; the usual trend of her thoughts when her position seemed more than usually hopeless lay rather towards a career of nursing, or some similar selfless benevolence, but this afternoon she was more than ordinarily dispirited.

"She's no use to me," Amy had said, later in the over-night conversation which had followed on Mr. Fatigay expressing anxiety about her eyes.

"I must declare," she had continued petulantly, "that, little as I like those two hobbledehoys you introduced as friends of yours, whose idea of mannerly behaviour seemed to be to brush aside every conversational opening I gave them, in order to chew to death their revolting reminiscences of what you were before I knew you, little as I liked them. . . ."

"But hang it all, Amy," Mr. Fatigay had

replied uneasily, "Grant and Thompson are excellent fellows. We were inseparable in the old days, and I hope we shall be again."

"Then you'll have to be separable from me." she had retorted. "No man can serve two masters, and if you choose to trample on everything I hope I stand for by introducing those clownish philistines into our life together—well, I'm afraid I can't bear with it. I blushed for your connection with them, and for mine with you, at every word they said."

"Oh, come!" he had replied, "Amy, you must admit they're not as bad as all that. They're not exactly highbrows, I'll agree, but two better-hearted fellows never breathed. They do their own jobs well enough, I can tell you, and that's more than can be said for the crowd of chatterers you're so fond of, and, as for your disliking them, you can't hate them half so much as I hate that wretched little Dennis Tickler who's always hanging round this place."

At this Amy had become very angry.

"Look here, Alfred," she had said. "My friends are cultured and intelligent people, and Dennis is one of the best friends I have. If you want to say anything against him, or any of them, whom goodness knows I'm always trying to get to like you, you can clear out."

"Well, why should you speak against *my* friends?" he had muttered.

"If I become your wife at all, Alfred," she had

said, piercing his heart with the words, "we must have our friends in common. I'm not going to be dragged into association with people of that sort, nor sit by on the shelf like a chattel and see you degraded by them. Friends, indeed! People you've not seen or heard from for years, and who came, anyway, only to make a butt of you. Perhaps you didn't see the glances they gave one another behind your back while we were talking, but *I* did. I'd like to know any *real* friends of yours, but these——! Alfred, you surely wouldn't put your relationship to them before your love for me, would you? *Yes or no?*"

Here Mr. Fatigay had looked sadly bewildered, for in such arguments the real tussle lay between his heart and his reason, rather than between Amy and himself; they were conflicts in which she played, from outside the region of stress and wounds, the decisive part of an Homeric goddess.

"And to return to what I was saying," she had said, when she had extracted a halting negative from him, and had lovingly transformed it into a gracious and chivalrous promise before storing it safely away in her memory, "I was saying that Emily's no use to me. She's either more stupid even than the rest of her species, or else maliciously sulky. To hear you talk of buying spectacles for her, as if she was human, makes me feel that the jungle must have turned your brain. The Zoo's the proper place for an ape, after all, where she could have the company of her own kind, and I really think we ought to send her there. I don't feel that I can stand her stupid dirty ways much longer."

Emily had here stared open-mouthed at her protector. She had already heard enough to furnish a sleepless night with new meditation on her folly in ever hoping that he would be disillusioned by hard treatment. And now he was being tried even nearer home. What would be the result, she wondered?

Fortunately Mr. Fatigay had here a middle course to resort to, and one which baffled for the time Amy's petulance at his over-scrupulous regard for the chimp.

"Why, of course, Amy," he had replied, "if you find Emily unsatisfactory, there's no need for you to keep her. I'd hoped she'd please you, but if she doesn't I can easily take her back now I've got a place of my own."

"Oh, don't bother," Amy had said crossly. "You'd only spoil her worse than ever. If she doesn't go to the Zoo, she may as well remain with me. I'll try to put up with her a little longer." For she could think of no excuse for insisting that Emily was to be sent into captivity, and, indeed, found her so cheaply useful, and so satisfying to torment, that she would not have suggested it, but for her annoyance at Mr. Fatigay's concern for the humble creature.

Thus the matter had been left, but Emily felt that she had escaped by chance rather than by

Mr. Fatigay's power to resist his love on behalf of his lover. This, as much because it augured so ill for his future welfare, as because it implied the nothingness of her claims beside Amy's demands, was the cause of her present depression, which, occurring as it did just when her access to the anodyne of study had been cut off, through no fault of her own, weighed so heavily upon her that her dream of a jungle hermitage now gave place to the more practical consideration of whether she would not, after all, be wise to seek as a cloister the very prison to which Amy had proposed sending her.

"After all," she said to herself, "the jungle would only be so much scenery. The greatest tragedies are played best in the severest of settings. Given peace and loneliness, what matter whether it is the innumerable trunks of trees, or the nearer austerer verticals of bars, which hem me in?"

"But," she added, "I had better go first and see what it's like, lest it should turn out in this case as it has with love and England, from both of which (despite their importance culturally) I would have fled as from the plague, had I but had a true glimpse of them before-hand." And wasting no more time on reflection, Emily set forth, putting up her parasol, which she had again brought down with her, not for vain display, but from a sincere desire to shelter herself from the casual glances of the masculine crowd.

A heavy thunder-shower, shortly after noon,

had discouraged the sightseers, and Emily, descending on the inner side of the fence, found almost unpeopled the wide and stiff-flowered spaces, into which, with their surround of skeleton domes, ringed craters and Giotto crags, with their watercress teas like memories of childhood, with not knowing which way to turn amid staccato cries of unknown emotion: into all of which one enters as into the excitement of a half-familiar dream. The white sun, which five minutes ago had burnt up the last glittering drop from the paper-faced asters, had heated to their widest and thinnest expansion the humid bubbles of scent risen from the flower beds and the various dung, and now these met and interfusingly burst upon the eye-aching paths, and the chimp, as she inhaled each new cocktail of brittle essences, was switchbacked dizzily over the peaks of jungle fears and raptures, and into the wide dips of its rich and scented ennui. A flamingo spread its rosy wings, the sun stared, a lion sprang in his hollow cage, thunder muttered in the bankéd west, bears, tigers, ounces, pards, gambolled before her; the unwieldy elephant, to make her mirth, used all his might, and wreathed his lithe proboscis.

"Back in Eden!" thought Emily, as she watched a child in a dyed frock reward the last-mentioned comedy turn with a bun.

She had not gone very far when she saw, in a quiet corner behind the small cats' house, an empty cage, the door of which was unlocked, and recalling the purpose of her visit, she congratulated herself on this opportunity of viewing the bars from their hinder side, and accordingly, with a wary glance about her, she nipped into it. But no sooner had she closed the door, when she saw two people advancing upon her from different directions, and a sudden panic seized her. "For," thought she, "they will surely be amazed at my costume, and will speedily attract a crowd here, and I shall either be advertised as a runaway, and ultimately haled back to whatever punishment Amy chooses to devise, or I shall be locked in before I have made up my mind whether I want to stay or not. I begin to feel that I don't."

The intruders, however, were still pretty far off when an idea occurred to the sagacious creature, which was, that the best she could do was to slip off her dress and pretend to be a true captive, dully asleep, so that she should attract no particular attention, and, when the coast was clear again, she could reassume her clothes and quietly emerge. This course she at once embarked upon, though not without a blush or two, and before the approaching pair had met outside the cage, her dress and parasol were hidden beneath the straw, and nothing more unusual was to be seen than a simian and reclining edition of *September Morn*.

"Darling!"

"Beloved!"

These words have an irresistible appeal to every womanly heart, and Emily, hearing them, could not restrain herself from raising an eyelid and taking a sly peep at the enthusiastic speakers.

She almost sat up in her amazement. The woman, though disguised in a tenderer smile than Emily had hitherto noted on her face, was well known to her as Mrs. Dunedin, a young matron of some few months' standing, and an intimate friend of Amy's. The young man, her interlocuter, was certainly not her husband, who was, the chimp remembered well, a tall and soldierly looking man, whereas this was as weedy and ill-looking a scrub as ever she had set eyes upon. But Mrs. Dunedin was clearly not of this opinion, for having sealed her greeting with a hearty kiss, she held his hand in hers, and eyed him with obvious gusto.

"Good heavens!" thought the chimp. "Can this indeed be Amy's twin soul, the most high minded of all her friends? Can it be she who complained so bitterly to Amy, not a fortnight ago, of the carnal side of passion, and the indecency of the male form? If neither the frigidity of his wife nor the inferiority of his rival can protect a husband's honour, why, no man, not even Mr. Fatigay, is safe!"

At that moment, their first raptures having subsided, they glanced perfunctorily into the cage, and:

"Why!" said Mrs. Dunedin. "What an enormous chimp! It's almost as big as that one that Amy Flint now has, and has trained, by sheer force of personality, she told me, to serve her as a maid."

"Well," said the young man, with a sneer, "it might very well be the other way round, for, if you dressed this one up in Amy's clothes, I'm sure I should find it hard to distinguish between them, except that the ape has the sweeter expression of the two."

"What? Do you say so?" said Amy's friend, with a titter. "To tell you the truth, there *is* a likeness; Amy being so small and dark. But I'm greatly surprised to hear *you* mention it, for I always thought you were deeply in love with her. In fact, she told me so."

"Not I," cried the young man. "It's true I visited her a good deal a few months ago, but then I got bored with her superior airs, and . . ."

"Oh, come!" interrupted the lady, with a slightly acid smile, "I know more about it than that. You can't deceive me."

"After all, why should I?" said he. "Well, if you want to know, I *was* rather keen at one time, and hung about her longer than any man in his senses would. But she's one of those who'll allow nothing but a soul passion before marriage, whatever might be the case after. So I withdrew, and left her to this African fiancé of her's. And, if he's the sort of person she hinted he was. . . ."

"Oh, he *is*," interpolated the lady.

"Well, he'll have a pretty thin time, if you ask me," rejoined the young man. "But enough of such a dull subject. Is there anything here that might amuse you?"

"Oh, do let's go and see Monkey Hill," cried his companion, and they passed on.

It was a grave-faced chimp that crept out of the cage and resumed her inspection of the gardens.

"A thin time!" she said to herself. "A thin time. . . .!"

Conscious that it was almost madness to hope that she could be of any assistance, unless the extreme thinness of his allotted time should cause the scales to drop at last from his eyes, she nevertheless felt, in some stirring of that instinct which prompts sea-captains to sink with their sinking ships, that she must stay by her beloved, though it might mean no good to him, and nothing but prolonged torture for herself.

She had made her decision in utter hopelessness, but such was her temper that soon afterwards hope began to flood in, and she felt more and more confident that Mr. Fatigay's pride and manliness would recoil, with a force greater than that which flexed them, after a little experience of what was hinted at in the tinny phrase, "a thin time."

Strengthened by these thoughts, she straightened her bonnet, and, first brushing a little straw off her dress, she reopened her parasol, and resolved to spend the remainder of her afternoon in innocent pleasure among the album of scents and sights about her.

From a quizzical inspection of the lions and

leopards, she passed to the softer pleasures of the hornbills and the cranes, which roused in her such a tide of soft remembrance (for all the anthropoids are fond of birds) that it was with suffused eyes and quivering lips that she turned away at last, eager to seek any others of her kind who might be in residence here. A few yards farther on stood a large double cage, in a sort of island on the wide path, and, as she approached this, she saw within it the form of a large female chimpanzee, busily engaged in certain little refinements of her toilet. Emily leaned against the railing. The captive, who apparently went by the name of Sally, cocked a supercilious eye at this new visitor, and was about to return to her occupation, when she gave a second glance, and then, hastening across the cage, she caught hold of two of the bars, and, thrusting her face between them, she stared in silent amazement at the shy figure outside.

"Good afternoon," said Emily, in the tongue of her kind, which, if it contains but few syllables, is rich in nuances of expression.

"Good heavens!" cried Sally. "What are you doing out there, walking about like the rest of the people ? Have you escaped or something ? "

"Oh, no," said Emily. "I'm living nearby in a little maisonette, as a sort of companion to an Englishwoman, and, hearing that you were here, I thought I'd come in and look you up."

"Living with an Englishwoman, indeed!" exclaimed Sally, in tones in which surprise, envy and scorn were pretty evenly mingled. "Well, there's no accounting for tastes. Some of the younger set here have gone native to a certain extent, and take *thé Anglais* with one of the stewards every afternoon. I don't myself. Perhaps I'm old-fashioned. When in Rome, they say. . . . Of course, I've *heard* of chimpanzees taking up life among the inhabitants, but I must say I've never seen one before. Still—if you like it. . . . But that dress—is it silk? And the bonnet, really—very attractive. I feel it's the sort of thing that might suit me. Would you care to pass it through the bars for me to try on?"

"Please excuse me," said Emily, "but if anyone happened to come along, I'd have a crowd about me in no time. You know what people are."

"Well, as you like," replied Sally, good-naturedly. "Living in the public eye myself, I can't say crowds bother me much. If it wasn't for this threatening weather, I expect they'd be two or three deep about the place now. They generally come to see me first. I must admit I didn't intend to give the bonnet back to you, as probably you guessed."

Emily shrugged her shoulders with a friendly twinkle.

"I wouldn't take anyone's banana," resumed Sally. "But one doesn't often get a new hat. If there's a drawback to this place, that's what it is. The clothes they offer one are very second-rate. I happened to be taking a sunbath just as you came along, and I'm not sorry either, my dear, for my wardrobe," said she, jerking a thumb to the inner apartment, where in truth nothing but the back sheet of a newspaper and a child's glove were stored, "my wardrobe being what it is, I should have looked a positive frump beside you."

"Well, clothes aren't everything," said Emily spontaneously. "Life's not all honey outside, I can tell you. I expect you have chosen the better part."

"I don't know about that," replied Sally. "It's pretty dreary, being cramped in this draughty hole with a pack of fools pointing and laughing all day long. And as for choosing—I was caught by bird lime myself, and that's that."

"But at least you've got company, haven't you?" asked Emily. "Isn't there someone living in the apartment behind ? "

"Oh, there's a poor mad fellow come to live there now," said Sally. "One who got mauled by a leopard, and now thinks he's dead and in Hell for his misdeeds. And as it seems that the chief of these was, well—being too amorous, he's got a highly inconvenient complex on such matters now, in addition to his insanity. I don't know if there's any chance of him being cured. He's a well-set-up young fellow enough, and it goes to my heart to see him in such a state. It seems such a waste, somehow. Go and have a look at him, my dear, and give me your advice."

Emily, a premonition stirring within her,

hurried round to the other cage, and there, sitting crouched in a corner, horribly scarred, and adorned with a copious millinery of straw, was Henry, whom she had left in the clutches of the leopard.

"Henry!" she cried in amazement. "Henry! Don't you know me? It's Emily."

Henry looked up dreadfully from where he cowered.

"Well, Emily!" he muttered. "Have you too come to haunt me? I know I was wrong to throw that banana skin, and, it's true enough, I meant to do worse still. I determined that, if I could get you on the rebound, so to speak, that day you ran away from the schoolmaster, I'd take it out of you for daring to love anyone but me. But I was punished, Emily, and I'm being punished still. When I was in the very act of making up to you, a leopard sprang on me—no doubt you saw it—and I felt his red-hot teeth and claws, and then all was dark, and I awoke to find myself in the hands of fiends, who bore me here—to Hell! Sweet Em, what shall become of Henry, being in Hell for ever?"

"But why," she asked in amazement, "should you think that you're dead and in Hell?"

"Look!" said he. "Look over there!" pointing across the wide space to where an end of the great cats' cages was in view. "Look! D' you see him? That's the leopard. Perpetually he crouches to spring. Perpetually I crouch in terror. If I hide inside, a fiend comes and turns me out and bolts the door."

"Ah! He's looking at me now. Oh! Oh! Oh!"

"Come, Henry! Be calm!" said Emily sympathetically. "He's not looking at you really. Use your reason. Aren't you safe behind those nice strong bars? And, as for this being Hell; it may be for the leopard, but it should be Heaven for you. If it *is* your leopard at all, which I very much doubt, he's certainly being punished for having hurt you. These bars, and those, are arranged to make you safe, so that you can laugh at him, while he longs perpetually to get you. No one gives *him* nuts: they only rattle on the bars with a stick, on purpose to make him roar. To you, they give apples, bananas, copies of the daily paper, cigarettes and small pieces of mirror. Is this the behaviour of fiends?"

"But . . ." said Henry.

"Don't keep on saying 'but'," she said. "Pull yourself together, man, and realise that you're in Heaven, and that you're being compensated for your ill-treatment by the leopard in being able to tantalise him for all eternity, and," she added with a sigh, "for your ill-treatment by me in seeing me as unhappy as when you saw me last, while for you, in the cage behind, lies the opportunity of eternal bliss."

Here Henry began to scratch himself vigorously, as was his habit during strenuous attempts to assimilate new ideas, and, as soon as he had grasped what she said about the leopard, the honest fellow's demeanour changed entirely, and he began to dance about the cage like one possessed, pausing now and then to shout insults at his distant foe.

Leaving him still rapt in this ecstasy, and trusting that her second hint would come home to him when his first transports were calmed a little, Emily slipped away behind the cage to where Sally was awaiting her.

"I think he'll be better now," she said. "Listen! He's making all sorts of fun of the leopard to his face. I've persuaded him that he's in Paradise, and I must leave it to you, my dear," she added archly, "charitably to preserve him in the illusion."

"Well, he's certainly a well-set-up young fellow," said Sally, "and I'm one of those who like the matrimonial state, I must say. The only trouble is, that if I've a contempt for one sort of person more than for another, it's for the sort who must always be either in Heaven or in Hell, and will let a few breathy words make all the difference."

"Oh, pray don't mention it," cried Emily generously. "The transition's nothing. It'll require more than words to keep it up, or to make the illusion a fact, rather. That nobler task is yours."

"Oh, I don't feel jealous, really," replied Sally with a smile. "It was just a twinge. Naturally one likes to do everything for the man one's set one's heart on. Look here, my dear: aren't there some people coming? I think he's knocking at the door. So long."

"Good bye, dear, and lots of orange blossom!" said Emily, rather vulgarly for her, and noticing that the sun was far declined, she hurried off in the direction of Haverstock Hill, feeling on the whole much stimulated by her eventful afternoon.

CHAPTER XI

I told my love, I told my love,
I told her all my heart,
Trembling, cold, in ghastly fears.
Ah! she did depart!

Soon after she was gone from me,
A traveller came by,
Silently, invisibly:
He took her with a sigh.

"DARLING! What marvellous flowers! Are they really for me ?"

"How wonderful you look!" returned Mr. Fatigay, with equal enthusiasm, for on this, the night of the party, Amy had abandoned the rather demurely period sort of frock she usually affected, with its tight bodice and full skirt, and had put on a far simpler garment of black and vermilion, which was, however, so up to date, so deadly Parisian, that its simplicity only lent it the final touch, the hint of the prematurely vicious little girl. Lipstick a shade hotter and drier than usual, startling as a gout of arterial blood coughed up into the midst of Amy's smiling features, added to the effect of sweet innocence playing the cocotte. The speculation aroused, of course, was on how far the game might proceed.

Taking her lover by the hand, Amy ran with him lightly, laughingly, madly up the stairs, drawing ahead a little before they had reached the top, in order to wait for him in an attitude of provocative welcome on her own landing.

"You won't mind just a scratch meal in the kitchen to-night, will you, dear ? Nothing's nicer than party clothes in the kitchen. Because the room is all ready for the people who're coming. Put your hat and coat in here." And she flung open the door of her bedroom, and, still prattling, followed Mr. Fatigay inside.

Now, whether it was the novel aspect of Amy in the new dress; or whether it was the touch of abandon she had put on in keeping with it; or whether it was that her chamber, which was to take on for this evening the cold and formal aspect of a cloakroom, was not thus petrified in our hero's eyes by his own entrance, but awaited some more alien garrison of hats and wraps before suffering the change, and was still the rosy, scented sheath of Amy's intimate life; or whether it was that tawny August, cruel oppressor of the long-engaged, had fermented Mr. Fatigay's blood, like Dante's, to a liquor pale and ardent as the most potent of dry sherries; or whatever it was, the fact remains, that after a minute or two the door slammed violently, and Emily, washing radishes in the kitchen, found that though she strained very hard to hear the urgent voices within, she could distinguish nothing but a throaty rumble from her master, and a few sharp and angry ejaculations from Amy.

Shortly the door was plucked open again, and Amy emerged with the expression of one who has been mortally hurt by a trusted hand, and her lover followed with chagrin and regret mixed on his face in the most hang-dog look that any lover can wear. Emily glanced from one to the other, and nervously dropped her eyes to the floor.

The meal was eaten nearly in silence, in one of those suspensions of emotional life in which a complex mixture of feelings resolves itself into its elements, each of which ebbs back to the breast to which it is most native, so that before they had finished picking at their food all the humiliation was centred in Mr. Fatigay and all the resentment in Amy.

"I suppose we may as well go into the drawing-room," she said, when Mr. Fatigay had heaved a despairing sigh or two across the narrow table. And she got up, leaving him to follow as soon as he could pluck up heart enough to do so. For some time he sat at the table, moodily pushing a match through and through a banana skin, but at last Emily tactfully removed his plate, for it was high time for her to get on with the washing-up. At that he sprang to his feet, and, with some appearance of resolve mingling with the self-reproach on his countenance, he marched across to the drawing-room.

To-night that apartment had something cold

and strained in its atmosphere. White wine and claret cup, and a bottle of whisky for gruff old Mayhew ("thoroughly unconventional"), whose shaggy exterior advertised a heart of gold, tempting sandwiches, seductive sugar cakes, the silver box full of Turkish and Virginian, the Cona and its cups: this chilly and powerful still-life exuded an air unpropitious to the heated demands and defences of an outraged intimacy. Mr. Fatigay, however, thought he was not to be quelled by a cucumber sandwich.

"Amy," he cried. "Amy."

Amy, stiffly reclined in a window seat, where she held a page of Vogue to catch the last pale light of the fading sky, looked up after a moment, and said:

"Well?"

"Look here, Amy," he said. "I know I behaved very badly, but after all it's quite understandable—I'm only flesh and blood, after all—and there's no need for you to be so furious about it."

"Indeed?" said she, "I'm glad you think so. I happen to think otherwise, but then my ideas are not the same as yours. But if you think that being engaged to me entitles you to behave like a brute beast,—Good heavens! I shall never forget the side of your nature you've shown me to-night —if you think that—then the sooner our engagement's at an end, the better."

"I heartily agree," he replied (and Emily, who,

though she could not bear these continual quarrels, had found it impossible not to creep out upon the landing to hear what transpired—Emily here pricked up her ears in surprise and pleasure), "I heartily agree, but not perhaps in the way that you mean. Here you've kept me hanging about for years—I only went and buried myself in Africa because you insisted on having time for self-development, as you call it, before you settled down—and now when I come back you keep putting me off till I go nearly mad, and then, when my feelings get the better of me for once, you look at me as if I was something unspeakable. Why! You can't love me a bit, really, or you'd be eager to end this miserable engagement by marrying me as you promised. That's what I mean." Emily here drooped a little.

"I'm sorry you feel it to be a miserable engagement, Alfred," said Amy. "If that's the case now, I don't know that marriage would make things much better. And, as for not caring for you, why, how *can* you say such a thing? I'm always thinking about you and your work, and I give up all my time to you. I scarcely ever see any of my friends nowadays, and it's ages since I've been to see mother, even; all because of the demands you make upon me."

"Of course marriage would make things better," he replied. "Do you think that I can be myself, or happy, living as I am, on the rack, so to speak? Do you think it's a satisfying life for a man to come round and spend a few hours with you in the evening, and to have to go off at eleven with nothing but a few kisses, to make him more wretched than ever? As for giving up your friends: you were out seeing them three evenings last week: to say nothing of the fact that they're always dropping in when I'm hoping we shall be alone together. No. If you love me at all, you'll make up your mind to get married, and at once, too."

"As for seeing my friends," she replied, "naturally I still see them now and then. You don't want an absolute *egoisme à deux*, do you? I don't ask you to give up seeing *your* friends, when they're worth seeing. I always encourage you to. Why should you ask me to give up mine? Why, Alfred, being married to you would be like marrying a Turk or Arab. I wanted us to be comrades, and take an interest in each other's interests. But I know now."

"Oh, come!" cried Mr. Fatigay.

"Don't try to deny it," said she. "You've shown me your true nature too clearly for that. You only want me for one thing." And at this terrible thought, her voice began to quaver, which threw Mr. Fatigay further into confusion, for it added yet another element to the argument, and in discussions of this sort he had the magpie limitation of being unable to count more than three.

"No, Amy," he said, catching at the nearest

thread, "I don't only want you for one thing."

"Yes, you do," she cried.

"No, I don't," he said. "But, after all, you're not a Victorian miss, and you know perfectly well that if *that* is unsatisfied everything else gets warped, and one's nerves get upset, and everything's spoilt."

"Only if you choose to let it," said she. "Other men, men I respect, use *some* self control. And they sublimate. Look at Dennis. I've known him for years, he's always been a sort of brother to me. Well—I could never have anything but a sisterly feeling for him, of course—but I happen to know—I tell you this in utter confidence—he told George, Susan's husband, and she told me—that he's cared for me for years. And he's never even hinted at it."

But here Mr. Fatigay began to curse and swear so very heartily against Dennis Tickler and all his ways, not without including some bitter insinuations against Amy herself, that she, feeling herself to have got on to rather uncertain ground, dissolved into tears in good earnest, hearing which Emily shrugged her shoulders in disgust, and retired from her post on the landing, for she knew well what the issue would be, and could not endure to listen to it.

Had she stayed, she would have heard Mr. Fatigay suddenly turn about, and forgetful of all his case, begin to blame himself bitterly for his lack of self-control, and promise to amend for the future, if only Amy would now dry her tears. This, when he had cursed himself very bitterly for having caused them, she at length consented to do, saying:

"Now you've made me cry, I suppose you're happy." And when this suggestion had been suitably denied, she withdrew to her room, in order to remove the traces of her emotion before her friends arrived.

Soon they came, descending from taxis into the rustling lamp-lit cave of the great chestnut tree which overhung the front gate, or walking through the bloomy electric dusk from their dwellings nearby. The men were the sort who have given up art for marriage, but, as if nature was scheming to restore the balance, many of their women appeared likely to give up marriage for art. Dennis Tickler, that shadowy and sinister figure, arrived, and was received very warmly by all. It may have been that what Amy had been told about him was true, or it may have been that he recognised his genius as flowering best in the fields of sentimental friendship, but he had not given up art for marriage, but only for a post in an advertising agency, which bitter sacrifice marked him from the outset as being a man of sorrows, and therefore well fitted to hear the sorrows of others. Beyond this, as Emily's discerning eye told her at a single glance, there could be nothing in it whatever, and she wished she could speak, that she might whisper as much to Mr. Fatigay, to clear his spirit of the pain and suspicion which was evident in the glances he occasionally stole at this young man.

It was a good party. Everyone took a glass and joined lustily in *Billy Boy*, and, by the time another song or two had been sung, all the characters, and at least half of the people present were characters, had opened exhalingly as evening primroses, and were being thoroughly characteristic. Inseparable friends got their heads together; Mayhew, who painted, demanded guts in a picture; Angela was brilliant and delightfully mad, Peter was clearly in one of his wild moods (it was probably the sight of Susan and Jack, whom he had not seen since their honeymoon, that upset him), Amy was prepared to live part way up to her frock, Simpson tried to teach Elizabeth his Russian dance, and Herbert Houghton's impersonations of everybody were better than ever. Mr. Fatigay had no character at all, beyond being set down as rather possessive by certain of Amy's confidantes. Emily, in her black dress and starched cap and apron, was almost constantly in the room, handing round the drinks and working the gramophone.

When the evening was fairly far advanced, a friend of Amy's arrived, bringing a stranger. Nothing could be more supercilious than the bearing of this young man, though he was as ugly as a toad, for he now found himself among people who did not recognise his name at a first hearing, though it had been on the backs of two or three very advanced booklets, and by the time he had overheard scraps of some of the conversations that were going on, he began to think himself among savages, and behaved accordingly; that is, he stared at the women.

It was not long before his wicked eye lighted on Emily, and conceiving her to have more blood in her than the rest of them, and, in view of her position, to be less likely to talk, he began to wonder how he could come at her, for he had no more breeding, manners or scruples than any of his set. This was about the time when the central light of the room had been extinguished, for Millicent to perform at the piano, and for one or two others to sing.

"You'd better wash up all that you can collect," whispered Amy, "and set all the clean things on a large tray. Then you can go to bed." And she sat down in a corner to listen to the music that was beginning, while the young man, who had heard what she said, took a chair very near the door.

"Do you know who that is, that Bella has brought?" whispered Angela, who had been asked by Bella to do so. "It's the Wagstaffe who wrote *Pandarus, or the Future of Bloomsbury.*"

"Ssh!" whispered Amy. "Yes, I know." And she eyed the young man with great interest, and would have gone over and sat by him, but Millicent was just beginning to play, and it would have meant scuffling out from among too many people.

Before very long the young man, having decided

the music was less amusing than the little dark-eyed maid might prove to be, quietly opened the door and slipped out, as if he was going to fetch a pocket handkerchief from his overcoat.

As soon as he stepped out upon the landing, he could see the light behind the patterned glass panels of the little scullery, where Emily was drying the glasses, and he had advanced so far as to have his hand already upon the door handle, when he realised that his presence in the scullery must be observed by anyone who might come out of the drawing-room, so feeling that he need stand on little ceremony with the humble maidservant, he thrust his head inside, and with a smile he indicated in dumb show that she was to make haste and finish her task, and join him on the attic stairs which mounted darkly from the landing. Emily, whose innocence prevented her from guessing at all his motive, and who, indeed, disliked this young man far less than any of the others there, nevertheless hesitated before joining him in the nook to which he had already withdrawn himself. "For," thought she, "whatever it is he wants of me at the moment, I am unlikely to be able to satisfy him, being a mere dumb and inexperienced chimp, and if I join him in that secluded spot he may end up by wanting the one thing I can, but will not, give. So it is safer not to go." And with a good-humoured smile the prudent chimp turned again to the sink.

Now it happened, a few minutes later, that Amy,

released by a momentary pause in the musical programme, came out to fetch a pocket handkerchief, and the young man, seeing her pass the foot of the stairs, mistook her for Emily in the dim light, and began to renew his inviting gestures.

"What can he mean ?" almost thought Amy. "Perhaps someone has told him I write also, and he wants a more sparkling *tête-à-tête*, more *risqué*, than can be held inside. Walter Wagstaffe! Bella will simply tear her hair." And she gaily ascended to where he was sitting.

"What ?" he began, noticing the difference in costume, but deciding to treat the encounter as if it had been fatally ordained since the beginning of things, "Have you come at last ?"

"Has it seemed so long ?" said Amy, inspired by her wicked new frock, and by her knowledge of his reputation, to adopt that bright tone of sexual gallantry which she understood to prevail in the glittering circles in which he moved.

"Eternity!" he replied, with mechanical efficiency.

"Ah! but," said she, archly, seating herself beside him, "Einstein has shown us that time is only a dimension of space, and space being no longer regarded as infinite, time surely can't be eternal. Only those who have quite the *worst* sort of back to the womb complex. . . ." And here she rattled off into a most informed discourse, now brilliantly playful, now very serious and grave, to which, though he only replied in very hackneyed sentences, the young man listened with great complacency. For though he held the Einstein gambit to be rather a colourless one, he had found it to yield such excellent results that he had come by a generalisation from it, which was: that while he had sometimes failed to understand a woman who spoke simply and on the A.B.C. of some everyday subject, the more abstruse her matter and the more involved her terms, the more easy he found it to take her.

"Besides," said he to those of similar kidney, "the nearer we approach those altitudes where words must fail us, the sooner comes the time to proceed to action, and for this reason, and no other, I hold that the achievements of science are the greatest blessing which has yet been bestowed upon mankind, for where should we poor bachelors be without Freud and Einstein, poetry having declined so far since Swinburne's glorious day ? "

"Why," he had been heard to exclaim on one occasion, to a young man who had come to him for advice, "I began as a poet myself, and had so little success that I developed a painful inferiority complex, which (Heaven bless the day!) prompted me at last to glance at a magazine article on psycho-analysis, and it is no exaggeration to say that I owe my present comfortable condition solely to that article, and to a few of the terms I found in it. *So that sport*, as Tennyson finely says, *went hand in hand with science*."

"Why," he went on, "your scientist, or his simulacrum, is to the poor, lean, busy shark of a poet as is the great whale which Donne describes: he has but to open his mouth and his prey flock in:

He hunts not fish, but, as an officer
Stays at his court, at his own net, and there
All suitors of all sorts themselves enthrall,
So on his back lies this whale wantoning.

"Ah! what a poem!" he added, for he was a good fellow at heart. "To forsake such methods for the ugly jargon of science is like laying aside the whole art of angling, and dynamiting a stream for fish. Still, we must move with the times, but I don't mind telling you life is the poorer for it, and if I had my choice I'd live in the days when one cast a fine line of Baudelaire or Dowson, for, if the fish were shyer then, the least of them was a thousand times sweeter than all the shoals which, at the mere reverberation of one exploded hypothesis, turn on their backs and . . ." But here he pressed the metaphor to a grossness beyond the limits of good taste.

This, then, was the young man before whom Amy was innocently displaying her intellectual plumage, and you may be sure that, though he did not much pursue the subjects she touched upon, he had no scruple in exhibiting a great admiration for her understanding of them, a measure which, in a country where the administration of a mere cigar ash in a glass of port wine is, I believe, heavily penalised by law, should surely be punishable by a long term of penal servitude. And so it is, in the sense that many who adopt the pose end by hypnotising themselves as well as their victims, and are ultimately distorted into a reverence sottishly real. But this, like other of the penalties of license, falls chiefly on the ingenuous amateur, while the practised libertine escapes unscathed.

"But, surely," he said, "you must write ? What is it—poems ? Brilliant essays ? Or perhaps on some technical, scientific subject ? How is it I've lived so long without coming across anything you've published ? "

"Oh," said she, "I have, tentatively, tried to catch an impression here and there. What I should like to do would be to experiment with form. But publication . . . well, hardly, in these days ! But you—you write a great deal, of course."

"Well, I have," he replied, "up till to-night. But now I'm going to *live*." And with that he took hold of her, and in a manner which showed he had no illusions as to the main purpose of vertebrate existence. But Amy, though shaken, and though terrified of being thought a suburban prude, found the transition a little too precipitate for her sense of balance. More words were required.

"Stop," she said. "Why, you hardly know anything about me. Supposing I happened to be fond of someone else?"

"Why," said he, "you may well be. For I'm not so blind as to think your loveliness can have failed to attract a hundred hearts, or that your gallant generosity can have failed to reward the best of them. But you don't think me such a Victorian fool as to mind that? After all, how contemptible it would be, to study science and not to live according to its discoveries! And if there's one thing which modern advances have shown us, it is that it is the best and not the worst person who can love many, and the truly moral rather than the immoral who has the courage to attain full self-realisation in this respect. Besides, matter flickering, as it does, in and out of existence, ensures that we are born again every second, so that I no more feel that you are part of your past at this perfect moment, than you, when you have gone on from it into some radiant to-morrow, need feel, unless you wish, that what happens now is part of you then."

"But," murmured Amy, blushing with very shame, "I'm afraid I have no past; not in that sense, I mean."

"What," cried he, "then all the more reason that you should have a present, and *here it is!*"

"Stop," said she. "But, you see, *he* may not think as you do, and I should hate to hurt him."

"What?" exclaimed the young man, glad to fall back on poetry again. "But you think as I do. *Let me not to the marriage of true minds admit impediments . . . to thine own self be true, and it must follow, as the night the day, thou can'st not. . . .* But how I run on! The thing is, that he can't be moved by you as I am, who could not bear to sit inside there and see you surrounded by a crowd of fools. Do you think he understands you as I do ? "

"I think he loves me well enough," said Amy. "Indeed, I should be a rotter if I let you doubt it. But," she added with equal, though widely separated, sincerity and truth, "I don't think he understands me as you do."

"Why, then . . .!" cried the young man, and clipped her closer.

At that moment Mr. Fatigay came out upon the landing to fetch a handkerchief from his overcoat and switched on a new light. Emily, who had by now ventured to creep out from her retreat, followed his glance to where the unheeding couple were just visible above, and her heart opened with pity and contracted with apprehension as she saw him grow white to the lips, and then clench his hands in a sudden gust of fury. The poor man had, by this time, however, well learned that whenever he was moved very violently he was pretty sure to be culpably in the wrong, and knowing, too, that Amy would never forgive any demonstration of possessiveness in front of her friends, he made a tremendous effort at self-control, and he turned on his heel and rejoined the company, where, as very few of them ever addressed a word to him, he thought he might sit quietly and try to see Amy's point of view in this unconventional behaviour.

For some time he sat in a corner with his glass in his hand, and this he very frequently replenished in hope to still the restlessness of his mind, which hovered constantly outside upon the staircase. And, as a certain boredom which had overcome him during the earlier part of the evening had then prompted him to drink rather more than was his custom, he was very soon tipped off his balance into a moody and reckless confusion, in which things began to seem rather unreal, and not to matter very much anyway.

It was at this stage that he was joined by a very close friend of Amy's, Bella, the young woman who had brought Walter Wagstaffe, in fact. She had noticed the strained look upon his face when he re-entered the room, and, going out shortly afterwards to fetch a handkerchief from her hand-bag, had quickly perceived the cause, and not without some feeling of injury. It occurred to this young woman that what was sauce for the goose was not only sauce for the gander, but also for any other goose who happened to be about, so that as her husband, who was a foolishly jealous person, happened not to be present, she thought it no harm to approach Mr. Fatigay and to embark upon a little flirtation with him.

"Why is it," said she, seating herself beside him. "Why is it that you never say a word to me?"

"Well," replied Mr. Fatigay, after a little conscientious consideration, "I didn't think you wanted me to."

"How too deliciously modest of you!" cried she, with great enthusiasm. "Whatever can have made you think that? Perhaps it's that I've always felt so shy of you, since you're so much the lion of the party, with your too thrilling Conrad sort of background. I should love to live alone in the jungle."

"The lion, indeed!" said Mr. Fatigay with a titter. "I thought people generally regarded me as a bear, rather."

"Well, only because you look as if you could hug so terribly," replied the lady, and then, as if realising that she had said something very foolish and indiscreet, she blushed and lowered her eyes in confusion, though not before those orbs had, in the merest fraction of a second, held a brief correspondence with Mr. Fatigay's, in which time they had come to a very perfect agreement, which only needed the ratification of their more cumbrous principals.

"When I was a child," she resumed, with the agility of a dancer, who, having just shown you that she can do the splits, returns in bewildering *da capo* to a remotely earlier and more formal movement. "When I was a child I used to dream of the jungle. My schoolgirl heroes were always Conrad's and what's-his-name's, men carrying on their work among savages and wild beasts and fever and loneliness. Tell me about *your* work."

Mr. Fatigay had already learned that there are only two sorts of women in the world: those who are interested in one's work and those who are not, but, like the rest of his fickle sex, as soon as he found himself in conversation with one of either sort, he wished she was of the other, so he tactfully changed the conversation.

"That's a wonderful dress you're wearing," said he.

"Do you think so. I'm afraid you wouldn't if you cared much about the fashion. The fact is I have to wear them rather longer than most people, because I've got a terrible scar half-way up my shin, where I fell on some rocks when I was young. It positively sticks out through my stocking."

"Oh no!" said Mr. Fatigay, utterly incredulous of this.

"Yes, indeed!" said she. "It's most extraordinary. Give me your hand. There—you see." And at this moment their eyes met to endorse the treaty which had been made before.

"Well, I know something about scars," said Mr. Fatigay rather hoarsely, and after a short silence. "The blacks practise cicatrisation a great deal, of course. I wish I could have a look at this. I believe it could be removed."

"Do you really ? " cried the charmer. "How interesting. I wish I could show it you. But I can't here, in front of all these people."

"I wish I could examine it," said Mr. Fatigay, with something of the annoyance of the thwarted specialist. "Look here; if you like, I'll wait for you in the room at the back, and give you my opinion."

"Well . . . I don't see why not," murmured the lady. "Very well, then."

And Mr. Fatigay, first taking a further deep pull at his glass, got up and walked very carefully across to the door.

Waiting among the hats and coats, the poor fellow found himself assailed by a host of painful reflections, among which, however, those concerned with Amy and her violent flirtation so strongly insisted on precedence over those connected with his own procedure, that he was still far from giving attention to the latter when the door opened and the young woman entered.

"Here I am," she unnecessarily whispered. "How absurd! Do you really understand these things?"

"I know a bit about them," muttered Mr. Fatigay, whose hands had begun to tremble a little.

"Well," said she, turning aside to pull down her stocking, "here it is."

Mr. Fatigay approached and examined it very closely.

"It's very small," he said. "How white your skin is! Is it as smooth as it looks?" And with a stern and scientific expression he put out his hand to make sure.

But at this the charmer let fall her skirt, and edged away half a pace, on which Mr. Fatigay, leaning towards her, caught both her hands in his, at the same time experiencing an electric shock throughout his flurried nervous system.

"You bewitch me!" he cried, and, slipping an arm behind her, he pressed her to him for a hungry kiss.

"Stop," said she, as soon as she was able. "Are you sure we ought to do this? Wouldn't Amy dislike it? I'd hate to do anything that would hurt her."

"Oh, *she* won't mind," said Mr. Fatigay, with a touch of bitterness in his voice. Here, however, he was mistaken, for at that moment the door opened, for Amy, who had found her gallant adventure advancing a little too quickly for her, and who had, also, seen from her point of vantage the entrance of first her fiancé and then her friend into the bedroom, had decided to follow them, and now entered just as Mr. Fatigay was embarking upon his second kiss.

Neither the advanced nature of the lady's ideas nor the clouded condition of the gentleman's were proof against such a conventionally dramatic situation, and they stood awkwardly, with faces as red as fire, while Amy, after a freezing glance, said in a small thin voice:

"Oh, pray don't let me disturb you. I only came to look for something." And she withdrew, closing the door with ostentatious firmness.

Mr. Fatigay and his charmer stared at one another.

"I think we'd better go into the other room,"

said she, making for the door. "I do hope Amy hasn't misunderstood."

"I feel rather inclined to hope she has," said Mr. Fatigay, "but I'm afraid she hasn't."

"What a fool I've been!" he thought to himself. "Still, it's Amy's fault, for if she hadn't behaved so wantonly herself—and especially after our quarrel before dinner—I'd never have dreamt of flirting with anyone else. Oh, dear!" And he, who had entered the room with the expression of a doctor, left it with that of an undertaker's mute.

CHAPTER XII

While, like a ghastly rapid river,
Through the pale door
A hideous throng rush out for ever
And laugh—but smile no more.

BEAUTY, which some of us experience (as opposed to noting it merely) only when we are distraught by love, awakens, as far as the all-night corner-houses and soda-fountains are concerned, at about one in the morning, and there she waits the pale and burning few who come to seek her consolations. I refer to beauty of the super-sensual kind, though the other sort is, I believe, to be found at the same time and place, but that is a matter of taste, and not mine, though if it is yours I shall not quarrel with you, but I mean abstract beauty, and of the sort that De Quincey digested out of his opium, beauty made out of the mysterious presence of monsters in scenes of frigid and marmoreal splendour; the apparition, for one is not the only lover in the world, of white and twitching faces, and the wringing of despairing hands.

As it is not on a diet of moonlight and night-dew only that the nicotinia expands its cadaverous sweet bloom, but, like the blushing bouncing rose, it is nourished fundamentally on a homelier product, so this insomniac atmosphere, whether you penetrate like a jetty beetle into the ruby air of some sinister saloon, creeping silently over red carpets, sitting on red plush, staring at the rich satin panels whence the spongey air absorbs the colour of pigeon's blood; or whether you advance into an arena walled by cliffy marble, which seems to have sweated immense nodules of pale ice in which the waxy lights gleam like reflections, and take your seat somewhere on the wide mosaic pavement, on a gilt cane chair incredibly small and hard and frail, and perhaps at the foot of a tall squat-looking pillar, cut nevertheless with such dash and smooth precision out of the once difficult stone, and so wantonly placed and crudely and effectively capitaled, that it has all the violent facility of a rough sketch, or of the decor of an opium dream; or whether you sit in some gilded mirror-hall, down whose illusory aisles your somnambulist image steps from space to space, lit, like the mind exploring Coleridge's caves of ice, by lights increasingly tangled, flickering and faint; whichever it is of these you may happen to choose, and a true lover is likely to be stung on from one to another till he has seen them all in the course of a night; whichever atmosphere it is, its beauty and its mysteriousness is derived largely from the fact that it was smaller twelve hours ago, when it was filled from wall to wall and from Eden to Apocalypse with the rosy or milky or golden faces, all shot with satin iridescence, of innumerable sweet girls, now poutingly asleep under their sheeny eiderdowns at Wimbledon, or Enfield, but then bright in the bright light, flashing it back in sudden bird refractions, while under the many-jetted iris-jetted fountains of the band they preserved their roses with the bitumen-dark interiors of steak and kidney puddings. Inheriting from these, fed on them as they were on the dark hearts of the puddings, your pallor and grief, and the Dantean frigidity or poisonous soft redness of your surroundings, are not desolate and evil only, which would be pretty, but are damned, which is a sufficient foundation for the beautiful.

He who tastes this peculiar beauty, however, or any that is seen when love's strong claws have, in getting at him, rent asunder the silken caul of trance in which most of us pass through the world, had better beware, lest he gets a craving for it, so that he, who found this one crazy flower staring out of the Upas tree which is killing him, may in the end find little satisfaction in laughter and inn fires, and actually seek again those poisonous shades for the sake of their strange glamour, as De Quincey did with his drug. Sooner or later such a one will find the dreadful stimulant beginning to lose its effect, and then he will be marooned far from all that Rupert Brooke greatly loved, and on an island speedily growing desert of all that attracted him. His fate then, such is the cruel power of passion, will be little better than that of a chronic dyspeptic, who can find pleasure in nothing.

Mr. Fatigay was approaching this condition, as he would have found out during his nocturnal wanderings after the party, but for the unfortunate chance that he belonged to the large majority of the amorous, who, though their contortions are as lovely as any, are conscious of nothing but their pain. These, like unhappy mules, blinkered, and bleeding from the goad, serve to carry the imagination through the rocky and romantic scenery to which they are native, where otherwise its frail foot might fail to tread.

Poor Mr. Fatigay had slunk out from Amy's flat without making his adieux, all his longing for an intimate half hour after the others had gone having been slain by two wounds, anger and fear, either of which alone might have proved mortal. At his own lodging, he found that sleep had been murdered by the same fell agents, and after spending an hour or so, partly in staring at the dingy appointments of his bedroom, which, from previous associations of something of the same kind, had grown extremely distasteful to him, and partly in reviewing the events of the evening and the prospect of the morrow, which were infinitely so, he sprang from the bed, where he had thrown himself still half-dressed, and, pulling on the rest of his clothes, he fled from the torture chamber into the empty chalky street, which ached under the sleepless lamplight like a row of rotten teeth.

Before long, the ennui of suffering in the void avenues and crescents of Hampstead had turned his steps, as unconsciously as, through his weariness, the down-hill streets had drawn them, towards the centre of the town, and soon he had passed one by one the long chain of lamps that swoops down to Charing Cross, much as a damned soul passes star after star on its way to perdition.

On such excursions there is a fine balance to be noted between the aching of the heart and that of the feet, and, while the second pain is the baser, its cause, after all, is a present and a cumulative one, while the cause of our heart-ache lies in the past or the future, so that it is not liable to immediate material increase. This being so, it is inevitable that sooner or later the feet must weigh down the balance, and that attention, sliding down the beam, must come to rest upon them. Then it is that the wise man cries out in joy, for the physical anguish is infinitely to be preferred to the mental, from whose dominion it filches the light of consciousness, and he at once sets out on a wider circle, which, to another, would seem to be a circle of red-hot iron, but which to him represents comparitive oblivion.

The foolish lover, however, has no sooner had attention distracted a little from the worst of his pain, than he conceives a hankering to examine it further, and he hastens to find a seat, where, it must follow, his feet soon become easier and his heart becomes hot and swollen again, till the balance is once more tipped the other way, and he springs up from his seat and stumbles out upon the next lap of his mad career.

Mr. Fatigay was not the wisest of lovers, his experience having been a schoolmaster of the tyrannous kind, who cow and bewilder rather than instruct, so that when the inevitable pain in his feet began to intrude upon his thoughts, he entered the next all-night café that he passed. It was a blood-red one. Disposed droopingly at the tables about its walls were the forms of other disconsolate lovers, their faces incredibly white and Beardsley-esque against their background of Edwardian satin, some reading and re-reading letters of dismissal, some gazing at photographs, and some staring at mental images in the vacancy before them. In the centre were one or two groups of night birds, whose appearance seemed, at this hour, finally to establish the fact that life was ugly and obscene, and that whatever dreams may once have possessed these lovers were but futile bubbles, foredoomed, by the mere pressure of normality, to fade and die.

Mr. Fatigay began to stare at a succession of images of Amy, each in a different attitude, like a strip of snapshots from an automatic machine. He saw her simply as herself, the star that had burned on his inner eye in the velvety darkness of every African night. Then, and apparelled in a frostier light, he saw her as she had stood a few hours ago, icily and bitterly thrusting back his feverish approaches. "You brute!" she had said. To him, after all these years: "You brute!"

"This next image, then," he thought, "cannot be true. I must be mad. After that, how *can* she have lightly embraced that ugly, sneering stranger? Yet she did. I saw it. And yet she said, 'You brute!'"

All this drew up his mind into an erect figure of accusation, which crumpled up suddenly, though, as if hit behind the knees by a beam, when the last image inexorably asserted itself.

There she stood, the witness of his folly and his shame. "Don't mind me," she had said. Mr. Fatigay broke into a heavy sweat. How could he explain? How could he express resentment? He began, for the fiftieth time, to compose a long speech, in which he made it clear that he had most to forgive, and at the end of which, his bursting heart relieved a little, he forgave freely and lovingly.

"It's only natural: we've been living an impossible life. Now it's all over. We'll marry and be all in all to each other." He fancied he caught a tremulous assent.

"Good God!" he thought, "Perhaps she's suffering now, just as I am." And, bemused by the last stage of his reverie, he hurried out to the telephone box in the entrance hall to ring her up and reassure her.

But there was no reply. Mr. Fatigay returned to his table in a state of stupefaction.

"She must have heard," he thought. "Why doesn't she answer? She must know it's me. Is it because she hates me? She's got no right to hate me: she began it, after all. It can't be anything but that . . . surely? I wish I'd not gone before that ugly fellow went. Good God!"

And, unable to sit still any longer, he made his way out to the street, along which he drifted from call box to call box, at each he was injected, by the agency of mere silence, with a jealousy more insidious, more fertile and more irresistible than could have been conveyed by the most venomous of positive slanders.

It was not until, not his feet merely, but his whole body was aching with an insupportable fatigue, that he staggered at last into a vast and polar hall and sank fordone beneath a marble pillar. From whose cold shelter he at length looked out across the wide spaces under the heavy ceiling, oppressively low as an arctic snow-cloud, to where at intervals a few exhausted lovers leant over the glass-topped tables, like corpses waiting to be hoisted completely on to those morturial slabs. On the farther side of the hall a little group of people radiated an edgey gaiety, like that of the moonlight picnickers under the gibbet of Montfaucon. They were by no means rollicking, but, in this petrified waste, the fact merely that they ate up their eggs and bacon, broke their rolls, raised coffee cups, and spoke, and looked at one another when they did so, lit them up with a stagey Dionysian light, and drew all eyes wearily and resentfully towards them.

Mr. Fatigay gazed awhile in the same vacant annoyance; then, as if his eyes, their glaze broken, had acted as fire-alarms, summoning his wits from nightmare to come tumbling down to deal with a fiery reality, he grasped at the edge of his table and half rose to his feet. For there was Amy (that was why she had not answered the telephone), taking an after-party breakfast with the abominable Tickler and her smart friends, Mr. and Mrs. Dunedin.

To collect himself, he leaned back behind the pillar. His worst surmise, then, had been a false and a ridiculous one. The sun rose, just over the horizon, on his arctic winter. Assuming, a little too readily, that it must ascend uninterruptedly to a summer zenith, melting all the black ice, he rose to his feet, and baring his bosom to its warm shafts, and to her shafts, he hurried towards the group, knocking over a chair on his arrival.

"Amy!" he said, with a look of naked, indecent rapture, "Well . . . Amy!" And the poor clown, tired and glad beyond all restraint, bent over to give her a kiss.

Amy, bright and dry as a calico rose, had come out to establish these qualities of hers in the minds of her friends, as an innoculation against the story they were bound to hear, of how Bella had raided her private possession. With deft touches, she had, she hoped, modified the tone values in their idea of her relationship to Mr. Fatigay, so that he and she should be felt to be a hard and frivolous couple, to whom such incidents were part of life's wit merely.

As she did so, a small tight resentment had hardened in the core of her heart, not so much at the necessity of doing this, as at its probable inefficacy. No remote hints, much less any downright statement, if that were possible, would persuade Mrs. Dunedin that Alfred felt like that, although she might easily believe that Amy herself did. He had too often behaved, when they had been drinking cocktails, with a clumsy and provincial fondness, more appropriate to high tea. And while her friends knew that Alfred was at heart crudely romantic and sentimental, her own reputation for modernity and cynicism was insufficient, for still it held that these qualities of his, valuable in a subject, had been, for a time at least, entirely subverted.

Upon her now, at the moment of greatest strain, advanced the palpitating Mr. Fatigay, positively with tears in his eyes, stretching out two shaking hands, uttering her name in the rich moo of Italian opera, bending over, while the others looked on observantly, to engulf the last vestiges of the character she had given him in a heavy tremulous kiss.

Amy darted into the advancing mass a kiss of her own, as swift, hard and destructive as the knife Hugo's hero darted into the centre of the octopus. Mr. Fatigay sank, punctured, upon a chair.

Amy saw, somewhere deep within herself, that there was nothing for it but to leave him to the part he insisted on. Her only protection against the smiles the Bella episode would provoke must, then, lie in the stressing of her own fairy-like capriciousness. People must say, "Amy doesn't care."

"Hullo, Alfred!" she said, giving him an appropriate smile. "Have you been with Bella? I hope she was nice to you. Isn't she too attractive for words?"

"Good heavens! no, Amy," said Mr. Fatigay heavily. "You don't think I'd do that, do you?"

"Well, why on earth not?" said Amy with an amused glance at her friends. "Why, you blundering old African Jumbo, you! You don't think I'd mind, do you, surely? Why, you'd find it the most delightful thing in the world, a little affair with Bella. I'm sure I could never resist her if I was a man. I don't know that I could even now, as it is, if she tried to flirt with me. Sometimes she looks so sweet one simply has to jump up and kiss her." And she gave a little laugh so frank and friendly in its confidential audacity, that it completely deceived one of its hearers, if not the other three.

Mr. Fatigay sat silent, trying to sum up the conflicting jumble of false and true impressions that heaved his tired brain; a task in which, as he did not allow for the plus and minus signs which should have qualified them, he found it difficult to arrive at a result which looked even possible.

"In the ideal world, of course," went on Amy, making the point a general one, "it will be with everyone as it is with us. In every set there'll be a number of these divinely desirable little animals like Bella, who'll carry their perfect irresponsibility like a flag of neutrality, under which heavy engaged couples may shelter for a space. I'm sure it makes us ever so much nicer afterwards."

"But why be engaged at all?" said Susan Dunedin, and the conversation proceeded on the usual lines.

Mr. Fatigay did not join in. His brain had almost stopped working. With his chin sinking on to his breast, and his mouth gaping like that of a dead codfish, he sat mechanically registering each blow that Amy gave to his old African dream. Every sally of hers, which was expressive merely of ideas, and very usual ideas, to the others, was to him related to the two great poles of his present agitation, her bitter repulse before the party and her behaviour with the ugly stranger. His dream world lay in ruins about his feet, and, when he heard her make a light reference to the fascinations of this particular man, and to an arrangement she had made to have tea with him, it began slowly to revolve around him, evoking a sensation not unlike (yet how unlike) that obtainable on the joy wheel at Wembley. He felt he must summon up fury, or die,

Suddenly he got up, lifting his forgotten body with a gigantic dreary effort.

"Excuse me," he said, and walked out across the enormous hall to the lavatory on the staircase.

"When I get there," he thought, as one makes plans for the end of a three weeks' journey, "I will hang myself, and write a note saying why. Then she'll be sorry."

When he had arrived at the chosen place, however, he found that he had no paper in his pocket, which made the second part of his project difficult, and no pencil, which made it impossible. His exhausted mind was halted on its single track. To die without saying a word—was it possible?

"I have only my braces to do it with," he thought idiotically, "and then my trousers, being loose at the waist (for he had fallen very thin of late) might fall down. I'd be bound to kick a little. And then I should look absurd. It would be in the papers. She might only laugh. Would she laugh? Laugh. Surely I'm going mad."

And he rushed out of the place, and, calling a taxi, fled to his lodgings, where he fell upon the bed utterly prostrated, and was soon deep in the sleep of exhaustion, for these Africans are not used to late nights.

CHAPTER XIII

Her warbling voice, a lyre of widest range
Struck by all passion, did fall down and glance
From tone to tone, and glided thro' all change
Of liveliest utterance.

When he awoke, it was already afternoon. He arose stiffly, and while dressing he moved aimlessly about the room, absorbing the blessed normality of his surroundings. Outside the window a bank of tangled Michælmas daisies bloomed starrily in the shade of a sooty tree. His walking shoes, well-worn brogues, experienced, rich and glossy, stood in a shaft of mellow light. A snapshot of himself on his horse, taken in Boboma, stood on the mantelpiece: through it he looked into a vista of the life that he had lost. Amy's photograph, set framed beside it, compelled his reluctant mind back to the nightmare it was instinctively avoiding. He saw, in a compound vision of all that had passed since his return to England, a series of inevitable corridors along which he had been lured and hustled to the crazy amphitheatre where he had finally collapsed. To be tantalised, bewildered and betrayed, this might be his fate. "But not," said his brown brogues, "not in an all-night soda fountain."

As his thoughts became more collected, they resumed the aspect of his last conclusions of the previous night, but with this difference, that he was no longer half dead physically. The choice between fury and death, therefore, was decided automatically in favour of the former, and calling for his tea, and for two eggs to be brought up with it, he paced up and down rehearsing expressions of resentment.

Swallowing the penultimate mouthful, and cramming the last into his mouth, he seized his hat and hurried forth to deal summarily with Amy.

The chimp opened the door at Haverstock Hill. She gave him a sympathetic look.

"Amy ?" he demanded. And seeing that she shook her head, he asked:

"Amy soon ?"

Emily, who would have preferred not to be addressed in this nigger-English, nodded with a friendly smile.

Mr. Fatigay ascended to the drawing-room. This, since Emily had spent the day in tidying up, had resumed its normal appearance. Mr. Fatigay threw down his hat, and began to stride about. He was so full of words that he could not restrain himself to wait for Amy's return before speaking, but began to unburden his mind to the chimp, little suspecting that she understood such complex utterances.

"If Amy was shocked at the way I behaved to her," he said, "and called me 'You brute' when she's supposed to love me, how could she go on like that with that horrible little literary beast? And if she went on like that, how could she give me that dreadful look just because I kissed that wretched little vamp when I'd had a drop too much because she made me so miserable by flirting with that dirty libertine? And if she gave me that look, how could she say before all her friends in that cursed all-night café that she didn't mind, and wouldn't mind if I'd gone home with her? And if she doesn't mind, how can she love me?"

The chimp, who would have been unable to answer any of these questions, even if she had been as voluble as humans of her sex, expressed her growing concern on behalf of her beloved in a heavy sigh.

"Alas!" she thought, "I wish I had stayed in the Zoo. How can I bear to see him suffer so? And when she does marry him, it'll be even worse, if her behaviour last night is anything to go by. If only I could console him somehow. Perhaps some day I may."

And, crossing the room, she laid a gentle hand upon his knee, and gazed mournfully at him with her dark and eloquent eyes.

"What, Emily?" he said. "Are you there? Ah! Emily, I begin to wish we were back in the old days at Boboma."

"Shall I," thought Emily—"dare I—press my lips upon his hand?"

At that moment the door opened, and Amy came in.

"Hullo, Alfred!" she remarked. "I hardly expected to see you, you behaved so strangely last night." And mentally she took up Mr. Fatigay's misconduct in her right hand, and her own new light attitude in her left, as if she were taking up sword and buckler. "Where did you get to, in the end?"

"Did you mean all that you said in that place last night?" said Mr. Fatigay, in tones of considerable momentum.

"What exactly do you refer to?" asked Amy, with a glance of surprise flung like a dart at his ill-mannered emphasis.

"You know what I mean," he said brutally.

"If you mean the various ideas I expressed about people enjoying a certain amount of freedom," said Amy, "what of it? Those are very usual ideas nowadays."

"Did you mean them for us—for you and me?" he demanded. "That's what I want to know?"

"I may have, and I may not," she replied loftily. "But supposing I didn't; supposing I think as you want to make me think: how are you going to defend your conduct last night?"

"And what about you and that dirty scribbler?" asked Mr. Fatigay. "How do you explain that, if you didn't mean what you said?"

"I haven't said I didn't mean it," said Amy.

"As a matter of fact, you won't get anywhere by being abusive. It wasn't at all the same as your behaviour with Bella. You showed me earlier in the evening what part of your beastly nature was dominant, and what you did later on was obviously the outcome of it, and in mean spiteful revenge because I refused to be treated like a common prostitute.

"No, don't dare to interrupt me," she continued. "I mean to say what I think. You showed clearly enough that you haven't an inkling of what finer feelings are, so I can't expect you to understand that a girl can be momentarily dazzled by contact with a great mind, and perhaps be thrown off her balance for a moment without having the same hateful motives as yours."

"Well," said Mr. Fatigay, even more rudely than before, and with the additional offensiveness of an apparent resolution. "Well, you could have had me, as you know, but, since you choose to react like that to what you consider a great mind, you'd better stick to it. I'm off. You've got too many bright friends for me ever to feel safe." And he walked towards the door.

Amy, though shaken by his insolent parade of firmness, might have let him go, had he not turned, and said:

"I know you don't want Emily, so I'll take her. Come, Emily!"

Emily sprang out of the scullery, to which Amy had banished her on entering.

"Wait a minute," said Amy. "You can't go like that. We must thrash this matter out first. Perhaps I only said I was dazzled to punish you. You began it, Alfred, by your brutal assault on me before dinner. I was never so overcome in my life. It made me feel that everything I'd trusted, every clean and decent thing, everything that made me prefer you to the average intellectual, was done for. I felt that what you stood for was after all a sham, and there was no chivalry and self-control anywhere. So I just didn't care what I did. I just felt that you ought to be punished for destroying everything good."

"Oh!" said Mr. Fatigay with a sneer. "That's what you call 'mean spiteful revenge' in me, isn't it? To say nothing of the fact that I've got the excuse of having drunk too much because what I saw made me so miserable, and of having normal desires which you don't seem to have, as far as I'm concerned, any way. And having them all pent-up, because of your tantalising tricks, which God knows you've never had to complain of in me. If you'd loved me, as you pretended to, we'd have been married by this time. And now we'll never be. I'm off." And again he started for the door.

Amy, who had contemplated very seriously saying the words, "Be off!" at her next meeting with Alfred, found that she could not bear the initiative to be taken by her worshipper. There seemed to be all the difference in the world.

"I suppose you're going to that hateful Bella of yours," she said bitterly, using the first thought that came into her head to arrest him. But as soon as it was said, she almost believed it, and at the idea of such a calamity she burst into tears.

Mr. Fatigay did not run to her at once to console her.

"What does it matter to you?" he said, with cruel duplicity. "If you drive me away by your conduct, as you'd have driven me away a long time ago, if I'd had the sense of a flea, just by your refusal to keep your word about fixing our marriage—since you've now driven me away, what does it matter to you where I go?"

"Don't go to her," bellowed Amy. "Please, Alfred. Even if you hate me now, and can't forgive me, don't go to her just to hurt me."

"I don't hate you," he said. "And I forgive you, if that's what you want. But I'm not going to be played with any longer, and I'm not going to make any stipulations as to what I do next."

"Wait, Alfred," said Amy, and for a few moments she did battle with herself.

"Alfred," she said, "I *will* fix it, if only you won't go. Only give me six months more."

Mr. Fatigay made a vulgar grimace of contempt. "You ought not to be married at all," said he, "and I wish I'd seen that from the first." And he made as if to turn away.

"Stop!" said she. "I *must* wait till mother comes back from Scotland. Would early in

November do? Please, Alfred. You know I love you."

Mr. Fatigay could withhold himself no longer. He saw only the piteous surrender, and pitied, and loved, not caring to think that such a surrender implied a siege; a war in which, as in all wars, there can be no victor, but only two losers.

"Truly, darling?" he cried.

"Truly, truly."

"Amy! My own!"

Outside, in the scullery, some crockery fell with a shattering sound.

CHAPTER XIV

The Violet invited my kiss,—
I kiss'd it and call'd it my bride:
"Was ever one slighted like this?"
Sigh'd the Rose as it stood by my side.

NOVEMBER arrived, and in its chilly heart, like the core of all its darkness, Emily thought, came the day of the wedding, appropriately dulled and muffled in an icy fog. At eight o'clock, Emily rose from a hot and sleepless pillow and shuffled miserably into the dark little kitchen to boil the water for Amy's early tea. Standing in the chilly dirt, among the soiled plates and glasses, staring at the evil gas-ring, she tried to review the situation for the last time. At first her benumbed mind, which had been locked in a rigid cramp all night, seemed like a galvanised corpse, capable of but one spasmodic movement—"This must not be," —but a sudden hateful stirring in the kettle, signalling the moment when the dreadful day's procedure must begin, painfully goaded it beyond its pain-wracked impotence, and she began wildly to catch at even remotely possible means of saving her dear protector at this eleventh hour.

In such mental disorder, the extremest conclusions usually present themselves first, so it came about that the desperate chimp, from the trough of dejection, whence she could see nothing to be done, was next flung up into a contemplation of the stormiest future, which seemed to justify the most violent measures.

"Murder!" she thought, aghast, and she turned the ill word loathingly in her mind, until, as if it were some wicked bright blade she was handling, she seemed to see in it her own anguished reflection. "Murder!"

Those whose virtue is but the negative outcome of the triumph of a little good over less evil, may here conceive an aversion to our heroine because she entertained such a thought, but to do so would be as unjust as to condemn a neighbour because his house has been entered by burglars, forgetful of the fact that such violent visitors come uninvited, and usually only to the richest establishments. And, moreover, while the general statement, that the more we know of our fellows the more ready we are to forgive and understand, may not be quite true in all cases, it may be confidently invoked in this connection, for he is singularly fortunate who has much acquaintance in the world and had not been seized by the same impulse as now possessed Emily, and that not once but many times, and on but a hundredth part of her grievous provocation.

For here she was, face to face with the final ruin, not merely of her own, but of her adored oı 's happiness. One by one she had seen her hopes crumble away at the acid touch of reality.

She saw herself, infinitely far off and long ago, standing in some moment, one of many, in Africa, standing as simple in her equipment and her intention as any figure in an old morality play, standing in a lion-coloured patch of sunlight at the doorway of some hut, and thinking, "When he sees the author of those letters, the enslaver of his boyish fancy, he will surely recognise the gulf between her as she really is and the vision of her that he has treasured all these years." At the thought of such simplicity, the poor chimp writhed in humiliation.

She saw herself again, as from outside the house here, she saw herself looking out over the flower pots on the window-sill, chocolate and beige behind the dusky scarlet of the geraniums, looking to see who was coming up the front door steps, hoping against hope that it might at last be that not impossible she, who (wise, kind and gentle) should set up in Mr. Fatigay's misguided passion the disintegrating process of a damaging comparison.

But all the she's who came were impossible, and at length Emily had come to understand that the awaited one who never came must be impossible also, and though in her eyes nine-tenths of Amy's circle were preferable to Amy, she realised that this impression was probably the result only of her ignorance of them; a display of commonsense which, if it were only emulated by the many discontented husbands who exist among us, and who imagine that they can achieve happiness by a change of partner, would save a large proportion of the expensive divorce suits which are rapidly robbing us as a nation of our reputation for fortitude and far-sightedness.

Turning in from the window one evening, she had thought despairingly, "But perhaps he will fly from her." Glancing out again at the bevy by the gate, she had murmured, "But to whom ?"

"Besides," she had gone on, miserably, "from what I have seen of the married couples who frequent this house, it seems that those men who are treated hardest find it hardest to tear themselves away, as wretched flies find that poisonous fly-papers are less easy to break free from than is nourishing jam or treacle. Part chained, part drugged, it depends on the fibre of the man whether he becomes a doting sot or a sulky slave."

Moreover, a certain *tête-à-tête* between Amy and her friend Susan Dunedin, only the previous evening, had made it more apparent than ever, to the chimp's way of thinking, that poor Mr. Fatigay, if the drunken and enervating pleasures of besottedness were to be his portion, must qualify for them by a blindness so absolute that he must fail to see that there would be no attempt at hiding, and, if he was to become a conscious but helpless slave, he would be one whose torments were even more exquisite than the ordinary.

"The trouble, of course, with men," Susan had said, staring pensively into the gas fire, "is that they are so possessive."

"And the trouble with women," she added, when Amy had hinted acquiescence in a sigh, "the trouble with women is that they let themselves be possessed."

"Not every woman," Amy had murmured.

"Practically every one," said Susan severely. "And I'll tell you why. When they first get married they let their emotions run away with them, and give themselves entirely, and promise to do so for ever. And once that's done, with all the tradition of servitude to back it up, a woman's made a chattel of herself, and the man keeps her so."

"Well," said Amy, "to-morrow I marry. What would you have me do ? "

"Not what *I* did, anyway. Not if you value your individuality, that is. Last April, on our honeymoon, I was so keen on *giving* everything that Jack began to regard me as a mere piece of property at once. He objected to certain of my friends. I gave them up. He objected to my trying to get a part in a film. I gave it up. And each demand and each concession only paved the way for more and more."

"Who *were* the friends he asked you to give up ? " asked Amy.

"Oh! there were enough of them. Dennis was one, and George was another. And there are one or two you don't know. Anyway, by going on like that, Jack has taken all the bloom off our relationship, for he makes it impossible for me to be frank with him, and it even spoils my relationship with the men concerned, besides making himself look ridiculous. Yet if he *will* insist on my giving a lot of promises, which are utterly impossible to keep without hurting people I like very much and who are part of my life, what can I do?"

"Yes," said Amy.

"Don't mention that to anyone else, though," said Susan. "I don't want it to get about—yet, at any rate. I should hate to hurt Jack."

"If ever I *do* marry again," she resumed, "and it's not unlikely, owing to one or two things . . . if ever I marry again, I shall begin as I mean to go on. After all, all this ridiculous jealousy is just a habit, and the only way to break it is to be firm at the start. That's what I advise you to do, though I suppose advice is no good."

"I don't know," said Amy. "Alfred certainly is terribly possessive, and he seems to be getting more so. He can't seem to realise that there are moments when one must be oneself. Still, I should hate to hurt him."

"I think Alfred's fond enough of you to be got to understand," said Susan. "Men don't like it at first, of course, because they're so bitterly opposed to progress. But I don't think Alfred would make trouble. Sooner or later he'd understand."

"Well, certainly I think things ought to be on an open footing between people," said Amy.

"Yes, it's a hateful life for a woman, otherwise," said Susan. "I know. You'll be careful not to say anything to anyone, won't you, because otherwise. . . ."

"Of course," said Amy.

Emily, who had been clearing away the coffee cups, had lost control of herself for a moment, and tossed her head.

"One thing I've already put my foot down over," said Amy, giving her a severe glance. "And that is, that that monkey is to go straight to the Zoo, immediately after the ceremony to-morrow. Clumsy thing!"

How far the conclusions Emily had drawn from all this were the illusory outcome of her limited experience of civilisation, who can tell? But the fact remains that her view of the position, and of the menace to which her beloved appeared to be helplessly exposed, was none the less terrible to her because, in estimating it, some knowledge of the Dunmow Flitch and of the domestic life of the Browning's did not form part of her data.

Now she stood in the kitchen. In her hand was the teapot, there the cup from which Amy would shortly drink. Powerful disinfectants stood officiously beneath the sink.

The cutlery was in the basket on the dresserette.

The bedroom window was thirty-odd feet from the ground, to say nothing of the area.

But no! Not from fears of the consequences to herself, for on these she never bestowed a thought, but because of the danger of breaking Mr. Fatigay's heart, and because (she was, after all, but young and ingenuous) of her conviction that it is fundamentally wrong to obtrude steel, spirits of salts or other such material arguments upon problems of the inner life, she cast the crude solution from her mind. She strangled the luxurious desire in her heart.

A partition as thin and as doubtfully located as that which divides genius from madness, is all that lies between the tragic and the ridiculous. Emily next thought of appealing to Amy by the only means in her power, pantomime and passages from the printed works of great minds.

"For," said she to herself, "the fact that she so despises me might here be not an objection, but an advantage. Who, impervious to familiar voices, would dare to disregard the dust if it should rise up in accusation? Why, even those haughty emperors who retaliated dire displeasure on receiving good counsel from those about them, have been known to tremble and turn back from their evil courses at the admonitions of filthy fakirs and the miserable mad."

But her native good sense admonished her at this point that there was, however, no case on record of an empress being thus affected, and the bubble collapsed into nothingness before heavier arguments had need be brought to bear on it.

"There is no hope," thought Emily, taking up the teapot, "and no resource for me but to suffer up to the limit of my capacity, and then, renouncing a guardianship which it was presumptuous folly ever to have thought I could fulfil, to seek tardy oblivion in a self-inflicted death."

Then, finding in the depths of despair a firmness to which she had long been a stranger, she took up the flimsy tray, and, spilling no drop from the brimming cup upon it, she crossed the narrow landing, knocked resolutely on Amy's bedroom door, and, entering, found that lady awake upon her pillow, with her hands clasped behind her head and her dark eyes fixed thoughtfully upon the ceiling.

Amy, who had awakened early, and to emotions compounded pretty equally of triumph and misgiving, was not displeased when the chimp came in to her, for the sight of one who had become somehow connected with the politics behind her marriage served to direct her thoughts to that successful quarter, and away from certain doubts which had been troubling her as to some of the deeper but *démodé* aspects of the affair. With Emily, though, she had some business in hand, and Amy owed much of her briskness and brightness to the fact that whenever she was attacked by what she called "mental dyspepsia," she took the first opportunity of thrusting the qualmy thoughts behind her and embarking upon some sort of action.

Leaning on one elbow, her teacup raised to her lips, she eyed Emily with what had been called, in her last year at school, her Mona Lisa smile.

Emily felt profoundly uneasy. Had she been a hundred times less intelligent, she would by now have recognised that smile with much the same discomfiture as does a performing animal the dainty loaded cane.

There is, perhaps, no fairer maxim among all the many which our national genius has brought forth, than that which advises us not to hit a man when he is down. For, apart from its implicit generosity, to which every true Briton must whole-heartedly respond, it is, like most of our more exalted precepts, full of the soundest practical sense, since, in mental as well as in physical combats, he who flings himself upon his fallen adversary, must needs stoop to a something similar position himself, and thereby run great risk either of exposing himself to some unconventional blow, or of being dragged down in the same grapple by which his enemy manages to rise. It is, as a matter of technical interest, far better to wait till the fallen man has half, but not more than half, scrambled to his feet, before rushing in to finish him off.

Amy, however, would have thought very meanly of herself if she had accepted schooling from a mere copy-book, and to the lessons of experience, of which she had not had a full course, she had brought rather too much prejudice to profit greatly by them, so that, in what she instinctively felt to be her hour of victory, as far as the chimp was concerned, she saw no reason to deny herself the contrivance of an artistic little *coup de grâce* to the poor creature's presumptuous though unspoken criticism.

"Emily," she said, speaking very slowly and distinctly, "I have a little surprise for you. It struck me that it might be amusing—and Mr. Fatigay, needless to say, has raised no objection—if you were to perform the part of bridesmaid this morning. Freak weddings are quite the thing in these days, and 'The Monkey Bridesmaid' will be very attractive to the gossip writers, if to no one else."

"Open that box," she continued, pointing an imperious finger. "There are two white dresses in it. Bring them here."

"This," she said, "is yours, and you may get into it, and lay the other out for me, while I take my bath. Unpack the hats also, which are in that box above the wardrobe. It's a pity mother's ill, and can't come, but she'll love the photographs."

And drawing a jazz silk dressing-gown about her shoulders, she went to the bathroom, leaving the poor chimp to savour the full bitterness of the cup now placed before her.

Emily drew a deep breath.

To say that fury at the manner in which Mr. Fatigay's kindly motives were broken in and exploited to further his bride's vindictiveness, was the single element in her anger, would be to exaggerate her selflessness into something not of this world, but it bore an extraordinarily high proportion to the hot personal resentment with which it was fused. There was room enough, in Emily's feeling at the moment, for an almost infinite quantity of each of these factors. And, as a stunned man may be revived by the sting of a new blow, her mental forces threw off the numbness into which despair had cast them, and began feverishly to act.

When Amy returned from her bath, she found the chimp arrayed in her white dress, and waiting submissively to perform her office of tiring maid.

"It's getting late," said Amy, "so please try not to be clumsy, and attend to what I say. Here, help me on with this."

With trembling fingers the down-trodden chimp pulled on Amy's robe of triumph, so similar to that victim's garment which oppressed her own frail form.

"Come, dress my hair," said Amy. "And be sure you do it well. Alfred adores my hair, and, apart from that, I always like to be well groomed."

The chimp obeyed. One by one the stages of the toilet drew on towards completion. The clock crept remorselessly on. Then—it brought a reverse so sudden that no words can express it—wilfully misinterpreting a humiliating but very natural request from Amy, the chimp handed her a certain volume of tales, and it was open at a page describing the simian *Murders in the rue Morgue.*

Amy took in the familiar passage at a glance. She felt the chimp's hand upon her shoulder, and her freezing gaze became riveted upon the carving knife, of which Emily had possessed herself a few minutes before, and which she now brandished at about the level of Amy's fallen chin.

"Ah! Good God!" cried Amy. "What are you going to do ?"

The chimp drew back a pace, and, smiling in bitter scorn, took up the bridal wreath and veil and clapped their flimsy finery upon her own brown head. Then she handed the bridesmaid's lowlier head-wear to the trembling Amy, and, with a terrific gesture, commanded her to don it.

Amy, scared out of her wits, obeyed in faltering haste.

When she had done so, her wrist was taken in an iron grasp, and Emily, first showing her that she had the knife in her right hand, concealed under a fold of her garment, then drew her out from the dishevelled bedroom, down to where the hired car waited below.

"What can I do ?" thought Amy. "What can I do ?"

She dared not scream, for she was too well aware that the resolute being beside her would plunge the gleaming blade into her shrinking flesh long before any rescue could be effected.

"It will be all right," she thought, as the car crawled through the foggy streets. "When Alfred sees us he will be prompt to act. The stupid beast has not considered that."

The car stopped with a jolt outside the little Bloomsbury church where the ceremony was to be performed, and still holding Amy by the wrist, leading her as if she were an heathen chimp who had never set foot in a place of worship before, Emily escorted her into the church.

A flashlight flared unhealthily into the fog as they ascended the steps.

"So *that's* the Monkey Bridesmaid!" said the photographer in audible tones. "Why, the bride's just the same height as she is. Myself, I like a good upstanding woman. . . ."

"Good heavens!" thought Amy. "Is it possible he didn't realise I was human ? "

How often her lover had had reason to conceive, on different grounds, a similar misapprehension!

A sudden cold fear seized on her heart as they passed up the aisle to where Mr. Fatigay stood awaiting them.

No one else save he, and now the clergyman, was in the dark little church. Amy's mother, who had insisted on a church, was confined to her bed with flu, and, as a result of their agreement to a religious ceremony, neither of them had invited friends to be present, preferring to enlist the verger, who now appeared, to their support in the procedure.

They were some minutes late, for Amy, who

had a strong objection to waiting herself, had ordered the car to call for her at the time appointed for the service to begin, in order to avoid any possibility of this.

As Mr. Fatigay advanced to meet them, Amy parted her lips to call for his help, but a sudden pressure on her wrist, and a sudden steely glance flashed at her from beneath the bridal veil, gave her pause.

'After all," she thought, "Alfred will recognise me, and she will then have no excuse from act of mine to murder me, nor opportunity neither, for he will overpower her in a moment."

But they were late, and the church was darker than a registry office would have been, and Mr. Fatigay slipped his hand under Emily's arm, and meeting an appealing look from the bridesmaid with that kindly smile with which he had responded to many such glances from (he thought) that quarter, he turned to face the waiting clergyman, and the service began.

The bridegroom's responses were clear and emphatic; the bride's, as is often the case, were the merest inaudible murmur.

His eyes misty with happy tears, Mr. Fatigay slipped the ring upon Emily's extended finger, and they were man and wife.

Emily's heart beat hot and fast.

They entered the vestry, and Mr. Fatigay had just signed his name in the register, and the chimp had tremblingly taken the pen in her hand, when a heavy fall was heard in the body of the church. Amy, who had been standing rooted to the spot, had fallen in a swoon, knocking over a rush-bottomed chair in her sudden collapse.

Mr. Fatigay rushed to the door of the vestry, to which the chimp followed him, when she had scrawled her illegible but characteristic signature below his.

"Oh!" said he. "It is only Emily, fallen over a chair." For Amy was already beginning to stir a little in the throes of a painful returning consciousness.

The ardent bridegroom, instead of rushing up to set his fallen pet, as he imagined, upon her feet, turned again towards his bride, and, lifting her veil with a gentle hand, he bent down to imprint a passionate kiss upon her lips. The chimp, in the tumult of whose consciousness all but her invulnerable love was lost, protruded these responsively.

A pause, an abyss in time, followed.

Then the astounded man, turning to where the clergyman was departing the church, cried out in the voice of agony:

"Hi, sir! Hi, sir! You've married me to a chimp!"

The clergyman, suave, debonair, equal to any emergency his rag-tag and bobtail parish could thrust upon him; conscious too, that standing in the carven doorway, haloed in his blondness against the murky air without, he must look rather like the St. George in his stained-glass window, especially with the bowed and writhing form of the verger cringing at his knee, replied in befitting tones:

"Well, sir, what of that? The Church, you should be aware, is inspired from on High, and is therefore always abreast with the latest discoveries of science. Marriage between cousins, though I never encourage it myself, is perfectly legal. You must excuse me, sir, but I am a busy man. Good day!"

Mr. Fatigay pressed both his hands to his brow, and sank upon a chair.

Emily stood irresolute. She felt a strong and very natural impulse to go up to the stricken man, and, taking his hand in hers, to endeavour, by loving glances and a consoling caress or two, to persuade him that things were probably not quite as black as they seemed. On the other hand, a subtle and penetrating feminine instinct warned her that this was almost certainly one of those moments in which, as young wives are warned in the articles on husband management in the daily press, "Hubby is best left quite alone."

Thus, like figures in a problem picture, they remained for many minutes, during which time the coughing verger, waiting at the door to lock up the church, wondered impatiently how long the queer party meant to be.

Then Amy, who, having regained consciousness enough to hear the clergyman's departing admonition, had on hearing it sunk into a deeper swoon, began at last to stir and sigh again, which brought Mr. Fatigay to his feet in an electric bound, and, forgetting his own anguish in his solicitude for her, he hurried anxiously to her side.

"Amy! Amy!" he cried. "Good heavens! What nightmare is this?"

"Amy! Amy! Speak! Move! You cannot be dead! Oh, Amy!"

Soon Amy's eyelids fluttered once more and her limbs made some feeble spasmodic movements. At these Mr. Fatigay evinced an uncontrollable joy, so small a fraction of what we usually take for granted is sufficient to raise us to transports of pleasure, if only we are first brought low enough to appreciate it.

"She lives! She lives!" he breathed ecstatically, turning a working countenance upon the verger, who by now had come up the aisle to see what it was that induced these people to keep him waiting so long.

"What? The bridesmaid having a fit?" said the verger. "Why, I've seen worse than that happen in this church, and to the bride too, and before the ceremony was over, sometimes." And, considering this often remunerative business to be his own particular monopoly, he demanded that the patient should be given air, and he pushed aside the bewildered Mr. Fatigay, who was reduced to utter docility by the conflict of his emotions, and proceeded with great confidence to apply his own methods of reviving the prostrate lady.

All this time Emily had hung doubtfully upon the outskirts of the action, anxious, in her kind heart, for Amy's recovery, and still more so for Mr. Fatigay's emergence from his unrecognisably distraught condition, that he might become once again the man she had known so long. Now, when the hypnotised fixity of his gaze began to slacken a little, its object having begun to sip water from a glass which the verger held to her lips, Emily could restrain herself no longer, and, creeping up, she laid her hand upon his arm, in hope of consoling him a little, and of winning some response, which, however heated, might contain some faint evidence that she was not utterly anathema to her adored one.

But Mr. Fatigay, as soon as he felt her touch, started away as if he had been stung by a serpent, and fixing upon her a gaze full of a cold resentment, heavy beyond all thoughts of revenge, he took thought as best he might as to how he could efface her forever from the lives of himself and the sweet being whom her action had stricken to the ground.

"Here!" he said at last, in a strained hoarse tone, and, lugging out his pocket-book, he drew from it the bundle of notes which he had obtained to see them through their honeymoon in Paris. "Here: take this hundred pounds. It's no good to me any more. And, since, you've shown yourself to be so intelligent, go, get yourself your passage back to Africa, and never let me see your face again."

"No! Never!" he exclaimed in a voice of thunder, as the chimp, who from a habit of obedience had taken the money he thrust upon her, extended towards him her pleading hands. "Go!"

And, stretching forth his right arm, he pointed inflexibly to the door, through which the poor chimp, her own arm bent upwards across her brow, staggered in unutterable despair.

CHAPTER XV

"*O my cousin, shallow hearted! O my Amy, mine no more!*
O the dreary, dreary moorland! O the barren, barren shore!"

Ere Emily's stricken figure had disappeared into the fog, Mr. Fatigay had turned, and, without a second glance, he had rushed back to where Amy was sitting up and beginning to moan.

"Come!" he cried to the verger, and, linking hands, they bore Amy between them, but a little lopsidedly, for the verger's form was meagre and bowed with age, out to where the hired car was waiting. Himself almost fainting, he took the seat beside her, and, rewarding the man with what loose silver he had, he bade him instruct the drive to proceed, not to the hotel where they had arranged to lunch, but back to Haverstock Hill. As the door closed and the car started, he turned to her with a countenance brimming with woe-begone tenderness, and made as if to take her drooping head on to his bosom.

"Amy!" he murmured. "What a catastrophe has befallen us! How on earth could it have happened? Dearest, don't look so pale! We are still ourselves, and we must face this together. Love me as I do you, and nothing can harm us. It will, *it must* all come right in the end."

But, as he said these words, Amy's form stiffened antagonistically, and, jerking her head away, she replied with a vindictiveness which equally surprised and wounded him.

"Don't touch me! Let me alone, I say! I hate you. I believe you did it on purpose."

"Amy! My poor darling! You are still overwrought, and no wonder. There! Close your eyes, and try to quiet yourself till we get back home."

"No!" cried she. "Let me alone! I'm well enough, at any rate, to see through the trick you've played on me, with your mean, revengeful nature. I suppose you did it to get your own back, because I wouldn't give in to you in everything. Oh! Oh! Oh! If only Dennis were here, to give you the thrashing you deserve!"

"What—*him*?" retorted Mr. Fatigay warmly, but he checked himself, and after a moment he said very earnestly:

"Dear, if you think for just a moment you'll see how impossible it is that I should do such a thing. I swear to you I did not. I was never more astounded or horrified in my life than when I found out."

"Do you mean to say that you didn't recognise me from the moment we entered the church?"

cried Amy, as furiously as ever. "It says a lot for the 'love' you talked so much about, that you should think I was that ugly murderous monkey you burdened me with. No, Alfred, I can't believe that even you could be as blind as that."

"But I never looked properly at the bridesmaid." said Mr. Fatigay miserably. "I was looking all the time at what I thought was you."

"And do you mean to tell me you didn't see that that creature, with *that* figure, wasn't me ?" retorted Amy. "It comes to exactly the same thing."

"I didn't," said Mr. Fatigay. "I was so agitated, I suppose. And you being the same height and everything. . . ."

"Well, if you *are* innocent," said Amy, "you must be the biggest and blindest fool on earth. What do you think my friends will say when they hear of it ? I shall be the laughing-stock of all London! Oh! Oh! Oh!"

And at this thought, her grief arose in her more agonisingly than before, and she collapsed in a flood of scalding tears.

Mr. Fatigay, to whom the sight of his beloved's anguish, and the revelation of the chief cause of it, were like a blow on the mouth, rendering him dumb, looked on in silent misery till the car stopped outside Amy's house.

"Come," said he then, "let us go inside and talk over this dreadful business more quietly."

And Amy, who had still much to say to him, suffered him to escort her up the stairs to where the disordered rooms were awaiting the arrival of the charwoman who was to have cleared up and taken away the key.

"Amy," said Mr. Fatigay, when he had lit the gas fire. "Tell me what happened, please. My head is in a whirl."

"And what about mine ?" said she. "All you wanted was to get married, and I don't believe you cared twopence who it was. Well, perhaps you've got a wife who'll be more a wife to you, in your beastly sense of the word, than I could ever be. I don't see what you've got to worry about. But I'm disgraced for ever. I shall never dare to look any of my friends in the face again. What does it matter to me whether you're a scoundrel or only an idiot. I never want to see you again."

"Amy," said Mr. Fatigay, "for God's sake tell me what happened. How could you have let Emily play such a trick ? I can't believe that you did it willingly, just to get out of marrying me at the last moment."

Amy, who could not stomach the least implication reflecting on her conduct, opened her mouth to deny this with an emphasis which lent something slightly canine to her expression, and was about to rebuke Mr. Fatigay for entertaining the idea even negatively. But suddenly she closed it again, for an idea had crossed her mind. There seemed an avenue of escape from the worst result of the catastrophe, the mockery of her friends. "Supposing," she thought, "I were in a position to imply at least that this came about through my own desire. Supposing I *had* made Emily play the part. It would be taken as a very dazzling, though unscrupulous, action. I could always find some way of justifying it. And I might even hint that some make-up was employed. I must think it over. I must admit nothing. I've already been too open in the car."

"Alfred," she said, with an expression of severe reserve, "I won't even trouble to deny such an infamous suggestion. I will make no statement at all. I'm sorry to have to say it, but I don't trust you enough."

Mr. Fatigay's chilled mind fumbled numbly at these sentences, as one's fingers do at one of those abominable Chinese puzzles, consisting of two interlocked nails which are supposed to be capable of disentanglement.

Amy quite pitied him as she watched him knit his brows and pace up and down the room, and stammer out the beginnings of half a dozen sentences. "But," she thought to herself, "I must be strong. He has brought it on himself by his ridiculous blindness."

"Well, Amy," said he at last, trying a new tack, "I won't question you any more at present, if that's how you feel about it. But what shall we do now? Surely, in spite of what the clergyman said,

this marriage can't be legal. There's a law against chimps."

"There's no law against marrying them, that *I* know of," replied Amy. "And if there was," she added, for she was determined to avoid at all costs any appearance of pledging herself to a course of action which might end in exposing her to the ridicule she dreaded—"And if there was, I couldn't go behind the marriage service on a legal quibble. It would hurt mother's feelings too terribly. She would regard it as no better than living in sin."

"What? Even if I could get a proper divorce?" cried Mr. Fatigay. "I'm sure she wouldn't. I'll ask her."

"Well, how can you get a divorce?" said Amy. "Where *is* the animal, anyway?" For she had overheard him dismissing the poor chimp to Africa.

"I've sent her away," said Mr. Fatigay. "I told her to go back to where she came from. But I could bring the suit, citing some chimp or chimps unknown, and she'd never appear to defend it."

"No, Alfred," said Amy very nobly. "I can't agree to anything dishonest."

"Everyone will say:" she thought to herself, "Isn't it just too uncanny of Amy to have got out of it at the last moment like that? She's like a changeling, or a piece of quicksilver, or something."

"Well, Amy," continued Mr. Fatigay, with a

hopelessly supplicating glance at her. "I know it's no good asking you to face it out honestly with me, and live with me openly? After all, our love should be stronger than any outside opinion."

"I'm sorry, Alfred," she replied, understandingly.

"And you won't consent to a divorce, or any sort of annulment," continued the unhappy man, no longer enquiringly, even, but in flat recapitulation. "Well, then, what *can* I believe but that you did it on purpose. How could you? Amy! How *could* you? And what's worse than all," he added in a keening wail—"what's worse than all is the way you put the blame on me in the car just now. *You* did it, and you put the blame on me! That's cold blooded. . . ."

"Cold blooded!" said Amy. "Look here, Alfred! That sort of thing from you just shows me what all this vaunted affection of yours amounts to in reality. I tell you, I'm not going to descend to reply to your insults. Since you've shown me what your opinion of me really is, you'd better keep to it. And keep to your monkey wife into the bargain. She'll put up with anything—I expect. She'll have to. You'd better go after her before it's too late."

"But, Amy, . . ." cried Mr. Fatigay beseechingly.

"No, don't touch me," she cried in disgust. "I'm finished. The best thing you can do is to go away. You've done me enough harm. I mean what I say. Can't you *see* that I mean it ? Leave me alone. Cold blooded! You can think whatever you like, and, whatever you think, I'll consent to nothing. That's final. Go."

And, stretching forth her right arm, she pointed inflexibly to the door, through which poor Mr. Fatigay, his own arm bent upwards across his brow, staggered in unutterable despair.

A little later, Amy took down the telephone, and dialled the number of an intimate friend.

"Is Mrs. Dunedin there ? " she might have been heard to say. "It's Miss Flint speaking. Oh, it *is* you, is it, darling ? I didn't recognise your voice. . . . Yes, I said Miss Flint. . . . Yes, the ceremony *is* over. . . . No, I meant to say Miss Flint. . . . Well, it's *too* ridiculous, but the fact is, your Amy got a little nervous at the last moment. . . . Yes, I said the ceremony was over. . . . Well, Alfred's very short-sighted, you know. . . . Yes, he nearly went blind in Africa. But don't interrupt. Well, there was that chimp hanging around, looking the very image of a perfect wife and mother, so with the help of the bridal veil—it covers a multitude of . . . wait a minute . . . and with the aid of a little make-up for the bridesmaid. . . . No, no, *I* was the bridesmaid. You should have seen me shuffle! . . . What ? . . . Yes! Yes! that's it. Darling, it went off perfectly. . . . Well, perhaps *un peu de chagrin* just at first, but really I think he was rather relieved. . . . Oh no, he can get out of it if he wants to,

I should think, but I expect he'll absolutely love it soon. She'll suit him far better than I would. . . . Yes, if you like. Any time this evening. Tell Deidre to come too, if you see her. Good-bye. Good-bye."

CHAPTER XVI

"*Who calls that wretched thing that was Alphonso ?*"

The snow's a lady . . . and, like the rest of her sex, though delightful in her fall (to those who enjoy her), once she has fallen her effect is depressing, particularly in Piccadilly. A heavy blizzard had begun at noon, and continued for a couple of hours, during which time it was whisked and beaten by wheels and feet and sweepers into a kind of stale and ghastly sundæ, edging, like Stygian spume, the banks of the stream of black and glassy traffic, which creaked along as slowly and uncouthly as a river of broken ice.

Mr. Fatigay, whose trousers and jaw, both terribly thin, had alike sprouted a short and ragged fringe, felt it enter over the tops of his shallow shoes, which gaped the more loosely about his piteous ankles because he no longer wore socks. For having in agony averted his face whenever the future rose before him, for he had found it too horrible to contemplate, he had prevented himself from observing one detail in which it resembled all other of the states of man, that it demanded money. So that he had not gone very far into it, when, his small supply running out, he found this one most ordinary detail to have developed into the most hideous part of all its aspect.

With Amy's last scornful word of dismissal ringing in his ears, he had gone out into the streaky opening clearing air, into whose sudden rifts of clarity, hard and colourless as a photograph, or as the inside of a crevasse, he had stared madly, as if he was seeing everything for the first time. His brain was numbed. Tensely and automatically he called for his bags, left his apartments, cancelled the address he had given, offered no other, and went out into his new and empty world, the brittle walls of which, cupping its devastating hollowness, began to split before sharp jags of pain, like those of a hollow tooth at which the dentist has failed, and to which sensation returns as the anæsthetic begins to wear thin. This pain was more than Mr. Fatigay could bear.

When a young man, almost alone in London, and, possessed of a modicum of intelligence and a small deposit account, is afflicted with pain greater than he can bear, he is likely to find himself, in obedience to an inexplicable law, in the company of artists. This was the fate of our unfortunate hero, who, only a fortnight later, might have been seen in a bar near the Tottenham Court Road, exchanging short nods with certain young men who wore black hats, and long glances with certain youngish women who wore none.

He had already been there three nights in succession, and might have been described as an habitué. The women, to who he politely offered drinks, found his politeness refreshing, and excused his lack of artistic outfit by saying that he was *real* and unhappy.

Mr. Fatigay's reality, however was fated to be but brief, for the fact is, that he was living upon his capital, having cut adrift from his employment in cutting adrift from the rest of the unbearable associations of his previous life. Whenever he thought of this, which he did the more often as his capital grew less, he ordered another whisky, and whenever he thought of the cause of it, which he always did when waiting for his whisky, he exchanged glances with one of the Bobbies, Billies, or Trilbies, who either painted, or were painted, over and over again as the old song says, during the hours that this public house was closed.

But this was but a passing phase, for, as he grew poorer, his reality suffered in the eyes of these charmers: he was discovered to be ordinary, which is quite another thing, and at last they found him to be dry, empty, a mere nobody, and were unable to see him at all. When he was finally exiled from this noisy limbo, and forced to keep the squalid garret he had descended to, because he was completely penniless, he found that the devil which had possessed him during the period we have been examining, had partaken of the general decay, and become a little unreal also; it appeared to have been a mere *poseur*, its place being taken by what seemed a larger and more genuinely menacing relative.

In short, while to love and not to be rich has been set down as a great misfortune, our hero, in loving hopelessly and now being hopelessly destitute, had discovered a far greater. He proceeded to explore it thoroughly.

It may well be wondered that he did not entirely sink under his distresses, and take his leave of a life which had become so inexpressibly bitter, either by precipitating himself from one of the many suitable bridges, or by the even less difficult process of merely waiting for a day or two longer, until grief, weakness and his cough should release him. But the fact is, that at the very depth and bottom of all his misery, at a moment when, having stood long beneath a railway arch because he could walk no more, and then having begun to walk to save himself from falling forward, he had suddenly felt, through a sort of rift in his waking trance, an overwhelming desire to enjoy once again the flavour of a cabbage stump, portions of which, he remembered, are occasionally to be picked up in the purlieus of Covent Garden Market, and, being then no further away than Charing Cross, he had bent his steps in that direction.

Before the end of an hour, he was already in sight of his goal, but had begun to doubt if his legs would carry him the few additional yards that intervened, when suddenly his eyes had fallen upon the very article of which he was in search, and resting for a space against the door-posts of a set of offices there, he began eagerly to gnaw at it, when there emerged a tall and stylishly dressed gentleman, who, observing with high good humour the gusto which our hero brought to his simple meal, had said to him, "Come, come, my good fellow, take this shilling, and get yourself something a little more tasty and nourishing."

The grateful tears which welled up in the poor wretch's eyes magnified the coin to the size of a half-a-crown. Nor did this entail any danger of an anti-climax, for to one in his condition of bitter necessity a shilling fences in the whole horizon with its milled edge, for his longest view extends no further than to the next meal, unless he is a person of exceptional foresight and intelligence, in which case he may glimpse a second repast, as one glimpses, it seems beyond the earth's rim, what is perhaps a further Himalaya, or perhaps only a cloud.

Mr. Fatigay had given evidence of these qualities, when after a moment's reflection he put the cabbage stump into his pocket, saying to himself, "I will keep this in order to make a light breakfast on it one of these fine days, so that I need not gorge myself now as if I were taking my last meal on earth, and, being satisfied at a lesser expense, I shall have some money left over, on which, if I decide to do so, I may start life anew."

He had lost no time in seeking out an unconventional little restaurant behind St. Martin's Lane, where, after some moments' deliberation, he had ordered an egg and rasher, with extra fat, three slices of bread, and a cup of strong tea, milky and with plenty of sugar. Leaning back luxuriously after this repast, he had decided to take up, temporarily at any rate, the extended lease of life which had been offered him.

"For," he had thought, "I cannot recollect, and, what is more to the point, nor can I imagine, any bliss arising from the love of woman at all comparable to the ecstasy with which I have just devoured this meal, from which, moreover, when I have paid my just sixpence, I shall depart feeling completely satisfied, and with my sixpence change clutched firmly in my hand. Is it possible that my values have hitherto been wrongly pitched ? To consider this thoroughly will take a considerable time, and, in order that I may eat and drink while I do so, I had better invest my remaining sixpence in the stock-in-trade of some modest business, for I am thoroughly tired of the ups and downs of Bohemianism."

"'I remember," he had continued, "that it was my custom in the old days, when buying matches from men who sold them in the street, to put down threepence or so upon the tray when taking up a box worth only a penny or three ha'pence. Now, I will buy six penny boxes with my sixpence, and hold them out for sale in some crowded thoroughfare, where, assuming some hundreds of people to pass by every few minutes, it cannot be very long before I have sold them all for, say, eighteenpence. I shall purchase six more boxes and repeat the operation, until, by the end of the day, I have quite a respectable sum in hand, part of which I shall devote to creature comforts, and part to a studs' and laces' department.

"Later on, when profits increase, I might consider taking on an assistant, or renting a suitable shop. But that is a decision best left till I know the ropes a little. It is mere foolhardiness to settle such things in advance. One way or another, at any rate, I should be proprietor of a very pretty little business in the course of a year or so, and, indeed, I might enter into competition with Garrods, from which all the Flints derive their incomes, and then, when Amy is reduced to utter poverty, I might drive up to her mean lodging in my car, and say, with a look of tender understanding which would melt away all thoughts of old scores, apologies, humiliation and such rubbish, 'Amy! I would say. . . .' "

But at this moment the voice of the waitress, demanding his sixpence, had aroused him from his reverie, and, stepping manfully forth from the shop, he had entered a tobacconist's, where he had made his investment, and then advanced upon the street, no longer a pauper, but a respectable tradesman.

Probably owing to the prevailing depression in trade, business had been hardly as brisk as he had anticipated. Indeed, two or three days later, when he carried out a postponed audit of his accounts, he found that he had sold only three boxes of matches, two of them at cost price, and one at a profit of a penny, so that he was in possession of fourpence in cash and three-penny-worth of unsold stock. With inflexible determination he had purchased three more boxes of matches, and had spent only the penny of profit on a piece of bread, to the proteids in which he had been enabled, by his display of foresight, to add the vitamines in his cabbage stump.

Two more days had passed, and our hero, whether it was owing to international complications, or, as he had begun to fear, to his having chosen a line to which he was naturally unfitted, had sold no boxes at all. With a care-worn look he had determined to go into liquidation.

"I will write," he had said to himself, "a little card, with the words: 'Great Bargain Sale. Business in Liquidation. Stock MUST be cleared at 25 per cent below cost', and thus I will be in possession of fourpence ha'penny before very long. I will spend three ha'pence on food, and the rest on apples, or bars of chocolate, or some other merchandise which can, if the worst comes to the worst, provide me with a meal if it remains unsold."

But, going out that morning with his little notice, he had been appalled to find that it attracted no attention whatever, and two o'clock found him trudging dejectedly along the gutter of Piccadilly, with so cold and heavy a heart that he began to feel that it must indeed be descended into his shoes, into which, as has been noted, the vile and icy slush slopped at his every step.

"Can it be," he thought, "that it is to-day that my burdensome life is to be demanded of me? God knows, I have no great fondness for it. On the day I received the shilling I was ready enough to let it pass from me. But somehow the gleam of hope which that coin shed into my abyss, or the high living to which I treated myself on getting it, has made me rather critical and high-stomached in this matter. If I am to perish, so be it: but let it be on a golden afternoon of late May, or June, rather than in this black repellent air, and, above all, not from cold and retchy hunger, but from a surfeit of lampreys, or green ducks of eight weeks old, with the first peas of the season."

For the poor fellow's mind was almost unhinged by his distresses, so that he wandered, and in a moment he was thinking himself a boy again, playing puff-puff through the gulleys of crisp leaves in frosty autumn, and, lost in the hallucination, he spattered up the slush to the left and right of him as he toiled along.

A few threatening words having burst this happy bubble about his ears, he mooned on vacantly for two or three hundred yards, when, as he was creeping by a famous taxidermist's window, he happened to raise his eyes, and seeing before him various life-like specimens of tropical fauna, he found himself, like poor Susan, momentarily gaping in a world precariously built from the wreckage of the real one about him. Taxi horns were transmuted into the cries of that creature, whatever it is, which barks loudest in Zoos and in equatorial film effects; two popular writers, threading through the crowd on their way to confession, joined as back and front legs of an elephant, parting the slim and dingy grasses on either side. There was a monkey-chatter of teeth in his head. Piccadilly. Piccaninny. The air was full of blacks.

"Ah!" said he, rapturously inhaling a rank and orchidaceous fume of patchouli from an antelope-eyed undergraduate who passed at that moment. "Ah!" said he. "Boboma! Boboma!"

"What's that?" cried the undergraduate with an angry look, and he gave the enfeebled Fatigay a hard and spiteful prod with his clouded cane, and retired petulantly down a side street.

The flesh, in retreating from the unhappy creature's ribs, had left the nerves, it appeared, stranded behind it, perhaps like helpless and self-conscious starfish upon the furrowed shore, and while to the ear of an outsider the blow would have seemed merely to be one upon an empty cardboard box, to the more intimate senses of the recipient its effect was agonising. A groan, attenuated to the keenness of wind whistling in a keyhole, escaped through his chattering teeth.

No longer under any illusion as to his whereabouts, he shuffled westwards, in more senses than one, he thought, along the squelching gutter.

When he had got as far as the Ritz, still without disposing of any of his stock, his tottering steps were arrested by the glossy backside of a gigantic Hispano Suiza, which had swept up to the imposing entrance to receive one of the favoured few who had been lunching therein. Mr. Fatigay peeped humbly out from behind the sumptuous car to feast his eyes with a glimpse of this happy being. The door swung, a commissionaire bowed respectfully, and our hero's eyes protruded from their hollow sockets. For there, smartly groomed and fastidiously fastening a glove, stood Emily, his monkey wife.

Mr. Fatigay blinked as if to clear from his gaze what must surely be a filmy vestige of his recent vision of Boboma. But no: there was the Ritz, and there surely enough was Emily. Her expression, though sweet as ever, was pensive, even melancholy, but perhaps on that account more spiritual even than before. She was a little thinner, but, such being the fashion, it suited her.

As she put forward a daintily shod foot to cross the pavement to her car, she hesitated, and, with a startled eye, she held one hand to her heart, as if perhaps that organ had halted within her, supersensually aware of its mate, fluttering in the crazy cage on the kerbstone. Her eyes met those of Mr. Fatigay, and with all her soul and sorrow melting in her look, she hurried towards him with eager outstretched hands.

Before she reached him, the strained axle of the whirling scene had snapped in his brain, and, pitching forward, he fell in a swoon at her feet. In spite of her tumultuous feelings, the chimp remained mistress of herself and the situation. Before a crowd could collect, she made a sign to the chauffeur, and, assisting his efforts with all the energy of her well-knit frame, she had the pitiful unconscious form gently lifted into the luxuriously cushioned limousine, where, following, she took his ragged verminous head upon her bosom, and they started for her little home in South Audley Street.

CHAPTER XVII

And she turn'd—her bosom shaken with a sudden
storm of sighs—
All the spirit deeply dawning in the dark of hazel
eyes—

Saying, 'I have hid my feelings, fearing they should
do me wrong;'
Saying, 'Dost thou love me, cousin?' weeping, 'I
have loved thee long.'

As, with the whitening dawn, the lotus holds itself less tightly shut and heavy to the bitter lifeless mud, and, rising through clear inky depths, breaks open into the sun languor of its life, which, though, is less energetic by far than was the strained blank intensity of its shutting into nothingness, so the spirit of Mr. Fatigay, having remained a long while tensely furled, in a sort of rigid anti-life anti-nightmare constriction, detached itself from the frozen black depths of his being, to which it had sunk, and rose into the pearly shallows of semi-consciousness, where the light was the light under the white ceiling of a day-shuttered room, into which this spirit diffused itself a little when finally it broke surface in the imperceptibly popping twin blossoms of his vacant eyes.

The street outside the green slats must have had its greyness enriched a little by the hazy sun of a February afternoon, for the light that percolated was not utterly cold, and joining with, diluting, the coppery radiance from an electric fire, it warmed, without much colouring, the milky dimness of the bedroom air. What colour there was in these two lights precipitated itself on the surfaces of various objects in the room, causing these to glow with a sombre richness, which, to one detached from the present, with the body forgotten in that tepid bed, and the eye forgotten in the ease of that tepid air, was evocative of the orient and immortal aspect with which simple objects are endowed by all of us in childhood.

Through this tender colourless translucency, which was no more emptiness than is the sweet light of the horizon at bedtime in June, into which one longs, and is nearly able, to bathe one's outstretched hand; through this, and with the intimate nearness of the youngest moon, the palely shining crescent of a spoon described a gracious arc, rising from somewhere behind Mr. Fatigay's head, and setting in a voluptuous kiss on that Endymion's lips.

Bouillon! Slipping away beneath the horizon of his languid gaze, it rose again, and again the silvern argosy, piled high, full moon, full spoon, bore its delightful freight to the invalid. Chicken jelly! Then, in its third quarter, lined with darkness, it rose and set again. Stewed mushroom! With that savoury, the tempting little luncheon came to an end, and the sufferer, as if the last of his liquid courses had been spooned up from a superior Lethe, dropped his heavy lids in a slumber inexpressibly sweet.

When he opened them again, he was more himself. Objects no longer leaned against his eyes, staring in, but were regarded through them as, when an empty house is tenanted again, the prevailing gaze shifts round to a course from within outwards, instead of fitfully from outside through the vacant windows to the dim and empty rooms within. And from the newly inhabited interior, curtained to a dark rich secrecy by personality, interest, suddenly awakened, advanced a pale and staring face to the pane. Mr. Fatigay looked out in bewilderment.

Something in the disposal of the furniture, though he was sure he had seen no individual piece of it before, reminded him strongly of his airy white room in Boboma. Every detail was slightly different, but no detail of furniture can, by being changed, alter the identity of a room. It was as if his salary had been raised in Africa, and he had gradually changed each chair for a better one of the same sort, and the table also, and added a bureau, and got a very much more comfortable bed. Some orchids scented the room. Something moved in the corner behind the bed.

"What is it that moves?" he wondered suddenly, for to him this room seemed to be his fancy, but he recognised the movement, which yet was in it, as real. "Look!" cried his awakening heart. "Look! It's Emily! Here she comes!"

Smiling, the chimp advanced, and, with a nurse-like air, she laid a kind finger on her kinder lips. "Calm yourself," this gesture said. "Don't try to think. Excitement will only make you worse." But Mr. Fatigay, staring out of his preconceptions, goggle-eyed and mouthing, as a goldfish seems to stare out of its glass globe, gazing at a familiar room which he was seeing for the first time, gazing at Emily whom, a few months ago, he had seen for the last time, rapidly retracing his experience till the long Elijah trail of footsteps in the slush of Piccadilly ended in nothing, outside the Ritz, he felt that all this, or even much of it, could not be, and falteringly he asked, in a sudden weak sweat of anxiety:

"Am I mad?"

At once the trim figure turned, and hurried to the bureau by the fireplace. Two or three quick clicks were heard. Mr. Fatigay rolled his eyes in further doubt and more dismal apprehension.

But then, returning with all the speed she might, the ministering chimp held up before him a sheet of paper, on which were typed the brief consoling characters:

"N.O,"

The poor man's bursting heart deflated in a long sigh of relief.

"Emily!" he said quaveringly, too weak and lost even to remember the part she had played in the events that had brought him so low. "Emily! But where am I? What does it all mean?"

Placing a cool hand on his brow, and with a pressure inexpressibly gentle, yet strong enough to restrain him from raising himself in the bed, as he was attempting to do, she enjoined patience with a tender gesture, and hurriedly slipped to the typewriter, whence soon she brought a sheet which said:

"All is well. Soon you shall know everything. But first regain a little of your strength. Eat and sleep."

And when he had read these words, she gave him what to the broken in spirit and body are the two best things in the world: a smile of infinite kindness and as much food as he could eat; and by repeating these benefits as often as he wakened during the next day or two, she cherished him at last to a condition of strength and calm sufficient for him to hear what she had to tell.

It seemed strange to her that his first questions were not concerned with the trick she had played upon him, for she was unaware, of course, of how Amy had taken over the chief responsibility for this, and of how Mr. Fatigay, who still greatly underrated her intelligence and initiative, had settled with himself that she had been Amy's uncomprehending tool in this matter, so that he felt little resentment and no curiosity as far as she was concerned. Had he known, at this juncture, that she had organised the whole coup, there is little doubt but that he would have raised himself from the bed and rushed from the flat, if only to collapse and perish on the doorstep. But he did not know as yet. If this, the turning point in Emily's fortunes, owes much to luck, let it be remembered that this is the case with even the best of us, for the most able and well-lived life is merely that which is prepared to meet and to receive the good chance, and to shoulder off the bad.

Mr. Fatigay, then, began to feel much restored, and:

"Now, Emily," said he, in a tone in which, though it was still weak, there rang something of the old Fatigay, to smite upon the taut chords of her heart. "Now, Emily, since you seem to have become literate: what I want to know is, what place is this, and whose, and whence came the fine clothes you were wearing when I met you, and the expensive car? You know you can be quite frank with me."

At once the docile chimp hurried to the typewriter, whence a few minutes later she drew a sheet on which was written:

"This place, my dear master, is a first floor service flat in South Audley Street, W.1, and until you entered it I have considered it mine, but upon that auspicious day it automatically became yours, with all else that belongs to me, including, needless to say, such trifles as my body and soul."

"Thank you, Emily, very much indeed," said Mr. Fatigay in the deceptively matter-of-fact accents of one who is dazed to a degree far beyond the shock of any further surprise.

"But," he went on, clinging to his own train of thought as if it were the only possible thread that might lead him out of this maze, and back to reality. "But tell me how you came by all these fine things. That's what I want to know."

The chimp nodded smilingly, as if to say, "Only wait and you shall be satisfied," and with that she began typing again and soon brought him a closely covered sheet of paper, which ran as follows:

"When you bade me begone, I was so miserable as to be unable to think connectedly for many hours, during which time I wandered about until I had at last overcome by physical weariness those paroxysms of emotion which tumultously prevented the voice of reason from making itself heard. When at last thought became possible to me, I applied it first to test a certain strong feeling which remained like a rock in the centre of my being after the raging tide of other emotions had shrunken back to its lowest ebb. This feeling was, that in spite of my reluctance to disobey you, I could not leave this country, either by a liner or by suicide, until I had ascertained that you were at least in a fair way to recover from the shock and disappointment for which I had been responsible. This feeling was endorsed by every rational consideration which I could bring to bear upon it.

"My first duty, it followed, was to return to you the hundred pounds you had given me for my fare to Africa, and I accordingly hastened to your lodgings that I might thrust them through the letter-box, but, as I crept towards the house, I saw your figure emerge and enter a waiting taxicab, and, remembering that you had spoken of giving up the apartments on the day of your marriage, I assumed it to be likely that you were now leaving them for the last time. I watched for some days, but you did not return."

(Here the paper was blotched a little, as if a reminiscent tear had fallen upon it.)

"I soon began," it continued, "to suffer acutely from cold and hunger, and resolved I must earn some money (for that which I had of yours I regarded as a sacred trust, which I have kept for you to this day. It is in the drawer of the little table by your bed.) Compelled by this cruel necessity, and unfitted, by physical and educational shortcomings, to earn my bread in any of the fields normally open to lonely spinsters in this city, I very reluctantly, and with many private tears and sighs, determined to sacrifice my self-respect and . . ."

Here the sheet came to an end, and Mr. Fatigay looked anxiously at Emily's stylishly draped back, where she sat industriously typing the next page.

"Good Heavens!" he thought. "What is she going to tell me?" And he began to twitch and stir in the bed, and to look uneasily about the room with an expression of quick distaste for its natty and expensive appointments.

"Emily fallen!" he thought, and he looked back across the dirty corpsey floodwaters that had drowned the last few months, back to what he suddenly realised had been the happiest days of all his life, dream days in Boboma.

And he stared aghast at two almost coincidental visions, one spoiling the other, as happens with snapshots superimposed upon the same film, first of the Emily of those idyllic hours

Wading in bells and grass
Up to her knees,
Picking a dish of sweet
Berries and plums to eat,
Down in the bells and grass
Under the trees.

and second, of a new Emily, fated, like Eve, to be considered a true woman only after her fall.

"Emily!" he cried, wondering a little at the tremor and huskiness of his voice. "Say—what *was* it you did? It wasn't—that? Say it wasn't that!"

The chimp, unable to comply with this request, dearly as she would have liked to, bethought herself quickly how she might allay his anxiety, and, pulling the next sheet, still uncompleted, from the typewriter, she tripped across and placed it in his hands.

"and go," it continued, "as an organ-grinder's monkey."

"Having been forced to this humiliating resolution, I wasted no time in putting it into practice. Making my way to an obscure corner of the town, I patrolled its streets until I came upon an organ playing outside a public house, and, entering the saloon bar, I removed my bonnet, and distorting my face into a smiling caricature of the monkey kind, I executed the little *pas seul* which you taught me, my dear master, for the fancy dress ball on the ship.

"The proletarians present seemed quicker than the first-class revellers had been to perceive the tragic humour in the little turn, for they accorded me attention and applause, and were by no means ungenerous when I passed among them with my bonnet extended in the style of an offertory bag.

"The pennies I thus received I unhesitatingly appropriated to my own use, they were so evidently given entirely as a reward for the dance, and, as I gave my unconscious accompanist a small douceur on leaving, I had no misgivings as to the honesty of this way of life, whatever were my regrets as to its lack of dignity. I must confess, though, to some qualms of conscience when, on looking back one day after leaving a public house near Hammersmith Broadway, I saw the unfortunate grinder, who had evidently looked in at the door to collect on his own behalf, being very roughly handled by two or three men who had already behaved most generously to me. After that I doubled the fee I had been giving.

"With the pence I thus earned I was able to purchase bananas from street stalls, and to receive a bed every night in a respectable women's lodging house, where I was treated with much consideration on account of being supposed to be dumb, and this life (which would have been more tolerable if only I could have discovered some trace of your whereabouts) continued until a day arrived, when, dancing in the wide lounge of a public house in St. Martin's Lane, I noticed that I had attracted something more than usual regard from an opulently dressed, but coarse and rather flashy man, who, however, had in his eye enough of a certain rough kindliness to compel a second glance from a creature as lonely as myself.

"Catching this glance, he beckoned me towards him, and what hesitancy I felt being counteracted by a sudden strong feeling, or hunch, that this meeting might mark a turning-point in my career, I joined him at his table.

" 'Baby!' surprisingly began this stranger. 'You're too slick a piece of goods to be going round with a wop and a lot of canned numbers. I'm going to take you right away from all that worry and strain. And now. Baby, I want you. . . .' "

Here, again, the page came to an end, and, when he had read the last words upon it, Mr.

Fatigay fell into the same feverish anxiety as before. It was, if anything, the intenser for a certain subconscious process of disentanglement, which had been set up by his previous alarm and relief. His emotions were not dissimilar to those that a poverty-stricken peasant of South Africa might experience, who having spurned peevishly a dull pebble in the road, sees a sophisticated-looking stranger pounce eagerly upon it, and disappear, all singing, all talking, all dancing, into the distance.

"Emily!" he cried. "How could you? Ah, the libertine! Did you? You couldn't! You didn't? Yes or no?"

At once the kind creature, to disembarrass him of his fears, drew the next sheet from the machine, and hurried to give it him.

"to take a big part in my new revue," he read, and experienced the relief of a peasant, similarly situated to the one previously described, who notices that the joyously bounding stranger has jolted the rough diamond from his pocket in his excited retreat.

"At this," continued the typescript, "I looked very doubtfully at the stranger, for I have a very strong antipathy to the theatre, and I had heard of strange developments following upon proposals of this kind. But I reminded myself that an increase in my earning capacity meant increased facilities in my quest for some knowledge of your condition, and an ability, also, to be of material assistance to you if you had been overtaken by misfortune, so I prepared myself to come to terms with the stranger.

" 'Come,' said he, looking shrewdly into my face, in which perhaps traces of my dubiety still lingered. 'What do you say to a level twenty a week?'

"It took some moments for the exact significance of this phrase to dawn upon me, and when I realised that I, a mere chimp, was being offered this sum, I was too overcome immediately to nod my acceptance. Before I could do so, the manager, for such was his rank, gave me a further shrewd look, and, addressing me as 'Chicken', said he saw that I was not a stranger to the theatre world, and, swearing that he hated equally meanness and taking advantage, proposed that we should be on the level straight away, and, as if to establish us there, advanced his offer in one bound to £50.

"At this I gazed at him with a certain degree of amazement, partly at the idea of being worth £50, and partly that so bluff and downright a man should speak so far out of character as to offer a novice what now appeared to be less than half her market value. You may imagine my surprise, when, again misreading my expression, the manager brought his hand down upon the table with a crash, and, laughing heartily, observed that I had him taped. He then expressed a determination that we should not fall out over the contract, and offered me the same as he had given the principal dame in his last production, that is, £100 a week. On that, he offered me his hand, which I shook with considerable enthusiasm, and then, with an appearance of the utmost satisfaction, he led me to his office, where a contract was immediately made out and presented to me for signature. I signed with a scrawl as nearly like human handwriting as I could manage.

" 'Ah!' said he, after a glance at it. 'Juanita Spaniola? Is that it? Spanish, I presume?'

"Thinking no harm of the white lie, I nodded, suppressing a smile.

" 'So I thought,' said he. 'Now that's what I call a very fair hand, for a ballerina. Say, don't you know English, señora? You seem to understand it all right.'

"I shook my head.

"It was not until after my first appearance upon the boards, where my success, for what it is worth, was prodigious, that my patron arrived at an inkling of my true species, which I had used every means to conceal, lest my exposure in a position entirely devoid of civil rights should render me a prey to the unscrupulous, and perhaps a slave to the immoral. This dreaded consummation did not follow, for my patron, flushed by the success of his undertaking, and genuinely grateful for my part in it, shook me warmly by the hand and swore that he would see to it that I had fair play, damning, incidentally, the eyes of all stars, leading ladies and chorus girls of human origin.

" 'For,' said he, 'with their everlasting chatter chatter chatter and grab grab grab they make my life a hell upon earth between them, while you, señora,' (for so he gallantly persisted in addressing me) 'say never a word, either jealous, quarrelsome or cajoling. You perform your steps without a lot of —— temperament, and you take your pay cheque at the end of the week without making a lot of fuss about the size of it.'

"I need not describe, my dear master, the various steps by which I made myself at home in the peculiar world I had entered. Suffice it to say, that I early acquired a proficiency on the typewriter, by means of which I gained all the advantages of communication with others. At the end of my contract with my good patron, I found myself able to bargain for the highest salary in my profession, and set myself up on the scale of luxury in which you have found me, and I have, moreover, accumulated a comfortable private fortune against the longed-for day when I should cross your path again, for knowing that your mind is concerned with more important matters than the mere acquisition of wealth, it appeared to me that it would be well for you if any property you owned (for such I hope I may still consider myself to be) should perform that menial function on your behalf. What luxurious display I have entered upon has been only in the interests of my professional status; the address, the clothes, the car, and the Ritz, for example, to which last, may I assure you,

I should have preferred the most humble of vegetarian restaurants, though now I shall ever hold it dear on account of it having been the point to which our paths converged.

"Now, my dear master, I have answered to the best of my ability the questions you put to me. Allow me, in return, to ask one of you. Is there any little dainty you could especially fancy for your tea ?"

"No, Emily," replied Mr. Fatigay, on reading this last sentence. "Nothing but a lightly boiled egg, and some slices of thin bread and butter."

When she had left the room to arrange for the preparation of these, he re-read the document she had handed him. Whether it was that his momentary apprehensions during the first reading had stimulated his general awareness of her personality, and of hitherto unsuspected depths in his feeling for her, or whether his long period on a restricted diet had had that effect of clearing the vision and sharpening the wits which those who indulge in voluntary fasts claim for the practice, it is impossible to decide, but the fact remains that he was not so satisfied with this mere record of events, from which, with rare selflessness, Emily had omitted so much of personal feeling and motive, as he would have been had he still considered her as an ordinary chimp, however talented.

After his last experience of the sex, this absence of egotism affected him with the new restlessness that a city dweller finds, when he retires into the complete quiet of the country in order to cure the insomnia caused by the cacophony of London nights. He wanted just a little of it in order to feel at peace.

"Emily," he said, when she came in bearing a dainty tray. "Is it true that you remained in England, which you hate, in order to be near me, who cast you out? And that you took up a profession which you abhorred in order to gain money for my assistance, when I had sent you away with nothing but your fare back to Boboma, and without even knowing that you were able to make use of the money? Why, you might have been robbed!"

Emily nodded, with a meek and tender smile.

"But why?" asked Mr. Fatigay. "And how, if your devotion is such, could you have brought yourself to wreck my life by upsetting my marriage to Amy?"

At this, the chimp began to tremble a little, for she imagined that he knew all, and thought the moment had now come when he would spurn her; but she bravely made her way to the typewriter, whence shortly she produced a sheet for his inspection, which said:

"The answer to both your questions, my dear master, is that which truth would have compelled me to make had you asked me the motive of even the least of my actions in Africa, almost from the day when I came into your possession. It is—because I love you."

"What I did, I did from cruel necessity. Was it wholly bad? Consider. Do you remember one happiness received from that affair for which you have not paid many times its value in pain? Which of your friends have you seen married to a woman without well-founded misgivings as to his future? Ponder these questions gravely, and, if you still wish it, I will, at whatever cost to my own feelings, give you grounds for divorce. You can then rejoin your fiancée, who, if she loves you as I do, will no doubt gladly receive you. I perceive that I have typed the last line with a certain degree of malice (which please forgive and discount), so I will say no more."

When Mr. Fatigay had read these words, he said nothing, but lay for a long time staring sadly into space, and every now and then he fetched a heavy sigh.

As with a drowning man whom mermaid hands draw down to what is probably, after all, far better than the life he has hitherto led, yet who kicks and struggles regardless of this consideration, until he sees his whole past unfold before him in a series of vivid pictures, when he folds his hands and fills his lungs and sinks without further protest, so did Mr. Fatigay rebel bitterly against Emily's invitation into reason, an element as unfamiliar and as fatal to lovers as is the sea to any land creature, and it was not until he had begun to review his past life in hard detail that he ceased his first instinctive resistance.

Oddly, perhaps significantly, it was not those pictures which might have been given such titles, if they had been shown at the Academy, as *The Rebuke*, *Waiting*, *The Green-eyed Monster*, or *So Near and Yet so Far*, that moved him most in this direction, but rather those in which a shadowy third appeared; a small melancholy figure, bowed by tyranny on one side and neglect on the other. When he thought of Emily at her most painful corner of that most painful triangle, a position in which she was thrust the farther from him, and to a more acutely pointed humiliation, by his own obtuseness, when he thought of what she must have suffered, and when he contrasted her constant good humour and control with Amy's pampered peevishness, he began to feel for her, not as a chimp, but as a woman, or, at the very least, as an angel.

"After all," he thought, "Emily had to do what Amy told her in that matter of the wedding, and her lesser part was actuated by love for me, though I neglected her, while Amy, whom I loved (and here he gave a groan) Amy invented that unspeakably cruel way of dismissing me."

Sheltered by this illusion from the cold facts which might at the present stage have easily destroyed it, a new feeling for Emily began to spring up in his heart, nourished equally by certain old memories, by his convalescent gratitude, and by some faint but ineffably thrilling hopes for the future: it sprang up much as a hedge does, sheltered for the first season or so by hurdles, which, when they rot, it will more than replace as a bulwark against the storm.

Every day this feeling made new growth, and yet without a word about it passing between them: it was too subtle and frail a thing, both of them felt, to be born save in a secure and holy silence, for, like the soul in Wordsworth, this love had had elsewhere its setting and needed repose and forgetfulness for its unencumbered delivery.

Not till Mr. Fatigay was almost completely recovered from the effects of his privations, and might sit, on the sunny March days, wrapped in warm rugs on the little balcony, did he make the remotest allusion to the past, and even this he did so vaguely that it was some time before the chimp realised the misapprehension which Amy had engendered in his mind.

When at last she understood, her heart stood still in her breast.

"Oh dear!" she thought, her whole life suddenly arrested, as is that of the cancer cure who one day feels, it seems, a twinge of the old familiar pain. "Oh dear! supposing everything goes wrong now? What will he say when he finds out?"

"Emily," called Mr. Fatigay from the balcony. "That, over there, must be the top of the Ritz, surely. To think that it was down there that I was trudging in the snow only last month! Now all that, and all that led to it, seems part of another life. It seems I died then, and am here with you in heaven. Let it always be so, Emily. We will live like the blessed angels."

Emily bowed her head.

As soon as she might, she withdrew into a back room to wrestle with the temptation that shook her.

"Can I bear it ?" she thought.

"Should I destroy his new-born happiness. Dare I take the dreadful responsibility ? Is it fair to him ?"

She sat for a long time, staring at the wall. Once, already, she had wrung the truth out of this last treacherous question, a pitfall which cowardly instinct digs for one sex, but which ultimately engulfs the other. Emily stared at the wall.

"No," she said, at last. "What grows between us must be based on truth, or, though it kills me, it must not grow at all."

And she sat down at the typewriter, to make a complete statement; but this, either because of the trembling of her hands, or because of a not unnatural impulse to express it in a rather finer prose than usual, she was a long time in completing, and she had not yet finished when the door bell rang peremptorily, interrupting her painful task.

CHAPTER XVIII

Fly a shadow, it still pursues you,

and so, adds the poet, does a woman. But he might have elaborated his conceit with the reservation that during the darkest hours both have a tendency to disappear, the pursuit being renewed only when the sun rises again, in the opposite quarter.

A woman who has sent a man about his business will hear very complacently that he is shunning all company and diversion and moping unprofitably alone, and if it is said that he has morosely flouted all his material interests, has flung up his job or has been thrown out of it for a display of sullen temper: "Why," says she, "a very little will suffice to keep a single man in comfort, and perhaps, for one so emotionally unstable as he is, it is better that he has no money, considering the temptations of the metropolis."

And if she is told that he is drinking like a madman, so that his best friends can no more have truck with him, she will show how the charity of love is superior to that of friendship, for she will say, "Poor fellow! It is as well we did not marry, clearly, but I can easily forgive him, for I know what he has suffered. He wrote telling me. . . .

After all, why should I grudge him an anodyne which may be a blessing in disguise, preventing him from turning to worse things ?"

But should it come to her knowledge that he has dared actually to go about his business, his business as a man, I mean, and is warming his starved heart in the new-risen sun of another affection, she will say nothing to anybody, but will at once go and pay him a visit; when in her first sentence she will propose, "Let us forget all that, and be just the perfect friends we were really meant to be." And in her next she will try to arouse his jealousy, and in the third, and the many that follow it, she will bitterly reproach him for desecrating all that has passed between them.

Amy, when she had recovered from her first chagrin at the sensation of defeat, found it possible to admit to herself that she had been prevented, after all, only from something which she could easily do without. Indeed, her relationship to her lover, for she still regarded him as hers, as kings and queens consider banished men as still their subjects, her relationship to him had never been more satisfactory. Registered letters, and some borne by district messengers, arrived continuously, and in reading these she was conscious of a receptiveness luxuriously free to devote itself to the writer's manner, and the pure feeling which this conveyed, instead of being bothered at every other sentence by the necessity for dealing with some point of fact, as might have been the case had she contemplated making an answer.

It was not long before these letters were written on a poorer paper than formerly, and the addresses from which they were dated became more and more doubtful, till the last of them, as she learned from a discreet enquiry of Dennis Tickler, who knew his London, was nothing but a slum doss-house, where a journalist friend of his had once spent a night in search of copy.

"Poor Alfred!" thought Amy that evening. "Yet perhaps such an experience as this is just what he wanted to make him pull himself together. He never had enough backbone." And she gave her thoughts a turn to: "How fortunate men are, to be able to go and live roughing it in the queerest, most thrilling places, whence women are debarred by a set of silly conventions. No wonder that men write all the best books."

"I quite agree," said her friend, for Amy had been thinking aloud, so to speak. "I quite agree. It's a part of a great conspiracy, which shows them to be conscious of weakness. Purdah! Absolute purdah!"

"But tell me," she went on, after a moment's bitter rumination on the guarded privileges of men, "tell me, dearest, unless you'd rather not—you've never told me, and I've never liked to ask—just what *was* it made you decide not to marry Alfred at the last moment?"

Amy stared into the gas fire as if in hesitation, or perhaps as if to collect her mind into a stark and unflinching sincerity. But, in fact, she knew what she was going to say, for she had said it before, and unflinchingly, to one or two other confidential enquirers.

"I don't know," she said at last. "I hate to seem to criticise Alfred: he was such a dear, and there was such a bond between us in one way—not mental, perhaps, at least, not exactly, our tastes weren't much the same, but that didn't seem to matter—I suppose it was spiritual. I think it was some instinct stopped me. Perhaps it was an awareness of certain deeps in me that Alfred never succeeded in arousing. I feel I ought to marry someone who could make me feel—*mad*. That's what it was, dear, in absolute confidence, of course; Alfred didn't attract me sufficiently in that way. So it seemed only fair to him. Supposing—afterwards—someone else—one might have been carried away, and he'd have hated it *too* terribly. He got terribly upset once, over something absolutely trivial. And yet—I don't know. I sometimes think I'm strange in that way. Have some more of this coffee, darling. Do you like it? It's supposed to be very special."

Amy's contentment survived another month or so, until a very extraordinary piece of news came to her ears. Mr. Fatigay, clad in a singularly sumptuous dressing-gown, had been seen sitting in the spring sunshine on the balcony of a certain house in South Audley Street. Beside him, and dressed up to the nines, Dennis Tickler said, the chimp had been sitting, and they had been actually holding hands.

Amy listened, aghast.

All this time, her sexual life had been balanced and satisfied by the vision of Mr. Fatigay suffering for her in an exile in which there were the fewest possible counter attractions to her image. She had felt inexpressively tender towards him. On many nights she had lain down to sleep in a warm surrender to the idea of a recall, and in a vision of their rapturous reunion. Though with each new morning's severer light there reappeared substantial reasons against it, the dream had become very dear to her, for it supplied all that she needed from marriage, and demanded nothing she was unwilling to give. And now this happy dream world lay in ruins about her feet.

"Really ? " she said. "Did you say that house with all that lovely ironwork ? How awfully lucky for Alfred! I've always thought that to live with that balcony must be perfect. Well! Well!" and with a light laugh she turned the conversation.

The next few days were perhaps the most emotional Amy had ever known. A burning resentment against her lover filled her heart. She felt stifled at the thought of the deceitful way in which he had been trampling on all the almost holy feelings that had grown up in her heart. This rebellion must be quelled at all costs, she felt, though it might necessitate the presence of her own person, temporarily at least, to effect a complete subjugation; a loan which Machiavelli advises to princes in their treatment of the unruly conquered.

At last she could restrain herself no longer; her heart, the chemistry of which had so long been giving off the mild vapours of an Heloïse part, seethed violently under the new acid, and emitted a stinging intoxicating gas which inflated her to the proportions of a Cleopatra cognisant of Anthony's marriage. Outwardly calm, she set forth one afternoon to reclaim the wanton Alfred, and it was her ring which interrupted the last sentences of Emily's confession, and it was her form that the disconcerted chimp beheld when she opened the door of the flat.

"Alfred!" cried Amy from the door mat, ignoring the lifted eyebrows of the chimp.

A faint sound emanated from the drawing-room. Amy, assuming a light and friendly air, made her way towards it.

"Hullo, Alfred!" she said, as he arose in confusion at her entrance. "I hope you won't mind my coming to look you up. You don't mind, do you? I thought, 'Even if our love affair did come to a horrible sticky end, yet there's so much between us. We may have been a misfit sexually, but nothing can destroy the fact that we are, underneath, the best friends in the world.' Isn't that so? Best friends, Alfred?"

And she extended, frankly and freely, a hand.

"Well, Amy," said Mr. Fatigay, giving it a

clumsy shake, "I don't know. I don't know that I bear any grudge. I must say, I've had a pretty bad time."

"A bad time? Poor old chap!" said Amy, giving him a look. "Well, I've not been too happy, myself, wondering what's been happening to you. I've missed your companionship and your . . . terribly."

A multitude of dead emotions rose from their graves in Mr. Fatigay's heart, like souls on the last day. In his tremulous surprise at seeing all these old friends again, he failed to perceive at once, that, battered by their violent end, they had become still more the worse for wear during their entombment.

"Amy . . ." he said, and halted.

At that moment, the chimp, in a simple afternoon frock of maizey green and yellow silk, entered with the tea tray. She placed it steadily on a low table, and, seating herself beside it, she glanced enquiringly at Amy, as if to ask, would she take tea?

"What, tea?" said Amy. "What a charming pot! Shall I pour out for you, Alfred, as in the old days?" And she began at once to do so, still utterly ignoring poor Emily, who exercised self-control.

Yet this was more natural than wise of Amy, for Mr. Fatigay, who had come to see Emily's early hardships with the same new eye which had lent perspective to his own, was inevitably reminded of both by seeing his sweet-natured benefactress thus slighted in her own house.

"Well. . . . Oh! Thank you," he murmured, taking the cup. "Of course, Emily usually pours out tea, you know."

"Yes, I see you've got Emily," replied Amy brightly. "And what a nice place you've got, Alfred. You *must* have prospered. But why do you dress the monkey up in that gaudy thing? Surely it's unsuitable for a servant? It would be for anyone, for that matter." For she meant to show how utterly impossible it was for any normal civilised person to conceive that the chimp could exist on any other footing.

"Emily isn't a servant," said Mr. Fatigay firmly. "If either was the servant here, it would be me. This place is hers, for she's now a well-known dancer, and she simply saved my life by taking me in when I was starving."

"Good heavens!" said Amy. "Well! Of course, I know that *legally* she's your wife. But. . . . Well, I suppose it's not for me to ask questions. Dennis told me that he'd seen you sitting together very intimately on the balcony. It was from him I found out where you were. I've been looking everywhere for you, though perhaps with a quite ridiculous thought in my mind. . . . I wish I'd questioned Dennis more closely now. I didn't like to, for I didn't want to hurt him. He's been *too* marvellous."

"I wrote to you often enough," said Mr. Fatigay, "till I got too poor and hopeless. You can't have been looking for me very long."

"It takes a woman some time to get over a shock like that," replied Amy. "That's the sort of thing you could never understand, Alfred. We might have been happy together now if you could ever have understood that."

"And apparently you needed the assistance of Dennis Tickler," rejoined Mr. Fatigay. "Good Lord! What a choice of a consoler! And goodness knows what shock you've had to get over. I should think I was the one who had the shock."

"Don't run down Dennis, please," said Amy. "I haven't *said* that he was my 'consoler,' as you call it. He's been perfect, absolutely. If anyone's consoler is to be criticised, it's yours, if you only knew," she went on, getting her trump card played as best she might. "And not because she's a filthy monkey either, but something far, far worse even than that. You don't know what she did about our wedding. I came round meaning to tell you, and put matters right between us, but, finding you living, God knows how, with this admirable wife of yours, dragging everything that was good and lovely between us—or so I was fool enough to think—in the mire, I won't. I expect she was your—your *creature* all the time, and you put her up to doing what she did. Good God! To think what I've given my love to! To think that I should have come round this afternoon, feeling and hoping what I did—to this!"

"You know perfectly well," said Mr. Fatigay, "that none of your insinuations about Emily and myself are true—Put that teapot down, Emily—either in the past or now. Whatever it was you felt when you came here, you've not gone the right way to bring it off. And vague accusations will carry us no farther. Why don't you say it downright?"

"Oh, I don't know, Alfred," she replied. "I'd better not spoil whatever happiness you seem to have contented yourself with. It wouldn't do any good. You've made it pretty clear that you hate me now."

"I don't know what I feel," said Mr. Fatigay. "But you owe it to Emily, and to me, and to yourself, unless you wish me to think you a mere slanderer, to say everything now you've said so much. Otherwise we'd better say good-bye."

"Well, if you force me to, I will," said Amy. "You don't know just one thing that may alter your opinion of your beloved wife. You don't know that it was she who threatened me with a carving knife, and made me put on the bridesmaid's hat, and would have killed me if I'd said a word—it was she who spoiled everything I'd been longing for—and on my bridal day, too."

"Good God!" cried Mr. Fatigay. "Emily! Emily, is this true?"

The chimp nodded piteously.

Mr. Fatigay sank back in his chair. His whole mind seemed shattered by this revelation. His thoughts raced wildly round from point to point of his riven firmament like the needle of an overturned compass. It was significant, though, that, when their wild oscillations settled at last into a trembling stillness, they should concentrate on Emily. Was she, after all, their true pole?

"Emily," he said hoarsely. "But how *could* you do such a thing?"

Emily laid an eloquent hand upon her heart.

"Of course," said Amy with a short laugh, "the ridiculous creature's been hankering after you from the first. Anyone could see that in her shameless looks."

Mr. Fatigay looked at the chimp more in sorrow than in anger, for even in his shaken state he found the motive thus indicated to be at least a possibly forgivable one.

"Poor chimp!" he said. "Even if in your ignorance you hoped to advantage yourself by such an act, how could you have deceived me now? I said only to-day that . . ."

"Why," cried Amy vindictively, "she's as deceitful as anything. She reeks of deceit."

Emily held up her hand arrestingly. Both stared at her. Quickly she bounded from the room, and in a moment had returned with the typewriter, in which fluttered the nearly completed page on which she had been making her confession.

Mr. Fatigay took it out and glance at it.

"My dear master," it began. "One or two

recent remarks of yours have made me doubt, and something you said to-day has made me certain, that you are under some misapprehension as to the part I played in preventing your marriage to Amy, and in marrying you myself. I had not thought it possible that she should not have told you, or I would have enlightened you earlier, though I know that it may make you hate me, and drive me from you into a still more hopeless darkness than before. I alone am guilty. I could not bear to see you engaging yourself for a lifetime into that cruel subjection under which I had myself suffered so often and so bitterly. That is what I meant when I said I had acted from cruel necessity. I had reason to believe that still worse lay in store for you, and, determined to save you from this fate, rather than from the least hope of gaining you for myself, I forced Amy to play the part of bridesmaid, while I, trembling, assumed that of the bride. I justified myself by the thought that I was only intruding upon a legal formality, and that if by some remote chance I had underestimated Amy's affection for you, this would have an opportunity to demonstrate itself in an acceptance of you in spite of what had happened, and in spite of the gossip and scandal which might ensue."

Mr. Fatigay looked up from this sheet, with a countenance which, after some seconds of utter blankness, began to work as a man's does when devils are being cast out of him, and after he had amazed Amy and alarmed Emily by the protracted violence of this symptom of internal conflict, he leaned back in his chair, with a countenance pale and bedewed with sweat, and spoke, in a pale cold voice, these words:

"It seems that Emily had no intention of deceiving me, Amy! Why did you deceive me, though? What excuse have you for poisoning my whole existence with a belief, compared with which the real event, and even your straightforward rejection of me after it, would have been nothing—nothing at all?"

"I never actually *said* that I'd made Emily do it," said Amy, and then, terrified by the expression on Mr. Fatigay's face, she added: "Oh, Alfred! I couldn't bear to be laughed at. *Do* understand."

"I understand one thing," said Mr. Fatigay, with cold vehemence, "and that is, that a man would be better off with any chimp in the world, much less Emily, than with a woman of your sort."

"No, Emily," he went on, "remain where you are. *I* will show Amy to the door."

"Well," said Amy with a dry sob of humiliation, "If you treat me like this, don't be surprised at anything you hear about me and Dennis, that's all. Or anyone else for that matter. You'll have driven me to it by your hardness." And she began to weep.

"Don't cry, Amy," said Mr. Fatigay. "The people in the street will see you."

And he closed the door.

"Emily!" he cried, as he turned back to where

the chimp stood, waiting with downcast doubtful gaze. "Emily! My twice preserver! My good angel! My consolation! My wife."

The chimp, drowned in happiness, heard his words falling like the sound of bells from an infinite height.

"Had he but said 'my love'," she thought, "my wildest, fondest dream would have all come true. But what a happy task, to spend the future years in winning that last dear epithet from his truthful lips!"

It was perhaps a train of thought following on this last idea, and confirmed by her careful consideration of what would be best for his future happiness, that led her, two or three days later, to suggest that they should leave the country in which they had both suffered so much, and return to the warmer climate and happier associations of Boboma.

"Yes, Emily," said Mr. Fatigay, when he had read the neat typescript in which she conveyed this proposal. "I'll see if I can get the schoolmaster's position again, and we'll start as soon as ever we can."

CHAPTER XIX

And I lie so composedly,
Now, in my bed
(Knowing her love),
That you fancy me dead—
And I rest so contentedly,
Now in my bed
(With her love at my breast),
That you fancy me dead—
That you shudder to look at me,
Thinking me dead.

THE dirty white boat train, its windows bedewed as if with tears, ran out from under the vast indigo cloud, which lowered and billowed saddeningly over a hundred miles of silvery khaki and darkly silvered green, and it drew up in a burst of pale sunshine at the harbour platform. The baggy cloud rolled off eastward over the glimpse of sea, leaving bright waters pitching in the south-west prospect, and on the horizon a glimpse of ultimate blue. Through gaps in raw planks, gangways and derricks were to be seen, and, high above them, and above a flash of white paint, the surprising funnels stood up to proclaim that all that was best and sincerest in poster art was true.

Mr. and Mrs. Fatigay were among the first to

descend from the train, and a glad haste winged their heels as they tripped, arm in arm, up the ridgey gangway. Several cameras clicked: it had been impossible to conceal the monkey dancer's romance from the Press.

"My message to your readers," said Mr. Fatigay, when he had escorted his shy bride to her stateroom, and was able to give his attention to the group of slick young interviewers who surrounded him, "is simply this. It is true my wife is not a woman. She is an angel. But though I believe there is no chimp like my Emily, I can heartily recommend my fellow men to seek their life's pal, so to speak, among the females of her modest race. My experience has taught me that they are unequalled as soul-mates, if that is the correct term, either when skies are grey or blue. Behind every great man there may indeed be a woman, and beneath every performing flea a hot plate, but beside the only happy man I know of—there is a chimp."

At these words, those among the reporters who were young and single, looked a little dubious, but those who were older, or married, nodded their heads as if more than half convinced, and eyed Mr. Fatigay with something of friendly envy in their gaze.

The klaxons then began to sound, and lover from lover, husband from wife, parent from child, the one was taken and the other was left. The gangways were withdrawn.

"Write soon."

"Yes, I'll write from Gib."

A strip of emerald water was there, widening, dividing them from England, the land slipped by them, sank to the appearance of a sandbank, and next day was gone: a sultrier coast smouldered to port, they drew in under the shadow of the Rock, some officers disembarked, three palm trees sprang up from a cluster of rickety white where the flat warm water lapped the sand. It was Africa. Some smallish whales were seen, Guinea lay beside them, hot as brass; then they ticked in their coloured circle of sea, passing, save for their frothy white or boiling phosphorescent wake, through time only, to a dull and steamy coast lagooned with islands of mud. On the shining shores of these, crippled dug-outs, the craft of splay-footed fishermen, were beached. Behind them, sunlit beyond mudflat after mudflat, more and more water was seen, paler than the sea. Emily's heart swelled: there was the Congo.

Mr. Fatigay's heart swelled also. He came softly up behind the almost childish figure that stood gazing over the rails of the foremost boat-deck, and laid his hand very very tenderly on hers.

"Well, Emily!" he said. "Here we are, so to speak, and I must say I'm happy to have arrived. I've quite a longing to taste a yam again."

Emily smiled up at him contentedly.

"By Jove!" he cried. "I vote we have a marvellous spread in Cazembe. We ought to be there in time for dinner. New picked fruit for you, Emily, and for me, well, it's hard to decide. Something with plenty of flavour to it, anyway. I hate the pallid food that most English keep to out here." And he proceeded to express some very decided views on this subject, every particular of which Emily noted, although in fact she had heard the greater part already.

Now a dead branch drifted past them, and they stood in towards the port. A broad boat advanced to receive the Fatigays, who were the only passengers landing here, and, with a quiet farewell or two (for they had elected to live in a happy seclusion on the ship, and so had made little acquaintance among their fellow-voyagers) they descended the side, and settled themselves in the stern, impatient to set foot again on African soil.

When the excellent evening meal was done, Mr. Fatigay lit a cigar, and suggested to Emily that they should stroll abroad a little and see the sights of the town. But she, with one or two of those quiet signs by which she managed to express to his now subtler understanding almost all that she desired to communicate to him (*my gracious silence*, he sometimes laughingly called her), with one or two such signs she indicated that she had seen enough of cities, and that they made her tired, so that she would be well content to await him in he hotel while he took a walk, and perhaps a little refreshment in any congenial company he might find.

Mr. Fatigay, having been smilingly reassured that the chimp would suffer no sort of loneliness during his absence, consented to wander about for an hour or so, and as he sat outside the principal café, comparing their present brand of lager beer with that which they had provided on his previous visit, four years or so ago, he mused contentedly on the singular difference between his circumstances now, and then.

"Was it indeed I," he murmured, as his cigar smoke oozed from his nostrils into the blue and gold of the lamplit evening air. "Was it I who sat here at this same table with my very bones aching with misery at the thought of three years' separation from the she who was all I held dear, and with my heart already broken, so it seemed, by the thought that it was herself who had decreed my exile?

"Was it I whose life in Boboma was spaced and divided, and with a punctuation which grew more and more modernist in its increasing infrequency, by those letters, which, when they came, sucked all my heart's blood to fill their emptiness of affection, as if they were cupping glasses applied to that swollen and exhausted member?

"Was it I who spent that agonising night in the Corner House, descending to the very verge of suicide because Amy kissed that fellow at her party; a reaction so extreme in this age, when men are what they are, and when so few women are what they were, that it must have been in itself an obvious symptom, to any rational mind, of a lunatic abandonment of all sense of balance and proportion ?

"Was it I," he thought, with his twentieth spicy sigh of repletion, "who was brought down to mixing with artists, and eating cabbage stumps, and wearing no socks, like a damned highbrow, by my despair at the trick Amy played on me ? And here's that poor fellow writing from Boboma full of gratitude for being bought out of his job, and asking if I'll mind if he leaves a week before my arrival, as he is anxious to get quickly home to be married! I wonder if he's got a chimp."

"A chimp," the very word was like a bell; one of those bells which, struck only once by the skilled hand of the trap-drummer, arrests the melancholy heart-searchings of the verse, and turns the treacly current into the richer rhythms of the chorus.

Mr. Fatigay arose, and, his feet moving as if to music of this luxuriously slothful kind, he made his way back to where, at the end of the now darkening palm-rustling street, the lights of the hotel glittered like a collection of fire-flies in a broken cardboard box.

"Good night, Emily," he said, thrusting his head through the door which joined their rooms. But Emily, though she was still awake, pretended to be sleeping. "For," thought she, "if he thinks I go to sleep quite normally when he stays out late, he will never feel constrained to leave his enjoyment earlier on my account. It is best to begin as one means to go on."

At last he blew out his candle, and with the extinction of that, the last resistant spark of humanity in Cazembe, the night flooded in, dark as water under the mighty trees, hard as sapphire where it wedged in the white alleys, and, high above, as dry and light and thin as spangled gauze. Reptiles moved in the river, and lions on the land, desires in the heart and dreams in the mind. Then, tearing through the light upper night, blowing it away, the sun came, and, in a moment, all values were reversed.

Nothing is more sudden than daybreak in the tropics. It is as when, in a village cinema, the screen vibrates again, after a pitchy break, with that compelling white light in which move images shallowly common to all. Stars, or cigarette ends, fade; screams and embraces cease. The close-up of the beloved's enormous eye fades out before the still more illusory close-up of the world's sweetheart—Apollo or Rudolf Valentino, it's all one. The business we are here for is suspended, as the great cats run home, and the business we all pretend we are here for now begins. All of us, that is, except our hero and heroine, whose only end is to get home to Boboma.

As the sun sprang up, the respective shutters of Mr. Fatigay and his Emily popped open simultaneously, and, as they thrust their heads out into the singing morning, they at once caught sight of one another, and were glad.

"Look! Look, Emily!" cried Mr. Fatigay, and pointed to where the scabby little boat was moored, which was to take them up the river.

The streets opened up into life, mats were shaken, breakfasts eaten at doorways, greetings shouted, merchandise spread out on the pavements. The cripples, crawling as if tangled in their own black shadows, like wet flies, made for the shady nooks in which they passed the day.

"Come, Emily," said Mr. Fatigay, "and I'll buy you a new parasol before we go on board."

The journey was delightful. The captain and his mate were enchanted by Emily's quiet charm, so different from the loud mixture of arrogance and querulousness with which the wives of other officials had so often frayed their nerves. Shyly, and with the manly delicacy characteristic of their profession, they hinted to Mr. Fatigay, during a pleasant game of Nap, that, if she had any sisters at home at all resembling herself, they would be more than honoured by an opportunity of making their acquaintance next time they put in at Boboma. The crew plucked water-lilies.

The river narrowed. They were nearing their own parts. Looking up, they saw a dark figure suspended from the overhanging branch of a gigantic tree, watching their approach with idle curiosity. But as they passed beneath, this figure showed signs of amazement, and ran out along the bending branch to get a closer view.

"That looks like a cousin of mine," thought Emily, and, standing up in the boat, she impulsively waved a handkerchief in greeting. The effect was electrical. The simple-hearted fellow performed a hundred superb feats in joyous trapeze. Finally, after nods promising his speedy return, he disappeared, swinging, with rustle and crash and low sweet bird call, from tree top to tree top through the haunts of his acquaintance and kin.

From that hour their progress was processional. Dark faces and flying limbs switchbacked along the sheer green wall of the jungle, scattering flocks of gaudy parrots like fluttering confetti. Rustic bouquets sailed through the air. It seemed as if all the chimps in the world were present at the carnival. Mr. Fatigay bowed right and left. Emily kissed her hand.

At last they rounded a bend and saw the landing stage before them. It was crowded with the young men of the village, come out to escort them home. A mighty cheer arose as they came alongside. Mr. Fatigay was now dearer to these honest hearts than was Livingstone, who had discovered Boboma, or any of the white men who had visted it since, for he was the only one who had ever come back after once having left it.

"*Au revoir!*" cried the captain and the mate, and the crew's faces were split with smiles expressive of all the good humour to which their humbler station forbade them to give voice.

The blacks gaily hustled the happy pair into a a state litter, which was raised upon the shoulders of the chief's bearers, music was struck up, Chinese lanterns, contemptuous of the day, were hoisted before them, and they set off back along the forest road.

"Welcome home!" said the head man graciously. "The residents of Boboma are unanimous in hearty welcome and goodwill and best wishes for connubial bliss. Accept the freedom of Boboma. Be pleased to attend a fête organised in your honour by the Corporation of Boboma and by her hearty healthy happy townsfolk."

As he concluded, the music struck up again, and the whole population began to dance and sing, even those who brought in the victuals to the high festal table at which the Fatigays were seated with the chief between them.

When at last the evening's merriment was done, and Mr. Fatigay and his bride had been escorted to the dear house in which they had first met, which had been swept and garnished to receive them, they sat a long while on the verandah, watching the lights in the village fade out one by one, and the moon rise like a clear and simple idea in a happily tired mind. Not a word was spoken. They almost ceased to think.

"Well, we must to bed," said Mr. Fatigay at last, and, rising reluctantly, he switched on the light. Home, with chairs and tables, sprang up about them, like a comfortable wooden cage for the nocturnal feelings, shy as birds, which the blue moon-silences had lured from out their timid hearts.

Soon afterwards, Mr. Fatigay came from his room and sat on Emily's little white couch, wherein she sat upright, dark and dainty as a Spanish princess.

"Emily!" he said, and was silent for a long time.

"Emily!" he said. "My Angel! My Own! My Love!"

At this last word, Emily raised her eyes, and extended to him her hand.

Under her long and scanty hair he caught glimpses of a plum-blue skin. Into the depths of those all-dark lustrous eyes, his spirit slid with no sound of splash. She uttered a few low words, rapidly, in her native tongue. The candle, guttering beside the bed, was strangled in the grasp of a prehensile foot, and darkness received, like a ripple in velvet, the final happy sigh.

THE END

OXFORD PAPERBACKS

Twentieth-Century Classics

Memoirs of a Midget

Walter de la Mare

Introduction by Angela Carter

'This book is an authentic masterpiece. Lucid, enigmatic, and violent with a terrible violence that leaves behind no physical trace . . . It may be read with a good deal of simple enjoyment and then it sticks like a splinter in the mind.' So writes novelist Angela Carter in her new introduction to Walter de la Mare's elegiac study of the estrangement and isolation suffered by the diminutive Miss M.

The Slaves of Solitude

Patrick Hamilton

Introduction by Claud Cockburn

'Mr Hamilton has the habit, the art, or the genius of writing in his novels, about the most familiar scenes, the most threadbare experiences, as if they were being observed for the first time' – Stephen Potter

A seedy boarding house provides a wartime haven for Miss Roach, a lonely middle-aged spinster. Romance, glamour, and finally tragedy enter her life in the shape of a handsome American serviceman.

OXFORD PAPERBACKS

Twentieth-Century Classics

The Village in the Jungle

Leonard Woolf

Introduction by E. F. C. Ludowyck

As a young man Leonard Woolf spent seven years in the Ceylon civil service. The people he met in Sinhalese jungle villages so fascinated and obsessed him that some years later he wrote a novel about them. It is his knowledge and profound understanding of the Sinhalese people that has made *The Village in the Jungle* a classic for all time.

'*The Village in the Jungle* is a novel of superbly dispassionate observation, a great novel.' – Quentin Bell

Ethan Frome and Summer

Edith Wharton

Introduction by Victoria Glendinning

Edith Wharton (1862–1937) is probably America's most original and important female novelist. This volume contains two short novels, *Ethan Frome* and *Summer*, both of which outstrip their predecessors in the genre of American realism.

OXFORD PAPERBACKS

Twentieth-Century Classics

The Unbearable Bassington

Saki

Introduction by Joan Aiken
Illustrated by Osbert Lancaster

Set in Edwardian London, Saki's best known novel has as its hero the 'beautiful, wayward' Comus Bassington in whom the author invested his own ambiguous feelings for youth and his fierce indignation at the ravages of time.

'There is no greater compliment to be paid to the right kind of friend than to hand him Saki, without comment' – Christopher Morely

In Youth is Pleasure

Denton Welch

Introduction to John Lehmann

Denton Welch's writing, so much admired by Cyril Connolly, Jocelyn Brooke, and Edith Sitwell, has a purity of style that is completely without affectation. In this, his best novel, he gives a profoundly disturbing vision of the world through the eyes of his adolescent hero.

OXFORD PAPERBACKS

Twentieth-Century Classics

Riceyman Steps

Arnold Bennett

Introduction by Frank Kermode

Bennett's reputation as a novelist waned after the publication of his great pre-war novels, *Anna of the Five Towns, The Old Wives' Tale*, and *Clayhanger*, but it was emphatically restored by the appearance in 1923 of *Riceyman Steps*, the story of a bookseller, Henry Earlforward, and his passion for money and for the widow Violet Arb. In a sinister and irresistible way his miserliness and 'extraordinary soft obstinacy' come to dominate the household – with terrible consequences.

Elmer Gantry

Sinclair Lewis

Introduction by Paul Bailey

An unforgettable study of religious hypocrisy in America. Lewis's *Elmer Gantry* is best remembered for Burt Lancaster's dazzling portrayal of the shameless barnstormer in the 1960s film of the same title. Just three years after the book was published in 1927, Lewis's important contribution to American writing was acknowledged when he became the first American to win the Nobel Prize for Literature.

OXFORD PAPERBACKS

Twentieth-Century Classics

Manservant and Maidservant

Ivy Compton-Burnett

Introduction by Penelope Lively

Ivy Compton-Burnett's novels are profound studies of family life that are both immensely funny and completely original. *Manservant and Maidservant* describes the petty tyrannies to be found in an upper middle-class Edwardian household, and shows Dame Ivy's wit at its sharpest and her characterization at its most memorable.

The Death of Virgil

Hermann Broch

Translated by Jean Starr Untermeyer
Introduction by Bernard Levin

Broch's magnificent novel describes the poet Virgil's last hours as he questions the nature of art, and mourns the death of a civilization.

'One of the most representative and advanced works of our time . . . an astonishing performance.' – Thomas Mann

'Broch is the greatest novelist European literature has produced since Joyce.' – George Steiner

OXFORD PAPERBACKS

Twentieth-Century Classics

Love and Mr Lewisham

H. G. Wells

Introduction by Benny Green

Mr Lewisham regards himself as a young man poised on the brink of dazzling academic achievement. With degrees and diplomas brandished like lances, he will smash his way out of the prison of class and poverty. And yet, on the very threshold of his advancement, all his fine plans are swept aside. For Lewisham falls in love – with Ethel, stepdaughter of the shameless confidence trickster Chaffrey – and before long he is made to realize that the world is a more tormenting place than ever he had supposed. A cautionary tale, *Love and Mr Lewisham* is one of Wells's most carefully planned novels and one of his most deeply personal.

Seven Days in New Crete

Robert Graves

Introduction by Martin Seymour-Smith

A funny, disconcerting, and uncannily prophetic novel about Edward Venn-Thomas, a cynical poet, who finds himself transported to a civilization in the far future. He discovers that his own world ended long ago, and that the inhabitants of the new civilization have developed a neo-archaic social system. Magic rather than science forms the basis of their free and stable society; yet, despite its near perfection, Edward finds New Cretan life insipid. He realizes that what is missing is a necessary element of evil, which he feels it his duty to restore.